MELTDOWN:
The Conclusion

RB HILLIARD

Editor: Christian Brose
Proofreader: Roxane Leblanc
Cover Model: Graham Nation
Photographer: The Glass Camera
Cover Designer: Rebel Edit & Design
Formatted by CP Smith

Dedication

This book is for the music lovers, the die-hard rock fans, and the Melties of the world.
Rock On!
XXOO,
-RB

Evan's ENCORE

MELTDOWN:
The Conclusion

CHAPTER ONE

"How's It Going to Be"

Evan

It was hard to believe my marriage was officially over. Then again, I couldn't really call it a marriage, could I? It was more like a sham or a joke, maybe even a farce. Farce sounded about right. My marriage was a farce. At least, it was to my wife, Mandy. To me, it was nine years of my life. Nine years of living with a woman I thought I knew, but didn't. Nine years of wasted time. The sad part was I loved her. At least, I'd tried to. She didn't make it very easy. Truthfully, she didn't make anything easy. I no longer loved her. Hell, I didn't even like her. Now, all I felt was bitterness and resentment. I contemplated this as I carried the last few boxes inside the house and up the stairs to my room. The house really was amazing. Then again, a tent in the Amazon jungle would be amazing compared to the hell I'd been living in. Carefully, I placed the boxes on the floor. My new room was impressive with its pitched ceiling and ornate fireplace. I dropped onto the bed and tried not to think about my pathetic excuse for a life. The mattress felt great. At least I'd gotten that right. With a loud sigh, I pulled out my phone and dialed my brother's number.

He answered on the first ring. "Are you moved in?"

"Somewhat," I responded.

"Shit, that was fast." Moving is easy when you had nothing to move.

"Yep. Listen, don't say anything. Not to Mom and Dad, not to Elaine, not to anyone. I need time...just to let it all sink in, okay?"

"You could have moved in with me, you know."

Of my two siblings, I was closest to my brother, Ehren. He was five years younger than me. He was also the peacemaker of the family and an all-around good person. My sister and I had never been close. Elaine was three years younger and the family princess. She was also a spoiled brat. I was the oldest of the three Walker children as well as the biggest disappointment. As much as I loved my little brother, I needed my own space, a fresh start, so to speak. Two grown men living in a one-bedroom condo, especially when one of them didn't believe in picking up after himself, wasn't my idea of fun. No thanks. I'd just crawled out of hell—had the scorch marks to prove it. I wasn't looking to go back.

Trying to keep it chill, I said, "Thanks, but my days of sleeping on sofas are long gone."

"What's the latest on bitch face?" he asked. Ehren greatly disliked my wife. He wasn't the only one. Our sister, Elaine, hated her to the point that four years ago, in a desperate ploy to split us up, she showed up at our house drunk off her ass screaming about how Mandy was cheating on me. The look of hurt on my wife's face gutted me. I didn't even question it. Instead, I got pissed at Elaine and kicked her out of my house. I never dreamed she would refuse to speak to me after that. If that wasn't bad enough, my brother also tried to tell me she was cheating on me over Christmas break. Of course, I didn't believe him. Just thinking about it made me feel all kinds of stupid. Hell, I was stupid.

"She's cheating on you," Ehren blurted. Our eyes met and held, his filled with anger and mine contempt. Not this again.

"Come on, little brother. If it didn't work the first time, it's not going to work now."

"Just listen. A buddy of mine, someone I trust, swears he saw Mandy at a bar in The Woodlands a few weeks ago. She was with some dude. He said they were...together."

Blowing out a disgusted breath, I asked, "Really, Ehren?"

"I'm not making this up, I swear—"

I held up my hand to stop him. "Were you there? Did you see it with your own eyes? Was your buddy drinking? Did he actually talk to her?" When his face clouded with doubt, I let up on the anger. "I know you want to protect me and I appreciate it, but not like this." I loved my brother, but he could be dense sometimes.

"You're an amazing musician, E. You always have been. Anyone who knows you, knows this. Anyone but her!" He'd gone too far.

"Don't go there," I warned.

After blasting me with a defiant glare, he said exactly what I didn't want to hear. "She should have supported you."

"Yeah, well, I shouldn't have left."

A snort of contempt shot from his lips. "When are you going to stop blaming yourself?"

"When she forgives me."

"When she forgives you," he repeated, his tone filled with

disgust. I knew he wasn't a big fan of Mandy, but I didn't realize how much he hated her.

"Look, I get that you don't like her, but to accuse her of cheating? You're better than that."

"Will you at least ask her about it?"

I asked, and of course, she lied. Everything about her and our life together was a lie...

"Did you hear me?" Ehren asked.

I slowly shook off the memory. "I heard. Bobby's supposed to call later today or tomorrow. I'll fill you in once I've spoken to him."

"Okay, well, not to be a dick or anything, but can I just point out that you're choosing to live with a woman you've known for all of three seconds over your own brother. I don't get it." That was just it. It wasn't his to get.

Scowling at the fancy gold light fixture above my head, I informed him that Quinn and I weren't living *together*, but that I was simply living in her house, and there was a vast difference between the two."

"I can't believe you let Mandy have the house," he grumbled.

"Good thing I didn't discuss it with you first," I shot back.

"It's just that...I find this whole thing odd."

"Call it what you want. The fact is, Quinn lives in a house, not a one-bedroom condo. She needs a tenant, and I need a place to live. If you think about it, it's really not that hard to grasp."

"Fine. I'll leave it alone." He didn't want to, though. He wanted answers, but how was I supposed to make him understand when I didn't understand myself?

"Look, I don't need your opinion on every aspect of my life. I just need your support right now. That's all."

"You know I've got your back. I just want you to be okay." I couldn't help but smile.

"You promise not to tell anyone?" I added.

"I promise, but for the record, I think you should talk to Chaz or Grant." I planned on calling Chaz, just not yet. When I didn't respond, he asked, "Now that you've moved in, what are you going to do?"

"Nothing," I lied. I knew exactly what I was going to do. I was going to find Quinn and collect on the free drink she owed me.

The minute I hung up with Ehren, I was out the door. On the drive to Margo's, I thought back to the first time I met Quinn. It was over that same Christmas break. I'd come home to patch things up with Mandy, and in an attempt to get my mind off my marriage troubles, Ehren, and some friends offered to take me out for drinks. The thought of going to a bar sounded great. There was just one small problem. I was no longer anonymous.

"I'll have to borrow a baseball cap," I told him.

"Not where we're going, you won't." Grinning at my questioning look, he explained, "Jason wants to get in some chick's pants. She works at a gen-u-ine honky-tonk. Get this, it's called Margo's." He laughed at the smirk on my face. "I kid you not. We're talking, a country bar in the middle of BFE. I doubt they'll know who you are, much less that you're even there. So, what do you think? Are you up for a little road trip?"

"Sure, why not?" What else was I going to do? It wasn't as if I could hang out with my wife or anything. Nope. She had plans and wouldn't be able to see me until tomorrow.

While Ehren made arrangements with the guys, I headed to the bathroom to get cleaned up. As I made my way down the hall, I couldn't help but smile. Little brother had done well for himself. After becoming an official member of Meltdown, I called and offered to help him financially. When he declined, I thought it was out of pride. Now I knew better. He was making his own way and I couldn't be prouder of him.

My heart kicked in my chest when I felt my phone buzz in my back pocket. *Mandy?* I thought, as I reached for it. When I saw Chaz's name scroll across the screen, I gave myself a mental slap. *You're going to see her tomorrow. Stop being such a pussy.*

Chaz's text read: *You coming to Austin for G's thing?*

Grant and his girlfriend, Mallory, were throwing a Christmas party at their house in Austin. Mallory didn't know, but Grant was proposing to her. I'd been invited but had declined.

"Hey, E! You ready?" Ehren called down the hallway.

"Be there in a few!" I called back, then quickly responded to Chaz's text—*No. Got shit to deal with here.*

As I opened the bathroom door, he responded back. *She ain't worth it, bro.* She, meaning Mandy. In a moment of weakness, I'd told Chaz about my failing marriage. To say the guy was opinionated was a gross understatement. Try a relentless dickhead. It was a damn good thing he was on my side.

Have you heard from Nash? I typed in response. Right before we went on tour, our lead guitarist, Nash, discovered his mother's cancer had returned. The prognosis wasn't good.

Chaz responded right when I reached the living room. *Nah. Gotta run.*

Later. I replied.

"All good?" Ehren asked.

"Yep. All good."

My brother wasn't lying about my not needing to worry about getting recognized. Somewhere between downtown Houston and nowheresville was a roadside bar called Margo's.

"You said off the beaten path, not in another country," I teased as we pulled into the gravel parking lot. Cars, trucks, and motorcycles were lined up across the lot. I heard the music as soon as I opened my car door. Little did anyone know, but I was a country music fan way before I ever got into rock.

While Waylon and Willie warned mamas about letting their babies grow up to be cowboys, we waited for my brother's friends to arrive.

"Why here?" I asked.

"I told you, Jason has a crush on one of the bartenders," he replied, right as his friends pulled into the lot. We waited for them to catch up to us before going inside.

"Holy shit!" Jason shouted. "We thought you were kidding when you said Evan was coming." He turned to me with an expression of adoration on his ugly mug and I couldn't help but feel like a bug under a microscope. Jerking his hand out, he gushed, "Fuck, you're like awesome, man."

"Thanks." I had a feeling this would never get any easier. Not for me, at least. I shook both his and Mike's hands. Kenny Chesney's "Summertime" was just starting up as we stepped inside. At first glance, the place seemed smaller than it appeared from the outside. A long, dark wooden bar took up the entire right wall, large metal booths filled the left, and in the middle sat free standing hi-top tables surrounded by barstools. Beyond the tables, bar, and booths, the floor opened up into a decent-sized dance floor. In true honky-tonk fashion, the floor was covered with straw and peanut shells.

Several sets of eyes watched as we wound our way past the hi-tops toward one of the empty booths. I held my breath, waiting for the onslaught. First would come the gasps, followed by the whispers, and last the shrieks. When none of the above occurred, I slowly released it.

"Told you," Ehren muttered as we slid into an empty booth. A giant mason jar filled with peanuts sat on one end of the table. While reaching for it, I became aware of a mouthwatering aroma.

7

"What's that smell?" I asked.

Jason's face split into a smile. "Sam's cooking."

Staring down at the cup rings on the table, I fought back a cringe. "Well, Sam sure could to do a better job of cleaning off his tables."

"Quinn's the owner," Mike informed me. As far as I was concerned, a dirty table was a dirty table, no matter who it belonged to.

"Well, then Quinn sure could use a new busboy," I corrected.

"Sorry, but Quinn is up to her eyeballs in customers right now," a sexy, throaty, very female sounding voice replied.

As I shifted my gaze to the woman standing at the head of our table, the apology dangling from the tip of my tongue stalled beneath her light blue stare. No, scratch that. They were light gray. Exotic. Striking. Gray. The face they belonged to was delicate...femininity at its finest. Both of these attributes were almost outdone by a wild, untamed mane of brown curls streaked with gold.

"What can I get you boys to drink?" she asked. Her gaze touched on my brother before moving to Mike and then to Jason. This gave me a moment to take in her tight black T-shirt with the Margo's logo in bold, red letters across her chest. Shifting my focus from her chest back to her face, I tried to place her age. Her body said early twenties but the way in which she carried herself said she was older.

"We'll start with a pitcher of Bud," Jason answered. "Oh, and some of those amazing nachos."

Two finely shaped eyebrows rose in question. "You sure? The nachos are good, but our burgers are better."

"Sorry, but nothing beats your nachos."

"I'll tell Sam you said so." Her eyes slid from Jason back to me and her mouth shifted into a smile. In a teasing tone, she said, *"I'll also make sure to get my busboy over here pronto."* It wasn't the sarcastic cut of the words that caught my attention, though. It was her smile. It lit up her whole face. It felt like an invitation to something deeper...something more.

"Uh, is Alex-Ann here?" Jason asked, his voice an octave higher than usual. My eyes sliced to my brother's friend. Someone needed to give the boy his balls back.

"She's off tonight, darlin'," Quinn responded. *"but I'll be happy to tell her you stopped by...errrr—"*

"Jason," he squeaked.

"Jason," she repeated in her sexy southern drawl. Then, winking at me, said, *"The busboy will be right with you."*

Five minutes later, long enough for us to properly harass Jason, Quinn returned with a pitcher of beer, four mugs, and...a wet hand towel. As I watched her clean our table, I felt like an ass.

"Sorry about the earlier comment," I muttered before she could get away.

"No worries, sport. They were just words." She hit me with that gorgeous smile before walking away. She wasn't wrong. They were just words, but if anyone knew the damage that words could inflict, it was me.

After a few beers and some of the best nachos I'd ever tasted, Jason and Mike led us off to a hidden corner room where we played pool and threw some darts. Ehren and I called it quits around midnight. With back slaps and handshakes, we said goodbye to his friends. On the way to the door, I searched for Quinn and found her standing next to a table with a pen and order pad in hand. She glanced my way and acknowledged my departure with a slight lift of her chin. I responded with a smile of thanks. For a brief moment I'd forgotten that my marriage was falling apart. I'd forgotten how good it felt to be able to *hang with friends and be myself. It felt good to forget...*

It was hard to believe that was eight months ago—back when life seemed rough but actually wasn't—back before the rug was jerked out from under my life.

Only two cars and a motorcycle were in the parking lot when I pulled into Margo's. Quinn wasn't kidding when she said Sunday was a slow night. I paused to roll up my windows before turning off the car. Music greeted me as I opened my door and stepped out into the night. As I made my way across the gravel lot, the hopelessness I'd been feeling began to lift. That's what music did for me. It soothed the raw edges. Fuck knows there were plenty of those.

Singing along with the Avett Brothers, I headed for the front entrance. "Satan Pulls the Strings" was the name of the song. Satan sure as hell pulled my strings when he led me to Mandy James. If only I'd known. Willing myself not to go there, I pulled open the door and immediately spotted Quinn standing behind the bar. Our eyes met and her lips turned up. Even though I shouldn't, I felt that smile. I felt it deep in a place that, surprisingly, hadn't been tainted by Mandy's betrayal.

"Hey, Rock Star," she greeted in that smoky tone of hers that made me think of dirty things.

Ignoring the rock star comment, I dropped down onto a stool in front of her and asked, "What's up, Country?"

Waving her hand in the air, she said, "Take a look around. As you can see, absolutely nothing."

"You weren't kidding when you said Sundays were quiet."

"Yeah, I'm seriously considering closing the place and giving everyone Sundays off from here on out."

"So, why don't you?" Her answer was a shrug.

One thing I'd noticed about Quinn, was her lack of sharing. The woman was locked up tighter than a bull's ass in fly season. Hell, a few weeks ago, I stopped by to ask if she was still interested in renting out a room and all it took was three drinks before I was spilling all kinds of shit about my life.

"You look sad, sugar," she'd said in her sexy, southern drawl, and like a dumbass, I blurted that my marriage was over. We got to talking, or more like, I got to drinking which led me to talking, she asked about what had happened, and that was all it took.

"It all started last year, when I kind of lied to my wife and told her I was playing a gig in Austin, when, in fact, I was auditioning for Meltdown. And before you judge, I knew if I told her, she would try and talk me out of it."

Her brow shot up in surprise. "Why? Your wife doesn't like music?"

"My wife, though we shouldn't really call her that, kind of likes music, but what she really likes is control."

Quinn nodded in understanding. "Ahhh, one of those." See? I knew she would get it.

I explained how our life together was steady. We both had decent jobs and I got to see my buddies and indulge my "little musical hobby," as Mandy liked to call it, at nights after work or on the weekends. Everything was all good as long as I was toeing the line. Mandy's line, that is.

"Wow, that sounds so...not fun," Quinn muttered.

"It wasn't, which was one of the main reasons I decided to audition." I went on to explain how, in all the years we'd been together, Mandy had never understood my love of music. She more than enjoyed the attention it garnered, but the rest she could live without. "To be honest, I didn't actually think I would land the job, so no harm, no foul. Mandy would never know and life would carry on."

"Only, you got the gig."

"Yep, not even a week after my audition, Grant called to offer

me the job." Just thinking about it made me smile. "When he explained that the band had chosen me, I thought he was joking, but then he started bombarding me with dates and times and shit, and I realized he was serious. He warned me that it was only for the tour, but I didn't care if it was temporary or not. To me it was the opportunity of a lifetime, a chance for me to prove myself, to make my wife and family finally understand that this was what I was supposed to be doing with my life. There was just one problem."

"Your wife didn't know," Quinn finished for me.

Nodding, I said, "The moment the call was over, reality set in. Mandy had no clue as to what I'd done. I should have talked to her first, but I was so damn pumped and honored...beyond honored they'd chosen me. Finally, I was getting the break I'd been searching for. If it panned out, she would be able to quit her job."

Sliding another beer my way, Quinn asked, "What does she do?"

"She sells pharmaceutical supplies to doctors in four different states."

"I take it she was less than thrilled with the idea?"

"She was madder than hell."

While Quinn made her rounds, I drank my beer and thought about my soon to be ex-wife.

After accusing me of betraying our marriage and abusing her trust, Mandy shut down. As in, she wouldn't even hear me out. She didn't care why I'd done it or that it was only temporary. She just wanted me to call Grant back and decline the offer. When I refused, she packed a bag and moved in with her parents. It took me a week to get her to speak to me. Needless to say, the conversation didn't go well.

"Are you still going?" she asked.

"Babe, just listen—"

"Are you going?" she slowly repeated, her voice tinged with bitterness.

"Yes," I finally answered. Her reply was to hang up on me. Talk about being stuck between a rock and a hard place. I didn't want to lose my marriage, but I also didn't want to give up my dream.

When Mandy finally realized she wasn't going to talk me out of going and that her silent manipulation wasn't getting her anywhere, she moved back home and immediately took up residence in the guest room. By refusing to acknowledge my presence and making me feel like a ghost in my own home, she only helped to strengthen my resolve. Finally, I gave up trying to appease her. She'd drawn the line in the sand. I was no longer interested in stepping over it.

I only told Quinn part of the story. What I didn't say was that the night before I left to go on tour, my wife paid me a little visit. Like a thief in the night, she slipped into bed with me. I woke to her working me over with her hand. Once she had me where she wanted, she took without giving, and trust me when I say she was quick about it. We're talking night shirt still on, three pumps and done kind of quick—so quick that I almost missed the finale. When she dismounted and scurried back to the guest room, I almost wished it hadn't happened, because now, instead of being left with the few memories of how good our life had once been, I was left with the bitter taste of what it had become. In choosing music over our marriage, I'd irreparably damaged the bond that held us together. Did that stop me from going on tour? No, but it should have.

Quinn let out a snort. "Let me get this straight, your wife, who isn't really your wife—whatever that means—wanted out of your marriage because you went on tour with a famous rock band? Wow, it must have been pretty tough to watch you make it to the top and all." Her words and the way they so carelessly flew from her pretty little mouth, sounded...judgmental. Judgmental enough for me to want to change the subject.

"Awww, Country, if I'd known you were feeling neglected, I would've let you go first. Now, what has you singing the blues this evening? Did someone skip out on their tab?" And just like that, her smile vanished and her eyes dulled...Quinn had shut down. I watched her move up and down the bar, full of smiles and fake platitudes for the handful of customers, and wondered what a woman like her had to be unhappy about. I knew I shouldn't care. I told myself I didn't care, but I was definitely intrigued.

By the time she finally made it back to me, I was seven beers in and done. Handing her my card, I said, "If the offer still stands, I can move in next week."

She stared at me for a long moment. "You're kidding."

"You said you needed help. Well, here I am." That I needed out of that house and wasn't quite ready to have my life splashed all over the tabloids, was irrelevant. Quinn needed a housemate and I needed a place to live. A place that was completely off the grid. That's what mattered.

Without a word, she snatched the card from my hand and disappeared to the back.

"That went well," I announced. The guy sitting on the barstool next to me gave me a strange look. I thought about saying more, but then Quinn was back with my card and her answer.

"Here's my number. Call and let me know what day you want to move in."

A week later I called, and now, here we were. I wouldn't exactly call us friends, but that would come with time.

"Are you all moved in?" she asked, handing me a beer. I watched as she pulled another from the cooler. She popped the top, lifted it to her lips, and took her first sip.

Ignoring the tightness in my lower gut, I asked, "Do you normally drink on the job?"

She smiled and that tightness increased. "When it's dead like this, I do."

"To answer your question," because that was easier than acknowledging the unwelcome boner in my shorts, "I'm more or less moved in. I hope you don't mind, but I kind of went exploring and noticed that the pool house is empty."

"Yeah, my mother was kind enough to clean it out when she left."

"That sucks, buuuuuut, since it's empty and all, I was wondering if I could use it as a music room?" She hesitated for a moment and I knew she was going to say no. "If you let me use it now, I'll buy new pool furniture when I leave," I coaxed.

"Well, shit. How can I say no to that?" Grinning, she took another sip of her beer.

"You can't," I told her, and we both laughed. I raised my bottle in the air. "Here's to new adventures."

"To new adventures," she repeated, and leaning over the bar, she tapped her bottle to mine. My eyes instantly dropped to her chest. Yes, I would be a liar if I said I wasn't attracted to Quinn Kinley. I shouldn't be...but I was.

CHAPTER TWO

"Cheeseburger in Paradise"

Quinn

I left Evan sipping on his beer while I cleaned up the tables. I couldn't help but think about what my dad would say if he knew I had a man living with me. I'd spoken a few times to Mom since she'd moved but had yet to mention my housemate. I already knew what her reaction would be. She wouldn't approve. Well, tough shit. She shouldn't have left.

"Shit happens when you least expect it." My daddy used to say this. I figured it was his way of explaining the unexplainable. Now, I wasn't so sure. Truthfully, I wasn't really sure of anything anymore. Before he died, I was happy...truly happy. I knew who I was and where I was going. Somewhere along the way, I'd lost myself. I was starting to think I'd never find my way back to the woman I was or if I even wanted to.

While Evan was busy talking to Alex-Ann, I slipped outside for my nightly cigarette.

Humming along to "Tennessee Whiskey," I thought back to the day Dad told us he was sick. When he called a family meeting, I didn't think much of it, as he was known to do this often.

"Doc found a spot on my left lung and wants to do a biopsy," he announced in his oh-so casual way.

Mom and I just sat there staring at him, completely stunned by his news. Minutes passed before she broke the silence. While she hammered him with questions, I remained frozen to my chair. My father, the backbone of our family, my best friend and hero, was sick. How could this be?

As it turned out, the spot wasn't just a spot, but a cancerous mass. Dad wasn't just sick. He was dying. According to the doctors, the tumor had metastasized to his aorta, which in turn, had rendered it inoperable. The doctors called it "terminal." Mom and I called it bullshit. After three months of us dragging him to every specialist known to man, Dad said no more. At the time, I didn't understand. Why was he giving up? Unable to see past the fear of losing him, I got angry. That anger drove me to pull back, to withdraw from my family and my friends. This, of course, lasted all of a week. Then my father came looking for me.

"You're upsetting your mother," he drawled in that good-ole-boy tone of his. Mom's not the one dying! I wanted to scream but didn't dare. No one, not even me, was allowed to speak ill of my mother in front of him.

Glaring at him, I blurted, "Don't you want to live?"

"Oh, Quinny. I want that more than anything in this world."

"Then...why?" I asked, desperate to understand.

"You were there. You heard them. How many doctors did I talk to, four, five? Open your eyes, girl! Aside from a miracle, there's nothing that can be done." He stood there staring at me with heartache in his eyes, and suddenly it hit me. Whether I liked

it or not, my dad was going to die. In a landslide of emotion, the anger that I'd been holding onto so tightly, crumbled into a gaping maw of pain.

"Daddy," I whispered, trying my damndest to fight back the tears.

"I would give anything to—" he swallowed deeply before continuing, "stay here with you and your mom, but I can't. I need you to understand this, sweet girl." His lips quivered, but it was the sound of his voice cracking that was my undoing.

"Don't die," I pleaded, knowing how unfair it was to ask, yet saying it anyway. He didn't need to answer. The painful silence spoke for him. When he opened his arms wide for me, a sob escaped. The second my head hit his chest, I broke. I was still broken...

"I wondered if you smoked." I'd been so deep in thought that I hadn't heard him sneak up on me. Hot rocker boy. My new roomie. My secret sexual fantasy.

"Busted. Just don't tell my—" I started to say mother.

"Don't tell your—?" he pressed.

"Nothing." Rock Star hadn't earned the right to my secrets.

"Come on, Country. I feel all exposed here. I've basically told you my life story. You've got to give me something."

"You've told me like three things," I pointed out.

"And now it's your turn. Fair's fair," he urged. Leave it to the ass to appeal to my sense of fairness.

"Fine. Let's see, my mom was thirty-five when she met my dad. At the time, she was running her own accounting business. According to her, Dad was a real entrepreneur. He was also forty and a bachelor, two things that were unheard of in that day and age. My father referred to it as dabbling, but Mom claims he had his hands in at least three different ventures. One of these re-quired her services. He used to joke about how he went looking for an accountant and ended up with a wife. After the wedding," I continued, "my parents didn't waste time getting pregnant with me. They tried for more children, but Mom said it wasn't in the cards. She called me God's little gift." The look on Evan's face was priceless. I bit back a laugh. Clearly, he wasn't expecting a history lesson.

"While I was hoping for something a little dirtier, learning about your family history will do. Keep going," Evan inserted. Laughing, I flicked the butt of my cigarette at him.

"I didn't realize how different I was from other kids until grade school when I was old enough to have sleepovers. I mean, I knew my house was big. I just didn't realize how big. It only got worse. In junior high I was picked on. The mean girls took to calling me rich bitch and snob. I can remember crying in my mother's arms, wondering why I couldn't live in a normal house like everyone else. And before you say poor you for living in a big house when people are starving in the world, I didn't get that then. I was just a kid trying to fit in the best I could."

"No judgment here," he commented.

"It was my father who taught me to be proud of my heritage. He told me how my great, great, great grandfather had traveled to Texas from far away. How he'd built his home with his own two hands so he and his wife could start a family. One of their three sons found a black, tar-like substance bubbling up from the ground and that was how he got his start in the oil business. When the family grew too big for the little house, they built the house we currently live in. 'Be proud of who you are, Quinny,' Dad would say. 'Be grateful for what you have and try your hardest to always be humble and kind.'"

"I wouldn't exactly call you kind. I mean, you did try to poison me and all," he teased.

"You deserved it," I told him. Just thinking back on that night made me smile.

"Either you slow your roll, Herb, or I'm gonna have to cut you off," I warned.

"I'm not even buzzed yet," Herb, *our resident drunk, whined, even though we both knew he was already half-crocked.*

"One more and he's cut off," I ordered *low enough for my best friend and fellow bartender, Alex-Ann, to hear.*

"Your old man would never have cut me off," Herb *grumbled into his beer.*

"Yeah? Well, he's gone. This is my bar now and these are my rules. It's high time you get that through your sloshy skull." The moment I said it, I regretted it. Not the words, but the harsh way in which I'd spoken them. Nights like these I really missed my dad.

Sensing that I was on the verge of ripping Herb a new asshole, Alex-Ann gave me a gentle shove. "Take five. I've got it handled." With a quick nod of thanks, I headed for the kitchen.

"Give it to me," I ordered *as I passed by Sam, my cranky but trusted cook. He opened his mouth to lay into me, but then took one look at my face, and with a loud sigh, handed a cigarette over.*

Hot, sticky air greeted me as I stepped onto the landing, making it hard to breathe. I loved Texas but could definitely do without the humidity. It did horrible things to my hair. Tonight, I didn't even bother trying to tame it. I just piled it on top of my head with a clip. With a simple flick of my wrist, the match flared to life. I could feel my body start to relax before I'd even taken my first drag. After a year of trying to quit, I was down to one cigarette a day. Smoking wasn't a physical addiction for me anymore. It wasn't even a habit. It was purely psychological; something that reminded me of my dad. Just like the bar, cigarettes had been our thing. Too bad they were also what killed him. Slowly exhaling, I lowered myself down to the concrete slab, and with an ungraceful hop, I plopped down onto my butt. The beat of an old Hank Williams, Jr. song drifted through the cracks of the door. "Country State of Mind" was one of Dad's favorites. With a contented sigh, I curled my legs beneath me and sang along. Not a day went by that I didn't think about him. It was hard to believe he'd been gone a year.

My phone buzzed in my pocket, jerking me from my thoughts. Her Royal Highness rolled across the screen and I laughed. Alex-Ann had struck again. We had this thing where we would swipe each other's phones and assign different names to certain contacts. Sliding my finger across the screen, I answered, "Hi, Mom. Whatsup?"

"Hey, darlin', how's it going?"

"Other than Herb already being half in the bag, it's pretty slow tonight. What's up with you? Everything okay at the house?"

"Everything is fine. I was thinking of stopping by but wanted to see how busy you were, first."

"Come on over," I told her on an exhale. Then I remembered who I was talking to and froze. Shit!

"Quinn Kinley, what did I tell you about smoking those damn cancer sticks?" she barked. The fear and anger infused into her tone made me flinch. What was I thinking?

"I'm not smoking. I'm just catching some air on the loading dock," I lied as I quickly scraped the remainder of the cigarette across the bottom of my shoe.

"You better hope that's the case. I'd hate to have to tan your hide."

"You'd have to catch me first, little mama," I teased, and smiled when she laughed. I loved making my mother laugh. After my father's death, laughter had been slow to come for the *both of us.*

"Oh, shooey, Verna's calling in. Listen, can you come by the house for breakfast in the morning? I have something I want to run by you." This got my attention. Ever since Dad's death, Mom had been running the house by herself. We'd hired help, but the old place was a lot for anyone, including my aging mother, to handle. I offered to move in, but we both knew that wasn't a good idea. I loved her, but we were too much alike and therefore tended to butt heads. It was always Mom's way or the highway.

"Wait! Tell me now," I urged.

"Tomorrow, Quinny. Make sure Sam walks you girls to your cars. Love you," she replied, and the line went dead.

I was seriously contemplating relighting my cigarette when the door behind me swung open.

"Bax is here," Alex-Ann announced. I barely managed to hold back a groan. "He's with her and she's wearing the ring," she finished on a harsh whisper. Great. Just what we needed to round out the evening; Alex's ex.

I held out my hand and waited for her to take it before remarking, "I thought you said the wedding was off?"

"It was! You saw what a wreck he was these past few weeks."

"Thanks," I muttered when she pulled me to my feet.

A few months after my dad passed away, Baxter Keen, Alex-Ann's ex-boyfriend, showed up at the bar with his new girlfriend, Amanda. Baxter was a suit-wearing, pop-music loving city boy who'd never, in the three months he'd dated Alex-Ann, stepped foot inside Margo's. At first, we thought it was a ploy to get Alex-Ann back, but soon we realized he couldn't give a rat's ass about Alex-Ann. It was all about Amanda, which made no sense because, even though she wouldn't say it, she clearly hated the place. We figured as soon as the shine wore off, Baxter would crawl back over to his side of town to his fancy restaurants and bars. *When he didn't, we began to question his motives. Alex-Ann thought it had something to do with Amanda not fitting into Bax's social circle, but I felt it was more. I just didn't know what that more was. Either way, I didn't like it. No, scratch that. I didn't like her.*

"Herb's passed out on the bar," *Sam informed us as we rushed by the kitchen.*

"Did you call Delia?" *Delia was Herb's wife. If you asked me, the woman was an absolute saint to put up with his shit every night.*

"Yep. She's on her way."

Old Dominion sang about tattoos and sand as we made our way across the bar floor.

"Where are they?" *I asked, low enough for Alex-Ann to hear. Before she had time to answer, I spotted them slow dancing in the back corner. At least, that's what I thought they were doing. At the moment, it looked like Baxter was more or less eating her face off.*

"Would you look at them," *she hissed in my ear.*

"They're kind of hard to miss," *I drawled, trying not to laugh.*

"Why here? He could take her to any bar in the universe and he has to pick this one. Whyyyyyy?" *Alex-Ann's whining got my attention. Baxter was a nuisance and Amanda a world class bitch, but we knew this. So why was she all of a sudden bothered by this now? After all, she was the one who ended things with him. Then it dawned on me. She slept with him!*

We stepped behind the bar, and before she could escape, I jerked her around to face me. "Tell me you didn't," *I whispered. Her guilty expression said it all.* "Seriously? You slept with him?" *Sometimes I wanted to strangle my best friend.*

"It's not like I planned it," *she defensively stammered.* "He was so heartbroken and...it just happened."

"When? Where?" I asked, even though I wasn't entirely sure I wanted to know.

"Last week in the back hallway after we closed," she sheepishly answered, and I felt as if I'd been kicked in the stomach.

"Oh my God, woman! You had wall sex with him here in my bar?" Alex-Ann was one of the smartest people I knew, but the girl had zero common sense when it came to men. She fell in and out of love on a weekly basis.

"I know. It was a bad idea. And now he's dry humping her in the corner. Just shoot me nooooow," she groaned.

I was about to lay into her when Herb's wife, Delia, suddenly appeared in front of us. While Alex-Ann and my other bartender, Will, helped Delia get Herb to their car, I loaded up a tray of drinks for Gretchen, one of my waitresses.

"I can't believe it," she whispered, her voice filled with excitement.

"Believe what?" I asked, still irritated at Alex-Ann.

"Chaz Jones and Evan Walker are here."

"Who?" I glanced over at her section and immediately spotted him. The guy from that night. The one I'd tried not to think about but couldn't seem to get out of my head. Well, Quinn sure could use a new busboy, he'd said in that hella sexy voice.

"Do you know him...I mean them?" I asked, trying to play it cool.

"Know them? Oh my God, Quinn! That's Evan Walker and Chaz Jones!" she softly exclaimed. After a moment of me staring at her with a blank look on my face, she added, "You know, Meltdown, the rock band..."

"Really?" I asked, swiveling my head around to get a better look. Even though I preferred country music, I wasn't opposed to rock. In fact, I thought Meltdown was a pretty decent band.

"The one with the beard is their keyboardist, Evan," she pointed out, and the hottie with the wild hair is their drummer, Chaz."

"No shit?" I murmured, continuing to stare at the table of famous people. Meltdown's keyboardist and drummer were in my bar. Who would have thought...

"Where's Baxter and Bitch-Face?" Alex-Ann asked as she and Will returned from the parking lot.

"Huh?" I replied, still busy staring at the two rock stars. Evan was as good looking as I'd remembered, maybe even better with the beard. He had the most amazing eyes—green with a blue-gray circle around the outer edges. He also had ink, and a lot of it, which I found intriguing.

Alex-Ann nudged me with her elbow. "Baxter and Amanda?"

"Yeah, what about them?" I shot back at her, my eyes scanning over his buddy. Chaz, Gretchen had said his name was. Well, Chaz was hot, but in my opinion, he didn't hold a candle to Evan. He, too, had ink, but his was much darker.

"They're gone!" Alex-Ann's exasperated tone finally caught my attention.

Dragging my eyes from the tatted duo, I asked, "Who?"

"Baxter and Amanda. Did you see them leave?"

"Don't tell me you're actually interested in him?" Because that would be a really bad idea. Baxter had a lot of money but no backbone. Alex-Ann walked all over that boy's ass and then some. He called me for two weeks solid after she dumped him and I finally had to threaten to block his calls if he didn't stop.

"What? No," she snapped. "I was just asking."

We both turned as Gretchen walked up. "Hey, Sam says I have a phone call. Can one of you handle table six until I get back?" Table six was Evan's table.

"I've got it," I told her.

"Thanks."

"Lawdy me, would you look at that," Alex-Ann drawled. I followed her stare over to the tatted table and smiled.

"That's Evan Walker and Chaz Jones."

"Wowza," she whispered under her breath.

"The keyboardist and drummer from Meltdown," I added for effect. Her eyes shot to mine and bugged with surprise.

"You're shitting me!" she exclaimed. Several sets of eyes turned in our direction, including those of table six.

"I shit you not," I replied before exiting the bar area and heading in their direction. On approach I noticed Chaz sucking face with the female sitting next to him.

"Welcome to Margo's. Can I get you another beer or some food?" I asked, focusing my attention on Evan.

Leveling that green gaze on me, he said, "Yeah, can I get a burger?" My pulse fluttered under his rapt stare. The man wasn't cowboy enough for me, but he sure was something worth looking at. His dark hair and beard only helped to accentuate those fabulous green eyes. Now that I was up close and personal, I also took note of his lips. They were full, perfect, and very sexy.

"Hello?" he called out in a somewhat irritated tone.

"Oh, uh, sorry. What was that?" I asked, embarrassed to be caught staring.

"Food?" he clipped.

I started to apologize again, but instead, found myself saying, "Yes, what about it?"

"Can we order some or are you going to stand there staring at us all night?" Talk about rude.

"Sure thing, honey. What would you like?" I asked in a sugar-sweet voice. His green eyes narrowed in on me and I smiled. Take that Rock Star.

"I would like a hamburger."

26

"On it?" I questioned.

"On what?" he asked, clearly getting more irritated by the second.

"What would you like on it?" I asked, carefully enunciating each word. His friends laughed.

"Cheese, Let—"

"Kind?" I interrupted.

"Huh?" he questioned.

"What kind of cheese, dude?" his buddy asked for me.

Catching the female's eye, I winked and she smiled.

"Fuck!" Evan hissed. "I don't care. Just give me a damn cheeseburger with the works."

Lifting my brows, I asked, "The works?" I wanted to make sure I'd heard him right.

"Yeeees," he replied in the same slow tone I'd given him earlier.

Tit for tat, I thought, but answered, "Sure thing, doll. One burger with the works, coming right up." This guy was a real twit. After taking the other orders, I quickly escaped to the kitchen.

"You're sure he wants the works?" Sam asked.

Somehow managing to keep a straight face, I confirmed that the customer did, indeed, want a burger with the works. I left Sam mumbling behind the stove and returned to the bar, smiling all the way.

"So, what are they like?" Alex-Ann whispered.

"Chaz and his girl are nice," I told her.

"And Evan?"

"I'm back," Gretchen interrupted. "Thanks for watching my table."

"Order up!" Sam called from the kitchen.

"That's for table six," I directed at Gretchen. Not even

two minutes passed before the bar was interrupted by a loud commotion.

"What the hell is on this?" I heard shouted from across the room. My inner bitch gave a silent whoop and a fist pump and I had to bite back the urge to cackle with glee. Serves the shit-heel right.

A minute or so later, Gretchen called out, "Quinn, you're needed at table six!"

Zeroing in on my smirk, Alex-Ann whispered, "What did you do?"

Ignoring her question, I slid out from behind the bar and made my way over to table six. Evan's face was no longer pale, but more like the color of a ripe tomato. That's what habanero peppers would do to you.

"What the hell did you put on this?" he wheezed between gulps of water.

"I'm sorry, you did say you wanted the works, didn't you?" I could tell the guy wanted to blast me.

"He did," Chaz chimed in, which earned him an evil glare.

"People are staring. Let's go," Evan grumbled.

"I'm sorry. Did I do something wrong?" I questioned, my tone filled with fake concern. Without answering, he scooted from the booth and walked out the door. I watched him leave and had to admit, the guy had one fine backside. Too bad his personality didn't match his good looks. Turning back to the table, I noticed both Chaz and the woman staring at me. "Oh, dear. I hope he's okay. Would you like for me to box yours to go?" A long minute passed before Chaz smiled.

"Your name is Quinn, correct?" he asked.

A pulse of fear sliced through me and I wondered if I'd gone too far. "It is," I answered.

"I'm Chaz and this is Olivia."

"Nice to meet you both. Let me get those boxes for you. When I noticed Chaz reaching for his wallet I told him it was on the house. Without waiting for him to respond, I turned and headed for the kitchen. Sam glowered at me as I grabbed the burger and boxes from the window.

"What?"

"You know what," he replied and I couldn't help but smile. For all I cared, Evan Rock Star Walker could kiss my lily-white ass.

"Here," I told Gretchen as I reached the bar. "This goes to table six. Make sure you pack their burgers in the boxes and thank them for coming in. Oh, and just in case the works were too much, I had Sam make their friend another burger. I'll cover you for the lost tip later."

On the way out the door, Chaz made a beeline over to me. Holding up some cash, he said, "This is for Evan. Believe it or not, he really is a good guy." When I refused to take the money, he leaned over and shoved it down my shirt. "I like you," he stated. Then he walked out the door.

"What the hell was that about?" Alex-Ann asked.

"She pulled another Quinn," Gretchen muttered, clearly disappointed to see them go.

Alex-Ann huffed, as if this happened all the time, which it did not. "What'd she do this time?" she asked, as if I wasn't standing right there with my hand in my shirt trying to fish out the money Chaz had just deposited there.

"She gave him the Dragon Burger," Gretchen answered.

Alex-Ann's eyes shot to mine. "I thought you took that damn thing off the menu!"

"I did, and you're welcome," I told Gretchen as I handed her the two fifty-dollar bills.

Two hours later, Sam walked Alex-Ann and I to our cars. I

told her about breakfast with Mom and promised to call her after.

That night, as I lay in my bed, I tried not to think of the rock star with the gorgeous eyes. I tried not to think about his colorful tattoos and the stories they told. I tried not to think about his perfect lips or his bad attitude. Or how one of his bottom teeth was slightly crooked and that he was no longer wearing a wedding ring.

I tried...but I failed.

"You have to admit the house is amazing," Evan said, his comment jerking me back to the present.

"Yeah, it is pretty awesome," I agreed. And it was. Growing up, we referred to it as "The House," but in reality, it was so much more. It was my family's history. Not just that, it was a testament to success. With six bedrooms, six and a half baths, and fifteen acres of land, it was a structure of unmitigated beauty. Too bad it was also more than any one person could handle. The interior had been modernized throughout the years, but the exterior, with its wrap around porches and broad columns, still had that antebellum look about it. My parents loved the history, whereas I just loved the house, which was why I was shocked when my mother told me she was moving.

"You're what?" I asked, assuming I'd heard her wrong.

"Verna's asked me to move in with her and I've agreed." Verna, my mom's best friend, had moved to Florida three years ago.

In an attempt to reason with her, I said, "Mom, you can't just up and move to Florida."

"I can do what I want," she stiffly retorted.

"But...what about the house? What about me?" The house was one thing. I understood how difficult it must be to maintain, but this wasn't just about the house. It was about what was left

of our family.

Throwing up her hands, she shouted, *"All I see is him!"* The words burst from her lips, as if she'd been holding them in for far too long. I blinked, in shock at her outburst. Slowly, she exhaled before calmly explaining, *"I see him—in every room, with every breath I take. All I see is him. He is this house, baby girl, and I feel as if I'm drowning in the memories."*

"I'm drowning, too," I lightly replied, not meaning to sound selfish, but wanting her to understand that she wasn't the only one who missed him. Suddenly, I had the perfect solution. Well, maybe not perfect, but definitely doable. *"What if I move in with you? We can redecorate, maybe spruce the place up a bit."* Eyes, the same color as mine, shifted to the side before hitting back on me.

"I'm going, Quinny. I've already made up my mind." Her tone was firm and resolute. One thing I'd earned from my mother was her bullheadedness. When the Kinley women decided to dig their heels in, nothing could budge them.

"You can't just leave!"

"I most certainly can!" she snapped back at me. *"Look, I know you don't like it and I'm sorry, but I can't live like this anymore. You have a choice. Either I sell this place to the state and let them set it up as a museum or you move in and take it over."* I couldn't believe what I was hearing. Was she for real?

Shaking my head in disbelief, I let out a groan of frustration. *"Do you hear yourself? This is our home, Mother! The Kinley legacy. Daddy is rolling over in his grave right now!"*

"Your father is dead!" she screeched. *"I begged him for years to quit smoking, but did he? No! And now he's gone and I'm alone! Don't pretend to know what I'm going through. Until you love someone more than you love yourself...until you build a life and have children...until you bury that person in the ground*

and have to live the rest of your life without them, you cannot understand! Now, whether you like it or not, I'm moving to Florida!" I just stood there gaping at her. "Come with me," she offered. We both knew it was out of guilt. If anything, I was an afterthought. Anger seared through me.

"No thanks." I knew if I spoke another word I would regret it, so I turned on my heel and marched for the door.

"You have a week to decide!" she called after me.

Of course, I didn't share this with Evan. Looking down at my watch, I said, "Story time's over, Rock Star. I've got to get back to it."

"See you at home?" he asked. The feeling those four words evoked made my heart skip a million beats.

"Sure thing," I breathily replied. His perfect mouth split into a smile, but before he could say another word, I was up on my feet and through the door. Evan Walker may be gorgeous to look at and easy to talk to, but he wasn't my type. At least, that's what I told myself.

CHAPTER THREE

"I Wish I Knew You"

$\mathcal{E}$van

On the drive back to Quinn's place, I thought about my earlier conversation with my brother. My reason for hiding out in some woman's house I barely knew instead of being with my family was pretty simple—my parents wouldn't understand. Even though they'd never said it, they weren't big fans of Mandy. They were, however, staunch believers in the sanctity of marriage. To them, divorce was not acceptable, which I found ironic, because my dad was now going on two or more years with his latest side piece. They already disapproved of me. Why make it worse?

Mandy wasn't the only thing my parents disliked. They absolutely hated my choice of professions. In the Walker family, we each had our thing. Dad's was the family law firm. Mom's was raising the three of us and lunching with her friends while spending Dad's money. My brother got off on making other people rich, while my sister flitted from job to job trying to land a wealthy husband. My thing was music. According to my parents, music wasn't a profession, but more of a hobby. That was the one thing they seemed to agree with Mandy on. Because I'd chosen to turn that hobby into a profession, I was considered the black sheep of the family and an embarrassment to the Walker name. Funny thing, though. My love for music had stemmed from the two of them.

Like most kids, I was forced to take music lessons from an early age. It was the socially acceptable thing to do and my parents were all about their social status. My siblings hated their lessons. Not me, though. I couldn't get enough. By the age of ten, I'd mastered the piano. My parents were proud.

"Look at Evan. Isn't he gifted?" my mom used to say.

When I was twelve, I took two years of saved up chore money and bought a used electric guitar. By then, my parents were beginning to see the error in their ways, but it was already too late. I was hooked. After weeks of shredding everyone's ear drums, Dad gave in and reluctantly paid for lessons. They thought it was a phase, but I knew different. Music was like breathing. It was an integral part of the person I was becoming, of the man I would grow into.

No, running to Mommy and Daddy with my tail between my legs because my marriage hadn't worked out wasn't an option.

The sound of my phone ringing pulled me from my thoughts, and I noticed I was almost back to Quinn's place. This time, I made sure to check the screen before answering, in case it was Mandy calling to harass me. *Bobby,* it read.

Pressing the hands free on my steering wheel, I answered, "Bobbbbby—tell me you've got good news for me." Bobby Preston was part owner of LASH Investigative Services. We met this past year through the band and had become good friends. Bobby was there the day I found out about Mandy. He offered to look into it as a favor. Once he'd confirmed she was indeed cheating on me, I put him on the payroll.

"I've got Tut and Adam on the job, but we're going to need a few more days, a week at the most," Bobby replied.

"Shit. You really think you're on to something? The court date is weeks away. I know I don't need to say this, but if we don't find something concrete, I'll be shit out of luck."

As far as divorces went, Texas was a no-fault state. This meant that it didn't matter if Mandy had cheated or not. It was also a community property state, so anything earned or bought during a marriage is subject to being divided. We would need to agree on a division of property, and since I hit it big with Meltdown while we were married, this could get complicated.

After I kicked Mandy out of the house, she hired an attorney. The guy was relentless. After weeks of badgering me, I finally agreed to let her move back in, but only because I hated the damn place. What my wife didn't realize, was that I was no longer willing to make the mortgage payments. My lawyer agreed with me, and until the court forced our hand on the matter, this was where I stood. I had no idea where I was going to go. I could rent a place. For that matter, I could buy it, but why do that when I wasn't even sure I wanted to stay in Houston. It was then that I thought of Quinn.

Mandy didn't just want the house. She wanted half of what I'd made...over the nine-year period we'd been together. Fuck that. The bitch had cheated...was still cheating. She wasn't getting a dime from me, not if I had anything to say about it. This is where Bobby came in.

"I'm onto something, but I need total confirmation before discussing it with you," he explained.

"Will it get me out of this mess without going broke?" I asked.

"If it pans out, it will," he answered.

"Do what you have to."

As I disconnected the call, I wondered, for the trillionth time, how it had come to this? A year ago, I was happily married. Our life wasn't perfect but it was good. How did we end up here? I thought back to when I first set eyes on Mandy James...

In the fall of my Sophomore year in high school, my buddies and I formed a band. When we weren't at school, we spent every available minute practicing. By our junior year we had a pretty decent following. This was when I landed on Mandy James's radar. Mandy was a year older and queen of the popular scene. With her long dark hair and firm little body, she was every jock's wet dream. She was also prim, proper, perfect...and not for me. We were like oil and water, two opposing forces. I was a rebel. She was a do-gooder. I bucked the system. She figured out how to manipulate it. Even though we didn't match up, she wanted me and I wasn't smart enough to refuse her.

Like most high school romances, it happened fast. One minute she was talking to me in the hallway and the next we were making out behind the gym. Our relationship didn't progress past second base until the weekend that our drummer, Dave's, parents left town and he decided to throw a party. Stoned out of our heads, we thought it would be cool to give an impromptu concert. While attempting to conquer Dave's nine-hundred-year-old piano, I belted out the lyrics to "Smoke on the Water." It was both epic and awful. Awful in that it sucked ass and epic because it got me laid by the one and only, Mandy James, who'd just so happened to show up drunk with three of her friends. Evidently, my mad piano skills were the key to her magic kingdom. Who cared if she was shallow and we had nothing in common? The girl was a fucking rock star in bed.

Mandy and I were together until the summer after my senior year, when I decided I was too cool to be in a committed relationship. I was college bound and there was pussy to be had. I was ready to take back my freedom. In a dick move, I showed up at Mandy's house one afternoon and told her it was over. She cried, I consoled her, and that was that. If only it had stayed that way...

As I pulled onto the mile-long drive that led to the Kinley Estate, I mulled over my conversation with Bobby and found myself thinking about the day I discovered Mandy was cheating...

The final morning of the tour, the band had one last breakfast together. Regardless of the three-month shit storm we'd just been through, everyone seemed in good spirits. Sean was dead but Olivia, thank God, was okay. Marcy's betrayal hit hard, but it was nothing compared to what Sean had done to Chaz and Olivia...to us all. At the end of the day, Meltdown was as united as ever, which made walking away one of the hardest things I'd ever had to do. No one came right out and said it was over, but we all felt it. At least, I did. For a moment in time, I'd been one of the guys. I'd gotten the chance to live my dream. Now it was time to go home and take care of my responsibilities— responsibilities I'd neglected for far too long. I wasn't the only one walking away. Grant was going home to take care of his pregnant wife, while Nash and Rowan were going home to plan their wedding. Chaz and Olivia were going to visit Chaz's mother before heading back to New York and I was flying home to Houston. It had been hard keeping the news from Mandy, but I wanted...no, I needed, for it to be a surprise. After I was home on Christmas break, we'd grown closer. I wasn't kidding myself. We still had a hell of a lot of work to do, but at least we were together, united, and willing to fight for the life we'd built. A life I'd almost thrown away.

My phone rang in the middle of breakfast. "Excuse me," I said to the table. On the way out the door, I checked the screen.

Smiling, I swiped my finger to answer, "Jonas, you fucker, what the hell's up?"

"I'm kicking my own ass for not taking you up on those free tickets," he grumbled. Damn, it was good to hear his voice. I'd made a million acquaintances along the way, but there were few people I could actually call my friends. My high school bandmates, Jonas and Dave, were definitely two of those.

"So...you called to bitch?" He laughed.

"How much longer is the tour?" he asked.

"It's over, man."

"Seriously?" He sounded surprised.

"Yep, the band is taking a break. Honestly, I'm ready for it." I didn't bother to tell him it was for good. There would be plenty of time for that later.

"Hey, man, that's great. I know we don't live in the same town anymore, but Dallas isn't that far away. We've got a spare bedroom if you need a place to stay."

Finding his statement odd, I asked, "Why would I need a place to stay?"

"Well, with things the way they are with you and Mandy, I just thought..." His voice trailed off into silence. His words and the tone in which they were delivered caused the hairs on the back of my neck to stand at attention.

"Exactly how are things with me and Mandy?" I asked, starting to feel uneasy. When all I got was silence on the other end, I repeated, "How are things with me and Mandy, Jonas?"

"Awww, fuuuuuck" he groaned, and the feeling of unease morphed into a tight band of apprehension.

"Talk," I ordered as the band wrapped around my lungs and began to cut off my air.

"Shit, man. Okay, okay," he chanted as if trying to gather courage. For some strange reason the conversation I had with *my brother over Christmas popped into my head. I dropped my eyes to the carpeted floor. I knew what he was going to say.*

"Some buddies of mine were playing at the Roundabout in Houston a few weekends back. You know, the place that used to be The Old Tavern. Anyway, I took Livy to see them and—" he paused.

"You saw Mandy," I finished for him.

"We did." Livy was Jonas's wife. Jonas and I wanted Livy and Mandy to be friends but neither of them had embraced the idea.

"You're sure it was Mandy?" I asked, thinking that maybe he'd seen someone who looked like my wife.

"Livy and I both agree that it was definitely Mandy. Look, we knew you two were having problems. When we saw her, I just assumed you'd called it quits. In fact, that's why I'm calling today. I wanted to check in and see how you were doing."

"Did you recognize the guy?" I asked, while trying not to choke on the giant fucking knot in my throat.

"No. Neither of us had ever seen him before."

"And you're sure they were together?"

"God, I can't believe this is happening. I'm so damn sorry," he stammered.

"Hey, man, none of this is your fault. I would have thought the same. Listen, I've got to run. I'll catch up with you once I'm back in town." Before he could reply, I disconnected the call. Then, tossing my phone onto the nearest table, I collapsed onto the chair, lowered my elbows to my knees, and dropped my head to my hands. My wife was cheating on me. I'd just bought her a house. The thought that she was nailing some dude behind my back and that she'd lied to my face about it, was just so... wrong. So unbelievably beyond fucked up. I couldn't even begin to wrap my brain around it. The Mandy I knew could hold a

mean grudge, but would she really cheat on me? A noise caught my attention. Lifting my head, I noticed Bobby standing in the doorway.

"You okay?" he asked. Bobby was one impressive dude. Hell, LASH as a whole was impressive, but especially Bobby.

"I thought you took off," I muttered, deflecting his question.

"Cas left this morning, but I still had some stuff to cover with Chaz and Olivia. I'm heading to the airport in a little while. I just wanted to stop by and say goodbye." Chaz had been through hell. The fact that he was making plans with his girlfriend and not cowering in a corner somewhere was a testament to his strength. Bobby stared at me for a long moment before asking, "You sure you're okay?" I was on the verge of blowing him off but something made me change my mind.

"I think my wife is cheating on me." His eyes widened in surprise. Clearly this wasn't what he expected me to say.

"What makes you think that?" he asked in his matter of fact way.

"Some friends of mine saw her out with...another guy," I barely managed to get out.

"Want me to look into it?" My eyes snapped to his. Did I want him to look into it? Did I really want to know?

"This is so fucked up," I whispered.

"But you need to know," he responded for me.

Yes, I needed to know...

Jonas had tried to reach out after that, but I wasn't ready to talk. *I should give him a call*, I thought as I pulled into the main drive. One of Quinn's three cats greeted me as I stepped from the car. With a light "Meow" and a leg rub, she followed me up the steps and onto the porch.

"Quinn told me not to feed you, little pussy," I murmured, smiling at my play on words. Whether Quinn agreed with me or not, I knew I was a funny guy. I would be even funnier when I was finally rid of my ball and chain. I never looked at marriage that way. I always thought of it as more of a union. A "together we stand, united we fall" kind of thing. I'd fallen alright.

After unlocking the door, I told the cat to stay. *These cats are ratters.* Quinn had said. *They may look domesticated, but don't let them fool you. They have wicked claws and are outside animals only.*

"Meeeeeeowwwww," kitty responded as I made my way inside. My parents were too sophisticated for pets. Elaine came home once with a baby kitten and my father made her give it to the maid. She cried for weeks. No wonder we were all so fucked up.

I glanced at the Kinley family photos on the way up the stairs. Quinn favored her father but she had her mother's eyes. The Kinley's were a nice-looking family. Then again, so were the Walkers. Behind every picture was a story. Some good. Some bad. All of ours were fake. Fake smiles. Fake happiness. Fake life.

My room faced the back of the house, while Quinn's faced the front. The two were divided by three other bedrooms and a large sitting area in the middle. I was curious about Quinn's room but snooping wasn't my style. Tomorrow my piano would arrive. Tonight, I would have to settle for second best.

After a quick change of clothes, I snagged my guitar from the stand. Then I headed down the back stairs to the pool house. I wanted to make sure the acoustics sounded as good as I'd claimed.

In the middle of playing a song Chaz and I wrote together, I heard the sliding glass door open.

"Playing in the dark?" Quinn's sultry voice bounced off the walls and hit me right where it counted. Yep, the acoustics were just fine. I paused long enough to take her in and noticed the bottles of beer in her hands. "I didn't know you played guitar." Her excited tone made me smile.

"I can do a lot of things," I replied, wondering if she'd catch the double meaning.

"I bet you can." Her dry comeback made me laugh. She'd caught it, alright. She held up one of the two beers, and with a challenging expression on her pretty little face, said, "I'll trade you a song for a sip." Damn, this woman was potent.

Reaching out my free hand, I grabbed the empty chair from beside me and dragged it around to face me.

Nodding to the chair, I told her, "If I'm only sipping, that could be a lot of songs."

With that electric smile on her face, she settled onto the chair. "I'm up for the challenge, if you are." Damn, but I did like a good challenge.

"Okay, but only if I get to choose every other song." There was only so much country music I could take.

"Deal," she said, handing me the beer.

Taking a swallow, I asked, "What do you want to hear first?"

"How about 'You Never Even Called Me by My Name?'" Shit. I knew the song, but couldn't she pick something a little more current?

"Wow, talk about old school. David Allen Coe's got to be at least a hundred and fifty years old by now," I teased.

Her smile faded into a shrug, and I thought, *Damn, Evan. Why don't you ruin it before it even begins, you dumb ass.* Out of the blue, a fleeting thought skittered across my mind. Was this why Mandy wanted out? Did I ruin all the fun for her? Then I realized what I was doing...again. The why of it no longer mattered. Instead of working through our problems, she'd cheated her way out, and because of that, she'd cheated me. So why was I still beating myself up about it?

"It was a favorite of my dad's. You don't have to play it." Quinn's murmured response snapped me back to the moment at hand. The sadness behind her confession felt like a punch to the gut and I suddenly had the desire to take it from her. To ease her pain in any way I could.

"For your dad," I said, and with a nod of my head, I started playing. The look of awe on her face was priceless. In all the years I'd been with Mandy, she'd never asked me to play for her and I'd never offered. Yet, across from me sat this wild-haired woman who I'd known all of three seconds and she'd already gotten to the soul of me.

Quinn's eyes widened in surprise when I started singing the first verse. By the time I hit the second verse, she was singing along with me. Neither of us knew the rest, so we just made up the words.

"Oh my God! That was so fun and amazing!" she exclaimed when the song was over. *Sadness banished*, I thought.

Winking at her, I asked, "What? You assumed it was all about the looks?"

"Yeah, that's it," she shot back at me and we both laughed.

I took another swallow of beer and smiled. "My turn. I heard this on the radio a few days ago and it made me think of you." I didn't tell her I'd spent three hours learning it. Some things were meant to be kept secret. I had a lot of those. With my eyes glued to hers, I began to play the Revivalists "Wish I Knew You." I didn't expect her to know the song. To my surprise, she joined in on the first verse. Pretty soon, we were on our feet—me singing and playing and Quinn dancing circles around me while chiming in on the chorus.

Her next song choice was Sam Hunt's "House Party" and I followed it with a dumbed down version of Meltdown's "Avalanche." After that, it was a free for all—her shouting out songs for me to play and me surprising her with a few of my favorites. A little after four in the morning, we decided to call it quits.

"Why aren't you the lead singer in your own band?" she asked on our way up to the house. "I mean, no offense, but I think you're a far better singer than Grant Hardy." Oh, the power those words could wield. Quinn's hit hard and burrowed deep, straight through the hurt and the heartache, until they reached the heart of me.

"I'll tell Grant you said so," I teased, while still trying to catch my breath from her comment.

"Don't you dare," she laughed. When we reached the top of the stairs, she turned and hit me with that smile. "Thanks, Evan. I really needed this tonight."

The urge to pull her in, to show her what this night and her kind words meant to me, to taste her, overwhelmed me to the point of almost doing something we would both regret.

"Goodnight, Quinn," I managed to say. Before she could respond, I was through my bedroom door.

"Goodnight," I heard her say as the door closed between us.

"Shit," I whispered to the empty room.

CHAPTER FOUR

"In Color"

Quinn

The moment I stepped inside my room, the adrenaline rush cut out. With a deep sigh, I shuffled across the floor and collapsed onto my bed. *Don't get attached, Quinn. He's married, and even though he claims he's getting divorced, he's not until he is,* I told myself as I nestled into the covers. That didn't stop me from thinking about him...or his voice, or those sexy as sin tattoos, or his lips, or those eyes...God, those gorgeous green eyes. I could drown in them.

I wasn't an overly spiritual kind of gal, but I firmly believed that things happened for a reason. Evan Walker wasn't here by chance. I knew this to the depths of my soul.

My eyes drifted shut as I replayed tonight in my head. The look of surprise on Evan's face when I stepped through the sliding glass door. His fingers as they danced across the guitar strings. The sound of his incredible voice. The way his body moved to the rhythm of the music. Dancing with him. Laughing with him. His shocked expression when I told him he was a better singer than Grant. He didn't realize it, but he'd given me a gift. For a brief moment, my world had stopped spinning. I wasn't thinking about my parents or worrying about the house or the bar. I was fully grounded in the moment and it felt unbelievably right. No, Evan Walker was here for a reason. I just didn't know what that reason was.

Pulling the pillow over my head, I let my mind wander to the night Evan showed up at Margo's to apologize for being such an epic turd. God, I was so raw that night. Mom had just dropped a huge bomb in my lap and I didn't know what to do. I loved my little apartment. I loved the life I'd carved out for myself, but deep down, I knew that if I let her sell the house, I would regret it. My memories of my father...my entire childhood, were sheltered inside those walls. To let them go would be like losing a part of me. I was so angry at her for making me choose and beyond hurt that she was choosing her friend and Florida over her own daughter. Couldn't she see how much I needed her? Did she not care? I was such a mess that night. And then he showed up...

"Look who just walked in," Alex-Ann murmured under her breath. Glancing over at the door, I spotted him. Evan Walker, the rock star. Tonight, of all nights, this was the last thing I needed. I'd rather scrub the bar floor with a toothbrush than to go head to head with king rude himself.

"I'll be back in a bit," I muttered, before slipping out from behind the bar. Jamey Johnson's velvety rich voice followed me down the hallway and past the kitchen, where I paused in front of Sam and held out my hand.

"Girl, when are you gonna learn?" he growled.

In no mood to listen to his griping, I ordered, "Give it to me, Sam." While Jamey sang about seeing life in color, our eyes locked in a mental tug-o-war.

"Fine, kill yourself for all I care," he finally barked before slapping the cigarette on the palm of my hand. With a nod of thanks, I slipped outside.

I'd barely taken my first drag when I heard the door open behind me. Seriously? Could a girl not get any privacy around here?

"If you're going to bitch at me, you're wasting your time," I chided, before taking another drag.

"Where, it is a nasty habit, I don't think I'm the one to preach," a sexy, deep, so-not-Sam, voice responded.

"Beer's inside, Rocker Boy," I dryly stated, while trying to get my heart out of my throat and back inside my chest.

"I've been called a lot of things, but Rocker Boy is most definitely a first." The sound of his laughter barreled through me.

"As I said, beer's inside." Please go, I thought.

"Thanks for clearing that up, but I'm actually looking for you." Of course, he was.

"Oh?" I asked, slowly swiveling my head around so I could see him. Yep, he was still the same mouthwateringly- fine asshole. It wasn't just one thing about him, either, but the whole damn package. Tonight, he was wearing a simple black T-shirt, jeans...and flip-flops. My eyes dropped to his feet. Hell, even those were sexy. I held my breath as he dropped down beside me.

"Look, I was a real dick the other night and I owe you an apology."

I took a drag from my cigarette and slowly exhaled. "That's sweet, darlin', but you don't owe me anything. No one owes me a damn thing," I added as an afterthought.

"Maybe not, but if you send me away feeling all guilty and shit, who knows what might happen."

"Fine. Apology accepted. Feel better now?" I asked.

"Not when you say it like that," he complained, and I couldn't help but smile. A smile that, seconds later, faded to irritation when I noticed his eyes lock on my cigarette. Here he goes, I thought.

"You know, those things really are bad for you."

"Really? I didn't know that, but thanks for the PSA. Are we done here?"

With a snort of humor, he brushed off my obvious annoyance, and said, "You look like you could use a friend. Believe it or not, I'm a good listener." However tempting his offer may be, secrets were meant to be kept and family matters were private.

"No offense, Rock Star, but talking about my problems won't fix a damn thing. And, in case you didn't know, you're kind of famous and I'm kind of not."

Smiling his deadly smile at me, he responded, "Fame is overrated, and just so you know, I'm also a person." Talk about relentless.

Smiling back at him, I gave as good as I got. "Whereas I appreciate the offer of friendship, my dance card is full right now."

"Ouch," he murmured, and I realized that, once again, I was being a bitch.

"I'm sorry," I said on a loud exhale. "That was really bitchy. I'm just having family problems right now and really don't feel like talking about it."

"You're not the only one," he muttered.

His response surprised me enough to actually call him on it. "What does a guy like you have to be worried about? I mean, really? Did you lose a couple of million on your latest tour?" The second I said it, I wanted to take it back. What was wrong with me? I had better manners than this. I opened my mouth to apologize, but he beat me to it.

"Wow, Country, you're just full of piss and vinegar tonight, aren't you?"

"Country?" I asked, rearing back far enough to look him in the eye. Big mistake. I'd forgotten how gorgeous his eyes were, how mesmerizing his tattoos were, how intrigued I was by his mere presence.

"Country," he repeated, more as a challenge than a statement.

Fine, challenge accepted. "No, seriously, what does a guy like you have to be worried about?" He leveled his green eyes on mine and I felt completely exposed. He'd come here to apologize. Why couldn't I just accept it? For the longest time, we sat on that ledge staring at each other. Until finally, he glanced away.

"Never mind. You're probably right." He moved to get up and suddenly I didn't want him to go. I really wanted to hear his answer.

Before he could get away, I reached out and touched his arm. "No, really. I want to know."

Slowly, he settled back beside me. Then he began to talk. He told me his wife had been cheating on him and that he was filing for a divorce. He talked about how stupid he felt for not seeing it. It wasn't so much the words, but his body language and the tone in which they were given. There was a sense of loneliness to him that called to me.

"My dad died last year and my mom is moving to Florida," I blurted. When he didn't respond, I kept going. "Either I take the house or she's selling it to the state."

"The state?" he questioned.

"It's more of an estate than a house," I explained. "The state will end up turning it into a museum of sorts."

"If you don't want it, let her sell it," he suggested once I was through talking.

"It's not that easy. That house is in my blood. It's where I grew up. It's my family's heritage."

"But you just said that you couldn't handle it," he pointed out.

"I can't handle it on my own," I clarified.

"Then get a housemate. Or even a live-in housekeeper." Mom had already tried to get our housekeeper, Lowis, to move in, but she didn't want to leave her house. That didn't mean I couldn't find someone else. Rock Star might be on to something.

"You looking for a place to live?" I asked, mostly teasing but kind of not.

"Shit no, Country. I got my own mausoleum to get rid of, but thanks for asking."

Evan and his brother, Ehren, stayed for beers, burgers, and a few games of pool before taking off.

First thing the next morning, I called my mother and told her I was taking the house.

The memory made me smile. My mind wandered to the night Evan showed up at Margo's and offered to move in. I'd all but given up on the idea. Alex-Ann couldn't get out of her lease and Gretchen lived with her sick mother. Hell, I'd even asked grumpy Sam. He just laughed. Then Evan stepped in to save the day. I accepted on the spot, but that didn't stop me from wondering. Why me? Where were his friends? Where was his family? Surely, with being a rock star and all, he had enough money to purchase his own place, so...why? This made me realize how little I knew about the man living under my roof. In the middle of mulling this over, I drifted off to sleep.

I woke to the sound of a truck coming up the drive. It took me a moment to get my bearings and then I remembered, *Evan's piano.* My phone rang right as I was exiting the bed. Plucking it from the bedside table, I headed to the bathroom.

The moment I saw the word "Bestie" pop up on the screen, I hit the button and said, "Girl, you are not going to believe what I did last night."

"Well, being that it's after one and you were supposed to be here an hour ago, I reckon it was good," Alex-Ann shot back at me. Damn, I'd completely forgotten about inventory.

"Shit! I'm so sorry. Let me get cleaned up and I'll be right there."

"Relax. Will said he'd inventory with me."

A few months back Alex-Ann and I decided to hire another bartender. Business was booming and neither of us had experienced a night off in months. I was planning on taking out an ad, but Alex and her make-shift sign beat me to the punch. Bartender Wanted, it said, and sat a total of three hours in Margo's front window, before Will Grange walked through the door. With his cowboy hat, alligator boots, and southern boy accent, he fit right in. After a brief interview, he had the job. Will and Alex-Ann hit it off from the get go. I thought she was going to go for it and then Baxter got dumped. Baxter. What a loser.

"Will said he'd work with me tonight if you want to take off," Alex-Ann offered. The thought of putzing around the house for the rest of the day and then making a home cooked meal sounded really good.

"I think I might take you up on that, but only if I can return the favor."

"Deal," she responded. "Now, tell me about last night."

I told her all about the sing-along. As usual, she romanticized it. By the time I was done, she had us married with six children. God love Alex-Ann and her romantic heart.

After a quick shower, I got dressed and made my way down to the kitchen, where I discovered a fresh pot of coffee. *I could get used to this.* Smiling, I poured myself a cup. I was standing at the sink when the movers strolled past my window. I waited for Evan to follow. When he didn't appear, I refilled my cup and went looking for him.

"I let the bitch have the house and she still won't grant me a divorce," I heard him say as I neared the pool house. His eyes met mine as I stepped through the open doorway. "Hey, Quinn just walked in. Can I call you back? Yeah, I'll be there Thursday," he added before disconnecting the call.

"I'm sorry. I didn't mean to interrupt. I saw the movers leave and thought you might need some help," I stammered as I took in the massive, glossy black piano parked in the middle of the room. He wasn't joking when he said it was big. To the right of the piano sat three metal stands, each holding a guitar.

"What's that?" I asked, nodding to the electrical tower thingy on the other side of the piano.

"That's a keyboard," he answered, pointing to what looked like a mini piano, "and this baby," he pointed to the second contraption, "allows me to record what I'm playing." The thought of him recording songs...in my house, did funny things to my insides.

While brushing the dust from the top of the piano, I asked, "Are you...uh... going somewhere this weekend?"

"Huh?" His brow furrowed in confusion.

"The phone call. You said something about Thursday?"

"Oh, yeah. That was Chaz. Well, first it was Olivia and then it was Chaz.

"Olivia?" I asked.

"Chaz's girlfriend and Meltdown's new manager," he responded. Seeing the confusion on my face, he gave me an eye-crossing story about managers betraying managers, Chaz getting blackmailed by a security guard, and Olivia almost getting killed. My eyes grazed over the brightly colored ink covering most of his body as I half-listened to his story. I was so absorbed by a particular design on his neck that I barely registered when his voice faded to silence.

"So...uh...Olivia is your manager," I stated after an abnormally long pause.

"You didn't catch a single word of that, did you?" he asked, his voice tinged with humor.

"In my defense, there was a lot to catch," I answered, and smiled when he busted into laughter.

"Okay, I'll dumb it down. Olivia is Meltdown's manager and Chaz's girlfriend."

"The same one from the burger night, correct?" His lip curled and it was my turn to laugh.

"Anyway, to answer your question, Olivia set up a benefit concert in Austin this weekend. You can come if you want." As much as I would love to take him up on his offer, I couldn't leave Margo's for an entire weekend. It wouldn't be fair to Alex-Ann or the rest of my staff.

"Thanks, but I can't."

"Margo's?" he asked.

"Yeah. It's kind of hard to get away for the weekend when you own your own bar."

I started to ask a question, but then his phone rang.

"I should get this," he murmured, his eyes on his phone screen. Before I could respond, he was already deep in conversation.

On the way back to the house, I remembered dinner. Smiling, I thought, *I'll just have to pay Rock Star another visit. Maybe he'll even play the piano for me...*

CHAPTER FIVE

"In My Blood"

Evan

"Hey, Stan, what's up?" I asked as I watched Quinn drift back up to the main house.

When I finally pulled my head out of my ass and decided to hire a lawyer, I chose not to go through my dad. At Chaz's suggestion, I called Grant. After explaining the situation to him, he hooked me up with the label's legal team and they steered me to Stan. I liked Stan as a person, but I wasn't sold on his legal abilities, just yet.

"I got a call from opposing counsel today and it seems that Amanda would like her car back," Stan drawled in his thick Texas accent.

"Yeah? Well, I'd like a divorce. Sometimes we can't get everything we want, can we?" My abrupt response gave him pause. *Good.* He should have told opposing counsel to go fuck themselves.

"I realize you're frustrated, Mr. Walker, but we might be able to use the car as a bargaining chip." We could, if I hadn't already gotten rid of it.

Over Christmas break—the same break my brother tried to tell me my wife was cheating and we ended up at Margo's for the first time—I flew home with the intention of fixing my marriage. My plan was to seduce Mandy into forgiving me by showering her with gifts, one of those being a candy-apple red Porsche Cayenne. The Porsche was such a hit that she forgave me on the spot. During the afterglow of our make-up sex, she informed me that she wanted us to make a fresh start. When I asked what she had in mind, she hit me up for a new house. New car, new home, fresh start. Why not? By break's end, not only were we back together, but we were the proud owners of a brand-new home. Yep, just slap a giant S on my forehead and call me "Sucker." My guilt for leaving had blinded me to what was really happening. Case in point—the car and the house. Not anymore...

"It's hard to negotiate with something you don't have, Stan. I guess Mandy will have to find another means of transportation." In an attempt to be funny, I suggested she borrow her boyfriend's car. Stan didn't laugh. Then again, Stan never laughed. I wasn't sure if he even knew how to.

"That's too bad," he commented. No, it wasn't. *I* should've never bought her the car in the first place.

"On your call to opposing counsel, did you happen to mention the phone calls?" The woman seriously needed to stop calling me. If not for the hassle, I would have changed my number by now.

"Did you block the number, like I suggested?" he asked.

"So far, I've blocked four different numbers, Stan, and she still keeps calling."

"I mentioned it to her attorney. She said she would advise

her to stop, but that's all she could do. It might behoove you to change your number," he advised. *No shit.*

Stan mentioned having another meeting to get to and ended the call. I was really starting to detest talking to him. All it did was dredge up the past. A past I wanted to forget...

Two days after Bobby confirmed my wife was cheating on me, I flew home to confront her. I didn't bother to call and tell her I was coming. Anything I needed to say had to be done in person.

The moment I stepped foot through the door, I felt like a stranger. New house? New start? Fucking bullshit. As I took in the ridiculously ostentatious living room, I tried to find a semblance of who we once were. Where were the framed pictures? What happened to all of the little trinkets and things we'd collected over the past nine years? Now that I thought about it, where was my fucking piano? It was as if everything that made us who we were had been erased. That's when it hit me. This was deliberate, her intention all along...this was my punishment for leaving.

"You're home." Her words floated softly across the expansive living room. I was somewhere, but it sure as hell wasn't home. Suddenly, the anger I'd been nursing for the past two days was gone and in its place was a bone-crushing hurt.

"Why?" I barely managed to get out.

I watched her head slightly tilt and her lashes flutter, both of which I used to think were sexy. "Why what?" she asked. And that's when I saw her. I mean, truly saw her. This woman, in her fancy clothing and frosted-blonde hair, the woman I'd tried so hard to love, wasn't my wife. She was a complete stranger.

"I gave you everything I had—diamonds, cars, houses— everything. I just want to know why?" Her brow creased in confusion as she took a step in my direction. My hand shot up to stop her. I didn't want her anywhere near me.

"Evan, what's wrong? You're scaring me." Her sweet voice,

the same voice I'd come to love, now sounded manipulative and calculating. The blinders were off and for the first time I was actually seeing her for what she was. I had to give it to her, she was good. Too good. My sister called it. My brother called it. Hell, even Chaz had called it. But not me. No, I'd been wandering around in the darkness, bound by vows, and blinded by feelings that didn't really exist.

"What's wrong?" I asked. "Tell me, Mandy, have you ever been to the Roundabout?" She blanched at my question, her face turning ghost-white. My heart seized in my chest. She knew. I could see it in her eyes.

"What's the Roundabout?" she asked.

"Hmmm, let me see. The bar where Jonas and Livy saw you... with your boyfriend," I harshly bit out. Her lips twisted as if she'd swallowed something sour. I don't know what I expected, a confession, maybe some tears, but certainly not anger.

"You had me followed? You have some nerve," she hissed. Stunned by her reaction, I just stood there staring at her. "You left me!" she shouted. "You think I don't know what goes on after concerts? You and your buddies all revved up and needing a place to stick your...dicks." She pointed at my crotch and let out a growl of frustration. "Why do you think I wanted out? Because I knew you were cheating on me!" Wait what? What the hell?

I was so shocked by her response that it took me a minute to react. "You've lost your mind. Believe it or not, you are the only woman I've slept with...in nine years."

"Liar," she snapped.

"I'm not lying. Ask anyone on the tour and they'll tell you." Her response was a glare. "You didn't want out of our marriage, you just wanted to see how far you could push me. If I say I want out, Evan will buy me diamonds. If I do it again, he'll buy me a

car or even a new house. I wonder how far the sucker will go?"
I mocked.

A caustic sounding laugh flew from her lips. "Yeah right,
blame this shit on me."

Was she fucking serious? "Blame you? People saw you with
another man, Mandy! I have proof that you've been cheating on
me for months! Hell, yes, I blame this shit on you!"

"You left me!" she screeched.

"I was on tour. That's my job. That's how we can afford
to live in this...house! And what do you do? You run out and
immediately cheat on me?" I shot back.

"You went behind my back and tried out for that band, knowing
that I wouldn't approve. Then you left me!" she repeated. She
may be pissed that I left, but she didn't deny cheating on me. Go
figure.

"I not only apologized, but I bent over backwards to make it
right, and you know it." The force behind my words brought her
up short.

Switching tactics, she said, "You're right. You did. I'm sorry.
Look, we're both in the wrong, here, but you're home now and I
forgive you for leaving. Let's just call the past the past and start
over." Was she kidding? She'd not only made the past year of
my life a living hell, but she'd screwed around on me. Fuck that
and fuck her.

"Get out."

"What?" she whispered, her eyes wide with surprise.

"Pack your bags and get the fuck out. We...this," I made a
circle with my finger around the two of us, "is over."

"You don't mean it. You're just upset." I could see her
mentally scrambling.

"I'm way past upset. I just want you gone."

"B-but this is my house," she sputtered.

"Which I paid for...with the job I took...when I supposedly left you. Don't worry, I'll let you buy me out when we finalize the divorce."

"Divorce?" she whispered, as if the thought had never crossed her mind.

"What did you think, woman? That I would just sit by while you fuck other men?" I watched as the reality of the situation began to sink in.

"But...I love you."

"Yeah? Well we clearly have two totally different ideas of what love is. Now, pack your things and get out." Tears spilled from her eyes and rolled down her face and I wanted to scream at her, at what she'd done to us.

"I don't want—"

"You don't get it, do you? I don't care what you want. I just want you gone..."

Mandy had left, but she certainly hadn't gone away. I thought that maybe she would chill if I let her move back into the house. If anything, she'd only gotten worse. The incessant phone calls added to her latest ploy with the car, was right in line with the rest of the shit she'd pulled. The woman just didn't know when to quit. Sick of thinking about my screwed up marital situation, I pushed back from the piano and headed for the house.

In my search for caffeine, I discovered Quinn. She was bent over with her head in the refrigerator and her ass swinging in the wind. An ass that looked damn fine in the shorts she was wearing, I might add. Mandy was all tits and no ass, but Quinn had both in equal proportions.

"Quit staring at my ass," she muttered from inside the refrigerator.

"I would never," I gasped. Laughing, she closed the fridge door. With creamer in hand, she turned in my direction. I tried not to stare at her tight as hell work out top, but seriously, the thing barely covered her chest.

"I was thinking about going for a swim. You want to join me?" she asked. *Quinn in a swimsuit? Fuck yes.*

"Sure," I managed to say, once I got my tongue unstuck from the roof of my mouth.

"Annnd, I'm cooking steaks tonight, if you're interested?"

"Does a bear shit in the woods?" I asked in my best country drawl.

"Hmmm, if no one's there to see it, then how would you know? Coffee?" she asked, holding up the pot.

Nodding, I teased, "Ahhh, so you're a 'didn't see it, didn't happen' kind of gal." When she lifted onto her tiptoes to retrieve a coffee cup and one of her tits all but popped out, I nearly choked on my own saliva.

"Creamer?" she asked.

"No, thanks." Although I considered my erection to be quite impressive, something told me Quinn might find it offensive. Locking onto her earlier comment about the pool, I murmured, "I'm going to change into my swimsuit. Meet you back here in fifteen."

"Sounds good," she muttered. I waited for her head to turn before slipping through the door and up the stairs.

Fifteen minutes later, I was back downstairs with my swim trunks on and the empty coffee cup in hand. Quinn was in the kitchen filling a cooler with bottles of water and beer. She looked amazing in workout gear, but the woman absolutely rocked a bikini. Even though Mandy looked good in one, she refused to wear bikinis as she claimed they accentuated her stomach pooch, whatever that meant. Last summer, I couldn't even get her to wear a one piece. I had to admit, it was refreshing to be around a woman who wasn't insecure about her body.

An hour later, we were on floats in the middle of the pool, listening to the local rock station when my phone rang.

"Shit, I should get that," I muttered. By the time I made it to the side of the pool, the call had gone to voicemail. When I realized it was Bobby and not Mandy, I called him back. He answered on the first ring, and after complaining about my not listening to his epically long voicemail that he'd apparently left, he got down to business.

"We need to meet. The earliest Tut and I can be there is Friday." Shit, this sounded serious.

"You found something?"

"Yeah, we found a lot of somethings." *Fuck!* Tension seized my muscles and I had to fight not to panic. I didn't want to wait. I wanted to know now. Taking a few steps back, I parked my ass on one of the pool loungers. *Think, Evan. Now, in front of Quinn, is not the time to discuss this.*

"I'm going to Austin on Thursday. You can either meet me there or you can meet me back here on Sunday," I told him.

"Sunday works. What time?" he asked.

"I'll be back by mid to late afternoon."

"See you then."

"Bobby?"

"Yeah?"

"How bad is it?"

"Bad enough for me to want to discuss this in person," he replied. Before I could respond, he hung up.

"You okay?" Quinn called out.

"No."

"Want to talk about it?" She was hanging on the side of the pool, her gray eyes watching me with a concerned expression on her pretty little face.

I didn't want to talk, but I also didn't want to be rude. "That was my PI, Bobby."

"And?"

"He has something on Mandy and wants to meet face to face. He'll be here Sunday." Then it hit me what I was saying. "Shit, I didn't even think to ask if that was okay."

"Pfft, this is as much your house as it is mine. Grab two beers and come float with me."

While Shawn Mendes sang about the walls caving in and giving up, I snagged two beers from the cooler and joined Quinn in the middle of the pool.

"I met him last year," I said, handing her a beer.

"Who, Shawn Mendes?" Her unenthused tone stated that she was clearly unimpressed by my confession.

"He's actually a nice guy. H—"

"Hey," she interrupted. My eyes found hers and I lifted my brow in question. "Tell me about the call," she urged. When I didn't immediately respond, she pushed the matter. "You look like you could use a friend. Believe it or not, I'm a good listener." She followed this with a smile. Super. Now she was using my lines against me.

"You remember that, huh?" I asked.

"Like it was yesterday." Her dry as hell response made me laugh. When the laughter subsided, I thought about what to tell her. Finally, I just gave in.

"Last Christmas, I gave Mandy a new car. When I found out she was cheating, I kicked her out of the house, and with the help of Bobby's firm, I hired a local PI to repossess the car. The night I got it back, I moved it into the garage, but before I headed back inside the house, I decided to search both the glove compartment and the center console. All I found were a few receipts. On my way inside, I casually glanced over them, expecting something like the grocery store or Dairy Queen. One was from 7-Eleven and the other was from a jewelry store in Spring. It was for a man's wedding band, size 8. Just so you know, I'm a size 10." Quinn's mouth dropped open in understanding. "I didn't recognize the credit card number and she signed it with her maiden name."

Filling in the blanks, Quinn said, "So you gave it to your PI and he found something."

"Yep, and apparently, it ain't good."

"Maybe it's not as bad as you think."

"Maybe not." But we both knew it was.

The conversation drifted to Meltdown and I spent the next few hours telling her stories about my adventures with the band. She was especially interested in the Melties.

"Oh my gosh! They're exactly like Kate Hudson in *Almost Famous*," she gasped, clearly excited by this.

"Who in what?" I asked.

"Please tell me you've seen the movie *Almost Famous?*"

"Shit, darlin', you just described my life," I joked with extra twang in my southern drawl.

Her gray eyes glittered with excitement. "You really haven't seen it?"

"I really haven't."

"Whoo-wee, Rock Star! We're having movie night tonight!" she shouted, and promptly fell off her float.

That night I ate one of the best steaks I'd ever had while watching a movie that was pretty damn true to my life and enjoying the company of a woman who'd made me feel more alive in one day than all nine years of my marriage. Go figure...

Thursday came fast, and before I knew it, I was on the road to Austin. I'd spoken to Chaz a few times since he and Olivia's visit, but had yet to tell him the latest news. I also hadn't told him about Quinn. Grant and Mallory had the bigger house, so we were all crashing there. We'd have plenty of time to play catch up.

I thought about Quinn on the drive to Austin. I also thought about Bobby. I could tell the severity of the situation by his tone of voice. He had some shit to tell me—some seriously not-so-good shit. Mandy was the one who'd ruined our marriage, so why did I feel as if I was the one paying for it?

The front gate was open when I pulled into the drive, so I continued to the house. Grant and Mallory had a killer pad, but I preferred Quinn's giant porches and antebellum style over their more modern Austin stone. I was halfway to the door when I heard the barking from inside. *Hellion,* I thought with a smile. I tried to think back on the last time I'd seen her. Had it really been a year?

The door swung open right as I stepped up to press the bell and before me appeared a very pregnant Mallory.

"Evan's here!" she shouted over her shoulder, then pulled me in for a hug.

"Hey gorgeous. Pregnancy looks good on you," I murmured in her ear.

"I want this baby out of me," she whispered back at me, and we both laughed.

"Get your grubby paws off my man," Grant told his wife. Mallory gave me another tight squeeze before passing me off to her husband. "Good to see you, man," Grant said, slapping me on the back. Hellion, who now looked more like a mix between a terrier and a schnauzer, circled our legs while barking like crazy.

An hour later, the rest of the gang had arrived, and I had to admit, I'd missed the hell out of them.

That night over dinner, after Olivia and Chaz had surprised us with Olivia's ridiculously large engagement ring, we'd heard all about Nash and Rowan's wedding plans, and Grant and Mallory's birth plans, all eyes drifted to me.

"Well?" Rowan asked.

"Well what?" I asked, pretending innocence.

"Talk, fucker," Chaz said, pinging me on the side of the head with a piece of bread. It had to come out sometime. It might as well be now.

"Fine. As I'm sure you all know by now, Mandy and I are permanently calling it quits."

"The bitch was cheating," Chaz interjected. I shot him a glare and smiled when Olivia smacked him on the chest.

I went on to tell them about the house and the car.

"You didn't tell me she'd moved back in," Chaz scolded.

"You didn't ask."

"You're living in the same house?" Olivia asked, clearly confused by this.

"Hell no."

"So where are you living?" Mallory questioned.

"With a friend."

"What friend," they collectively asked.

"Yeah, what friend?" Chaz pressed.

Here goes nothing, I thought, and answered, "Her name is Quinn."

"Quinn!" Chaz and Olivia both exclaimed.

"I so called it!" Chaz shouted, while pumping his fists in the air like an idiot.

"You did not! You said Quinn was too cool for Evan," Olivia argued.

"Thanks, dick," I muttered to Chaz's howl of laughter.

"Quinn?" Grant asked, and Chaz and Olivia both launched in, telling the table all about burger night at Margo's.

"I knew you were into her," Chaz stated, still laughing.

"I'm not into her. I'm simply living in her house and helping her when she needs it," I argued.

Olivia giggled. "Uh-huh"

"Think what you want, but I can't be into Quinn or anyone else until those divorce papers are signed, and after talking to Bobby, I doubt that's going to happen anytime soon," I informed them. The room instantly sobered.

"What's up with Bobby?" Nash asked. It took another ten minutes for me to fill them in.

"No more leaving us in the dark," Mallory scolded when I was through talking. "We're all family here and you, my dear, are a major part of it." Scanning over the table, she said, "You all are. Just because we're doing separate things right now doesn't mean we aren't still a family."

"About that," Grant said, giving his wife an indulgent smile. "I don't know about you guys, but I'm going insane. Mallory is sick of me moping about the house. Hell, I've written at least a dozen songs."

"Same here," Chaz and Nash both confessed. I hadn't written dick.

"Here's what I'm thinking," Grant said. "After Nash and Rowan's wedding and the baby comes, we get the band back together here at the house for a series of recording sessions, like we did before. We won't tell anyone about it until the album is complete."

"Then you can announce a new album and a surprise tour!" Olivia exclaimed, clapping her hands. "Oh my God, this is brilliant!"

Grant laughed at her obvious enthusiasm, then turning to us, he asked, "What do you all say?"

Nash stared at his wife to be. "Rowan?"

"I say yes, but only if I can go this time," she answered.

"I'm taking the baby!" Mallory chimed in.

"Well, you know I'm there!" Olivia exclaimed.

"If she's there, I'm there," Chaz cut in.

"Evan?" Grant asked. It was then that it hit me. My dream wasn't over. It was just beginning...

Meltdown was going back on tour.

CHAPTER SIX

"What Ifs"

Quinn

My mother called the day Evan left for Austin. I'd been avoiding her calls, partially because I was still mad at her for leaving and partially because I hadn't yet told her about Evan. Mom and I hadn't always seen eye to eye on things, but I'd always respected her. She lost some of that respect when she left, and I wasn't sure she would ever get it back. It was like Dad's death somehow freed her, and at the same time, it caged me. I was trapped in a house filled to the gills with memories of my father, our family, and the life we'd built together. Yes, it was my cage, but it was also my comfort, if that made any sense. I wasn't sure it did. As angry as I was with her, though, I had to admit that I missed the old bat.

"How's Florida?" I asked.

"Quinny, girl, you would love it here. Everything blooms and it's so tropical. You need to come for a visit. Verna has an extra bedroom facing the garden with your name written all over it."

"I'm sure I would love it," I unenthusiastically responded, while at the same time rolling my eyes. "Unfortunately, I'm a business owner, which means I can't take off at the drop of a hat, so Florida will have to wait." If I could take off, it sure as hell wouldn't be to Florida. It would be to Austin with a sexy, tatted rock star.

She sighed loud enough for me to hear. "Oh, don't be mad at me. It's bad for your blood pressure and causes premature aging. And, I know you can't leave the bar, but that doesn't mean I can't come to you."

"To Texas?" I asked, hoping I'd misunderstood her.

"No, to Africa. Yes, to Texas." *God, she could be such a smart ass.* I'd put off telling her about Evan, but only because I knew she'd give me grief. It looked as if my time was up.

"A visit sounds great, Mom. By the way, I've been meaning to tell you, I have a new housemate. His name is Evan Walker. He needed a place to live and I needed help with the house, so it was a win-win for us both."

"Evan who?" she asked.

"Walker, I answered, and before you ask, he's no relation to Ethel and Obid. He is, however, slightly famous." I smiled when I said the last part. My mother did love a good story.

"Oh, famous how?" she bit.

"Well, he's the keyboardist for a rock band."

"What?" she gasped, and I secretly laughed.

"Yep, he plays for a band called Meltdown."

"And he's living in our house?"

"No, he's living in *my* house," I replied, making sure to stress the word my.

"Is it safe?" she asked on a huff.

"Yes, Mother, it's safe."

"And, please, for Heaven's sake, tell me he's not staying there for free," she added. He definitely wasn't. In fact, he was doing quite the opposite.

The day Evan called to give me a move in date, we discussed rent. I thought a thousand or so a month sounded fair. That would go far with groceries and monthly utilities. He decided that four thousand was better. I argued, and he laughed. I figured I'd have time to talk him down, but his first night here, I found a check for four thousand dollars sitting on my desk. When I approached him about it, he said he needed to do this. I wasn't sure what this was, but something told me it had nothing to do with the check in my hand. I decided to let it go...for now...

"Yes, he's paying rent," I answered.

"Good. Well, I have to say I'm rather curious, now." Of course, she was.

"He has tattoos," I warned, knowing how she felt about them. My mother disliked anything that made anyone look different. When I was in college I came home with my hair dyed blue. You would have thought I'd shaved my dang head. By the end of the weekend, my hair was brown again and all was right in Marsha's life.

"He's a rock star, Quinny. That's expected," she responded in a don't-you-know-anything tone of voice. I didn't bother to reply. We talked more about Verna and what was going on around the house before she broached the subject of visiting again.

"I was thinking of coming next month. I could help you plant some fall flowers." A pang of nostalgia rolled through me. Mom, Dad, and I used to plant flowers together at the start of every fall. It would be nice to continue the tradition.

"I'd like that, Mom. You could even cook your famous beef stew."

We talked a few more minutes before she had to go. Apparently, she and Verna were into Hot Yoga and were going to be late for their session. I ended the call with a smile on my face. So maybe I was more than marginally over her defection.

That afternoon, I felt slightly out of sorts. It was strange being alone. Our housekeeper, Lowis, wasn't due until tomorrow, which meant the house was all mine. In the past I would have thrown on a suit and floated around the pool, but that just made me think about Evan. Then again, everything made me think about Evan. Last night before bed I almost Googled him. Not because I wanted to stare at pictures of him—even though I kind of did— but because I wondered what his wife looked like. What woman in her right mind would cheat on a man like Evan Walker? Not a sane one, that's for sure. And one only had to guess why she was buying a man's wedding band. Cheating hussy. If it was me, I would have gone on tour with him. That thought hung in my brain for a minute longer than necessary. Would I really quit everything to go on tour with my rock star husband? I kind of think I would. Well, it was a good thing I didn't have to worry about that.

I ended up spending the afternoon curled on the sofa, listening to the local rock station, of all things, and reading one of my mother's Victorian love novels.

That night, work was unusually slow. Alex-Ann and I were in the middle of wiping down tables when she mentioned that Baxter had paid her a little visit on my night off.

"Was Amanda with him?" I asked. If she was, I probably would have heard about it by now.

"No, he was alone."

"Why didn't you tell me?"

"It was busy, and you needed a break. I didn't want to bother you," she replied with a shrug. I could tell by her tone that something was off.

"Hey, Will!" I called out.

"Yeah?" he answered from the other end of the bar, where he was busy flirting with a woman who was old enough to be his grandma.

"Alex and I are taking a break. If you need anything, send Gretchen out back to get us!" I told him. Then, grabbing Alex-Ann's hand, I dragged her through the bar. When we passed by Sam, I noticed a cigarette sitting on the ledge. "Thanks, Sam!" I shouted. Not bothering to wait for an answer, I continued down the hall and out the door with my best friend in hand.

"Talk," I said, once we were both settled with our butts on the stoop.

"I love this song," she murmured, clearly evading my order. Truth be told, I liked it too. Kane Brown had one sexy, deep voice. Evan's had more rasp to it, but it wasn't near as deep. Once again, I was thinking about Evan. *Stop*, I told myself.

"I can't help if you don't talk," I coaxed.

"I'm in trouble, Quinny," she said in a defeated, barely- there tone of voice. This got my attention. Alex-Ann was a fighter, if there ever was one. No matter the situation, the girl had a solution for it.

"Are you in trouble with Baxter?" I asked, thinking that I would wring that boy's neck, if she said yes.

"He came to tell me that he and Amanda were back together, and the wedding was back on, as if I didn't already know that," she scoffed.

Pulling her in for a hug, she murmured, "I'm sorry."

"He threatened me," she whispered against my shoulder.

I pulled back in order to see her face. "What do you mean, he threatened you?"

"Not threatened as in an I'm-gonna-kill-you, kind of way, but more of a don't-tell-my-future-wife-I-nailed-you-on-a-dirty-bar-floor, kind of way," she amended. Forget about Baxter's neck. I was going to wring Alex-Ann's!

I yanked my arm back so fast she nearly toppled over. "You said you had wall sex, Alex-Ann."

"That was before the floor sex," she admitted on a sigh.

"Shit, girl! How many times did you two do it?" At the rate she was going, I was going to have to fumigate.

"Twice, but that's not why I'm in trouble."

"Oh, lawdy. Do I even want to know?"

"I'm late, Quinn. I was supposed to start last week." It took a moment for her words to register.

"Oh, God, Alex, noooooo," I groaned, dropping onto my back. Neither of us said a word. We just listened to Kane singing about his what ifs. Shit. This was bad.

When the song switched to Keith Urban's, "John Cougar, John Deere, John 3:16", Alex-Ann asked, "Is this song about the bible?"

"Not sure, but Lord knows you could certainly use a little Jesus right now," I muttered.

"Ha-ha," she mocked, smacking my leg. As she sang along to the song, I decided that I liked Keith Urban. The line about being baptized in rock-n-roll reminded me of Evan. I needed to stop thinking about Evan.

"I guess I need to take a test," she finally admitted, once the song was over.

I patted the pavement next to me. "Come down here with me." When she dropped onto her back beside me, I stared deep into her eyes, and asked, "Why didn't you use protection?"

"I don't know. We were already there before I even thought of it, and then it was too late." Neither of us needed to say more. The damage was already done.

My hand found hers and I gave it a squeeze. "You need to

take the test, but please, know that you're not alone. Whatever happens, I'm with you all the way, okay?"

"Okay. I love you," she whispered.

"I love you, too."

We discussed her taking the test sometime over the weekend before heading back inside.

It wasn't until the drive home that I thought about the cigarette. Today made three days in a row that I'd gone without one. Evan was rubbing off on me.

The next day I made sure to keep busy. I grocery shopped and paid bills in the morning and helped Lowis around the house in the afternoon. When she asked whether she should clean Evan's room or not, I had no idea how to respond. At her suggestion, I sent him a text. *—Hey, Rock Star, do you want Lowis to clean your room?*

His reply came immediately — *Is this your way of saying you want to snoop?*

A humor filled snort shot from my mouth— *I did that the day you left. I like the sexy unitard, by the way. You'll have to model it for me some time,* I replied, laughing like a goof.

—I'll wear it at our next pool date, he replied. My laughter died at the word "date." Shit. What was I doing? Flirting with my married housemate, that's what.

—So, should Lowis clean your room or not? I typed.

—Tell her to wait until next week when there's more to clean, he wrote back. A minute later, my phone pinged with another message. *—See you Sunday*, it said. I didn't bother to reply.

Saturday morning, Alex-Ann showed up with donuts and a box of pregnancy tests. With a donut in hand, I followed her to the bathroom. Now came the hard part.

"Promise you'll help me through this?" she asked as she squatted over stick number one.

"You know I will."

While waiting for the results, she told me that she wasn't planning on telling Baxter.

"Don't you think he has a right to know?" I asked.

"Not when he's married to her, he doesn't. That woman is toxic. Lord knows what she'd do to my baby." She was right about Amanda being toxic, but I disagreed. Baxter should know he was going to be a father. I didn't mention this to Alex-Ann. She already had enough on her plate.

While she paced back and forth in front of the bathroom sink, I parked my ass on the floor in the hallway outside and finished my second donut. I'd just swallowed my last bite when she picked up the stick and let out a shriek.

"What?" I gasped, jumping to my feet.

"Look!" She shoved the test in my hand. "I'm not preggers!"

My eyes dropped to my hand and I noticed I was holding the pee end of the thing. "Ewww, Alex-Ann! Now I have pee fingers," I whined, tossing it back at her.

"I'm not pregnaaaaaaant!" she sang from the tops of her lungs as she chucked it in the trash. While she serenaded me, I hauled it to the kitchen to wash the pee off my hands.

That afternoon, in celebration of Alex-Ann not being with child, we put on our swimsuits, cranked up some music, and floated in the pool.

Margo's was slammed that night and we were down a waitress. If that wasn't bad enough, Baxter decided to make an appearance. He claimed he was supposed to meet Amanda, but I knew the truth. He didn't just want to eat his cake. He wanted Alex-Ann's, too. Well, he wasn't getting it. By midnight, he was too drunk to drive. I was about to call a cab when Amanda walked in. Wearing all black, she looked like she belonged at a Goth concert.

"You're late, and he's drunk," I said when she stepped up to the bar.

"Hey baby," he said, though it came out sounding more like Bailey.

"Sorry, lumpkins, traffic was worse than I expected," she told him. Then turning to me, she asked, "Can I get a glass of water."

"Sure, and then you need to leave," I told her. I felt her glaring at me as I filled the glass.

"Why?" she asked, staring at Alex-Ann who, thankfully, was busy with other customers.

"You know why, but if you'd like me to spell it out for the entire bar to hear, I can."

"Let's go," Baxter said. At least one of them had some sense.

"No, she can't kick us out. We didn't do anything," Amanda argued.

Baxter turned to me and said, "I'm sorry. I shouldn't have come here tonight."

"No, you shouldn't have, and if you're smart, you won't be back in the future," I warned.

"Are you kidding?" Amanda shouted.

Baxter nodded that he understood. Then he pulled his screaming mad, bitch of a fiancée across the floor and out the door.

"Don't let the door hit ya where the good Lord split ya!" Alex-Ann shouted after them.

By the time I got home that night, I was barely functional. That's what a day of sun and a night of drunkards would do for you. As my dad would say, I was done tuckered out.

"Hey, Pookie," I murmured to the orange tabby hunkered by the garage, while unlocking the kitchen door. Normally, he was all over my feet. *Something must have spooked him*, I thought as I stepped through the door. After locking it behind me, I dropped my purse in a chair and crossed over to the cabinet, where I grabbed a glass and filled it with cold water from the fridge. On my way past the living room, I noticed a cushion on the floor. It took a second to fully register. Why was the living room sofa cushion on the entry hall floor? I picked up the cushion, took a step inside the room, and froze. My heart shot into my throat. The room had been turned upside down. Someone had broken into my house. For all I knew, they were still here.

"Shit," I whispered. Then I was on the move. Within seconds, I had my purse in hand and was running to my car. Once I was safely inside with the doors locked, I pulled out my phone and called 9-1-1. The dispatcher kept me on the line until the police showed.

Two officers went inside while a third stayed with me. It didn't take them very long to search the place. Apparently, the burglar only hit two areas of the house; the living room and Evan's bedroom. I walked through the house with them and didn't find anything missing. At least, as far as I could tell. The police thought I had probably scared the intruder before they had a chance to do any real damage.

When I explained that Evan wasn't due back from Austin until tomorrow—or rather later today, being that it was after three in the morning—they suggested I either sleep somewhere else or call a friend. They would come back sometime later in the day to talk to Evan.

On my way to Alex-Ann's, I called Evan.

"Hlo," he groggily answered. I'd clearly woken him up. Just hearing his voice made me feel better. It also brought on the tears. Pretty soon, I had to pull over to the side of the road. The entire time I cried, Evan chanted in my ear.

"Talk to me. Please let me know you're okay." After a minute or so of listening to me sob, he shouted, "For fuck's sake, woman, you're scaring me!"

"S-s-someone broke into the house," I managed to get out through the tears.

"What? Are you okay? Please tell me you weren't there?" Surprisingly, the panic in his voice is what calmed me.

Inhaling deeply, I replied, "I was at work and I'm fine. They ransacked the living room and your bedroom, but nowhere else. The police felt they might have been looking for something. They didn't want me to stay by myself, so I'm heading to Alex-Ann's."

"I'm leaving now. Text me the address and I'll drop by and pick you up at Alex-Ann's when I hit town."

"What? No, don't leave. I'm fine. It just scared me. I'm good now."

"Text me the address, Country. I'll see you in a few," he replied. Then he disconnected the call.

Evan was coming home.

CHAPTER SEVEN

"I Feel Like I'm Drowning"

Evan

The minute I hung up with Quinn, I began packing. It took no more than ten minutes for me to shove my things in my bag and get out the door. By the time I reached my car, I was physically shaking. Quinn's call had rattled me. Someone broke into her house. Just the thought made my blood run cold. She was somewhere on the side of the road, scared out of her mind, and crying, while I was miles away and helpless to do anything about it.

"Fuck!" I shouted, slamming my hands on my steering wheel. I needed to get my shit together. No, what I needed was to get to Quinn as fast as humanly possible.

It wasn't until I hit the main highway that I realized I'd forgotten to tell someone I was leaving. I shot Chaz a quick text saying I was headed home and to let Grant know. I shouldn't have left Quinn this weekend. I knew it was the panic talking, but bad shit seemed to happen when I wasn't around, like my wife deciding she wanted another man.

Quinn. From what I knew of her, she was a woman who didn't easily give into emotion. Her tears told me exactly how scared she was. It ate at me that I wasn't there for her when she needed me. What surprised me more was that I even wanted to be, especially with all the shit that had been going down with Mandy.

Mandy. I knew in my gut she'd done this. She was pissed about the car and even more so because I wouldn't give her the time of day. A part of me wanted to talk to her, to try to appeal to her better side, but that was just it...she didn't have a better side. I was beginning to think she'd never had one.

Mandy and Quinn couldn't be more different. Had this been Mandy, she would have demanded I drive home immediately and then would have proceeded to punish me for months after. Not Quinn. Quinn wanted me to stay with my friends, which only made me want to leave that much more. The irony was not lost on me.

I thought about Chaz and something he'd said this weekend. He pointed out that Mandy didn't want out until after I'd made it official with Meltdown. He was right. She claimed it was because I'd lied to her, but Chaz thought it was about the money. I wasn't so sure. Chaz wasn't there the day I left for the tour. Mandy's anger wasn't about money then. She was mad she wasn't getting her way. The fact that she then went out and cheated on me is what blows my mind. Was this the first time or had she been cheating all along?

My mind wandered back to the money thing and how furious she'd been when I told her I'd hired someone to help manage the finances. Up to that point, she'd been doing it. I thought she would be happy, if not relieved, but she didn't act relieved. She was furious that I would allow some stranger to handle our money. Could this really be about money? Or was it about control? The woman definitely liked her control.

Fuck! I was going to go insane trying to figure this shit out. One thing was for sure, Mandy was a game player. When she didn't get what she wanted, she wasn't afraid to pull off the gloves and throw punches. If I could go back in time, I never would have touched her, but I couldn't, and now, here we were...

The summer after I graduated from college, I put together a demo of songs and hit the pavement looking for restaurants and bars to play. My sole focus was music.

My father, however, had a different plan. He wanted me to follow in his footsteps, to one day take over his law firm and become one of Houston's top litigators. He honestly thought I would just fall in line with his plan, that I would give up on music once and for all. What he didn't take into consideration were my feelings on the matter. I didn't want to go to law school. I would rather tend bar for the rest of my life. At least then I would be living life instead of spending it sitting behind a desk while kowtowing to a bunch of greedy assholes and cheating on my wife. Unlike my old man, my kids would know me.

That summer, when he offered me a job at his firm, I took it. Not because I gave two shits about him or the job, but because it allowed me to do what I wanted—to pursue music. For three months, I worked days and gigged nights. It was the perfect setup.

It was one of those nights that I ran into Mandy. We'd gone our separate ways after the break up but had crossed paths a time or two over the years. It was apparent we'd both changed. She was still as gorgeous as ever, but in an older, more mature way. I was the same, but slightly more serious and a hell of a lot more driven.

"It's so good to see you, Evan. Why don't you stay and have a drink with me?" she'd asked. For old time's sake I took her up on it. One beer turned into too many and by the time we landed in her bed, I was hammered. That night we had sex. That night I also, apparently, forgot to use a condom.

The next morning, I bailed, leaving her still asleep in her bed. It was a dick move, but I shouldn't have slept with her in the first place. I had no intention of rekindling our high school romance, nor did I have time for women or dating. My plan was to get my music noticed. Until that happened, I needed to stay focused.

That focus lasted until the very next week, when I saw her again. This time, she was front and center, wearing a barely-there sundress and a smile on her face. Once the show was over, she found me, and like the week before, she asked if I wanted to have drinks. I politely declined. Seeming cool with my answer, she offered to help me load my gear into my car. I wasn't stupid. I knew what she wanted, and after explaining that I wasn't looking for a relationship, I gave it to her. That night, it was in the backseat of my car. At least I remembered to use a condom that time. The week after, I nailed her behind the building and the one after that we did it in the men's bathroom. After the bathroom incident, I told her it was over and that's when she told me she thought she was pregnant.

Three weeks later, the pregnancy was confirmed. Mandy and I were going to be parents...

It was hard not to think about all the years we'd spent together. All the times I'd given into her and the ugly fights when I hadn't. I'd tried to be a good husband. Even when I'd wanted to give up on us, I still tried. If only I hadn't slept with her that night. If I'd listened to my brain instead of my dick, I wouldn't be here now. I would be racing back to a woman I could actually have. A woman with more integrity in her little finger than

Mandy had in her whole body. A woman who would never in a million years settle for being trapped inside a loveless marriage.

Thinking about what should have been was getting me nowhere, so I focused my thoughts on Bobby and Tut and our pending meeting. I almost didn't care what they had to say. I just wanted out. If I had to go broke to get rid of her, so be it. I could always make more money.

I pulled up to Alex-Ann's house a little after eight. She met me at the door with a troubled look on her face.

"What happened? Is Quinn okay?"

"She's fine. She's sleeping. She's just...worried that she scared you."

"Fuck yeah she scared me," I replied.

"No, like worried that she scared you *off*," she whispered in a conspiratorial tone. I wanted to discuss my feelings for Quinn with her best friend about as much as I wanted to get back together with Mandy—as in, not at all.

"Where is she?" I asked.

"Evan—"

"Where. Is. She." I repeated more forcefully. After an impressive eye roll and a loud sigh, she led me to Quinn, who was out like a light, and from the sound of it, sawing some seriously big logs.

"Pretty, ain't she?" she asked, her tone laced with humor. Quinn Kinley was beyond pretty. Even in sleep, with her mouth open and that God-awful sound coming out, she was gorgeous.

As if sensing us standing there gawking at her, Quinn's eyes opened.

"You're here," she sweetly murmured. Her husky, sleep filled voice and the way in which she was looking at me, as if my being there made everything in her world okay, was like a shot of ice water straight into my veins. And that's when it hit me.

I cared for this woman. Not just as a friend, but as more. She felt the same. I could see it in the way she was looking at me. *This can't happen*, I thought. Whether I wanted it or not, I was still married, and Quinn deserved better. Red hot anger surged through me.

"Let's go," I snapped. Her sleepy expression turned alert.

"Is everything okay?" The concern in her voice made me feel even shittier.

"It's fine. I just want to see the house before the police return to question me. Also, Bobby and Tut should be rolling in this afternoon and I need your help getting their rooms ready."

"Bobby and Tut?" Alex-Ann inquired.

"His PI's," Quinn told her.

"My friends," I corrected. My harsh tone stopped the conversation in its tracks. Without another word, Quinn scooted from the bed.

"I'll close Margo's tonight. Come by for dinner," she murmured to Alex-Ann on the way out the door.

"You go with Evan. I'll bring your car to you later," Alex-Ann responded.

"Don't," I said, once we were secured inside my car.

"Don't what?" she asked. I could feel her staring at me—those beautiful gray eyes, searching, questioning, wondering what was going on inside my head.

"Don't close the bar tonight." I started the car and pulled onto the main road.

"Why?"

I thought about what to say, but couldn't come up with anything good, so I settled for, "Just...don't."

"Sunday's are slow. Plus, your friends are in town. It's really no bother."

"Fucking go to work, Quinn!" I snapped in a much harsher

tone than I meant.

"Fine, I'll go." She sounded...defeated, and I suddenly wanted to punch something. No, what I wanted was to pull her to me and kiss the hurt from her lips. Taking a deep breath, I turned to find her staring out the window. *Shit.*

"Hey—"

"Leave it," she responded in the same dull tone. I didn't want to leave it. I wanted to push, to prod, to crack her wide open... just like she was doing to me, but I knew if I did, I wouldn't be able to stop. Fucking hell. What was I doing? Why was this happening now?

Ten minutes later, I turned onto the drive that led to the house. Before I had a chance to come to a complete stop, Quinn was out of the car. I'd messed up. I was frustrated and had taken it out on her.

Slowly, I got out of the car and retrieved my duffle from the back. Then I followed her. Instead of confronting the situation, like I wanted, I decided to give her a moment while I checked out the damage. The living room had pillows on the floor and drawers pulled open, but Quinn said nothing was missing. My bedroom was a mess. Drawers had been sifted through and clothes scattered, but again, nothing was missing. Then again, the only shit that mattered to me was sitting in the pool house.

The pool house.

"Fuck!" I shouted as I shot out the door and raced down the stairs.

Quinn stepped out of the kitchen as I passed by. "What's wrong?" she asked.

"The pool house!" I shouted back at her.

"Shit!" I heard her respond. My heart seized in my chest when I saw the sliding doors standing wide open.

"No. No. No. No. Nooooooo!" I shouted as I reached the

entrance and saw the destruction.

All three guitars, including the one I'd purchased with my chore money, the one that I rarely played anymore but loved beyond words, were scattered in pieces around the room.

"Oh my God," Quinn whispered behind me.

Whoever did this didn't believe in God, that's for sure. I took in my piano, my pride and joy, and noted the deep grooves carved into the shiny black surface. Scattered on the floor next to it were the remnants of my electric keyboard and recording unit. All of it had been destroyed.

"Who would do something like this?" she asked. I knew exactly who'd done this. Mandy had done this, and all because I wouldn't give her what she wanted. As I stared at the grooves gouged into the piano, I thought about the similar grooves I'd made on the brand-new hardwood floors, the same grooves I'd refused to have repaired. Yes, I knew exactly who had done this...

My very first view of our new home consisted of me following my wife from room to room as she packed her bags to leave, the entire time sobbing about how sorry she was. Then why? I wanted to scream. The why of it no longer mattered. Mandy knew how much I valued trust. Next to love, trust was the most important thing in our relationship. By allowing another man to touch her, to be inside her, she'd irreparably broken that trust. Somehow, I managed to hold it together until she was gone. It was one thing to think my marriage was over and another to know it.

Eventually, I ended up in the master bedroom. As I took in the rumpled bed sheets, I wondered if this was the first time she'd cheated or if there had been others. If so, how many? I felt as if a part of me had died. In a way it had. Why now? Why when I could finally give her everything? Wasn't I enough? No. I'd never been enough, and she'd never stopped reminding me of it. I stood there staring at that bed for who knows how long before finally giving into the grief.

Much later, I made my way across the hall to the guest bedroom, where I crashed in an exhausted heap on top of the bed.

The next morning, I woke up angry. When had I become so blind? How did I not see what was happening right in front of my face?

A shower and two cups of coffee later, I called a locksmith. Then I redecorated. I wasn't planning on keeping this place. I meant it when I'd told Mandy she could buy it from me. I thought about tossing her things onto the front lawn but couldn't bring myself to do it, so I moved them off to one corner of the living room. As a nice fuck you, she'd had the piano placed in a room adjacent to the living room. Not only was it too small, but the acoustics were nonexistent. Reverently, I stroked my fingers over the shiny black surface. At the same time, I gazed at the creamy white walls and dark wood floors. Mandy had come from nothing. I'd tried to give her the world, but no matter how hard I'd tried, I could never seem to satisfy her. In her attempt to make this place fancy, she'd erased the heart of it. Now, all that remained was a lonely, sterile existence.

Over and over, my mind kept coming back to the same thought: This never would have happened had our child survived.

I would have been a great dad, I thought as I scanned the piano for scratches, all the while fuming that she'd put it in such a crappy place. Mandy knew how much it meant to me, yet she'd shoved it off to the side—just like she'd done to me, to our marriage. I should have divorced her years ago. Why did I stay? After moving the piano bench off to the side, I attempted to roll the piano from the cramped room but couldn't get it to budge. What the hell? My eyes dropped to the legs and a growl escaped. Of course, she'd taken the rollers off, probably out of fucking spite.

The wheels were nowhere to be found, however, in my search through the kitchen drawers, I discovered some old muslin cloth. After placing it under the feet, I managed to successfully drag the piano through the open doorway and into the living room. As I reached the final destination, I noticed the muslin cloth strewn across the floor and the giant gouges left in the wake of my efforts. Oh well, there was nothing I could do about it now...

As payback, the vengeful bitch had scratched my piano. Bobby better have something good for me.

"God, Evan, I am so sorry," Quinn whispered. So was I. She waited for me to make a call to the police before following me back to the main house. On the way there, I asked about the security system.

When she explained that they didn't have one on account of her father being old school, I said, "That'll have to change. I'll get Bobby and Tut on it."

"Evan—"

"And don't worry," I continued, I'll pay for the whole thing."

"Stop."

I stopped long enough to growl, "What?" Couldn't she see that I was three seconds away from coming unglued?

"I'm sorry," she repeated.

"Don't be. This has nothing to do with you—"

"I know," she cut me off. "But I'm still sorry." She pulled me in for a hug, and I let her. I might have even hugged her back, but my mind was somewhere other than Quinn. My mind was on a woman I'd once cared for but now hated and the realization that there was a much finer line between the two than I'd ever imagined possible.

"Nash had a security system installed this past year. Bobby knows the guy who owns the company. I'll get him on it this week. This won't happen again," I said, pushing back from her touch. Before she could respond, I turned and walked away.

I was sitting on the front porch when Bobby and Tut arrived. They'd barely stepped from their car when the police pulled up. *Might as well kill two birds with one stone*, I thought as I led them through the carnage that had once been my music room. They agreed with me. This was personal. After answering their questions and receiving assurances that they would investigate further, the officers took off. By then it was well after lunch and I was running on fumes.

Bobby wanted to use the bathroom, so I showed him and Tut to their rooms. On the way downstairs, I stopped off in the kitchen and found Quinn making sandwiches. Her eyes lifted to mine and her mouth tilted into a smile when she saw me standing there. As gorgeous as it was, I saw through that smile. I saw the hurt in her gray-eyed stare...the hurt I'd put there by being an ass. Mandy deserved my anger, but this woman did not.

"I'm sorry. I was a dick. I would love it if you would take off work tonight and for all of us to do dinner together." Her brows shot to her hairline and I couldn't tell if she was irritated or surprised. Either way, it was funny to see.

"You were a total dick, but I appreciate the apology." Her dry tone and blunt delivery turned my smile into laughter. Believe it or not, I could actually admit when I was wrong.

With the tray of sandwiches in hand, she headed my way. "And, I already called and closed Margo's for the night," she whispered as she breezed past me. I followed her, laughing all the way.

While Quinn passed the tray around, Bobby jumped right in. "The receipt was legit. Amanda James purchased a man's gold wedding band, size 8, with a credit card issued to a Baxter Keen," he explained. Quinn, who was sitting next to me, started coughing.

"You okay?" I asked.

"Swallowed wrong," she wheezed. She made several hand motions indicating her need for water and bolted from the room.

"Does that name ring a bell?" Tut asked once she was gone.

I shook my head. "Never heard of the guy."

"Baxter is a yuppie financial planner who makes a decent living, owns his own house, and drives a nice car. Mandy didn't pop up until I searched his social media accounts." I watched as he typed something on his iPad. Holding it out to me, he said, "Have a look."

Shit. I didn't want to see the guy my wife had been nailing. My eyes, however, seemed to have a mind of their own, because I suddenly found myself staring down at a middle-aged man with light brown hair and a weak chin. Baxter Keen looked nothing like me. I didn't know whether to be relieved or offended by this.

"Look at the photos," Bobby instructed. I clicked onto the photo section of the page and frowned when Mandy's face popped up. As I slowly scrolled through picture after picture of my wife—all in various poses and smiling happily with her new boyfriend—I felt sick.

"Great, so you found the guy she's nailing. How does this help me?" I asked, holding out the tablet for him to take.

He nodded towards my hand. "Keep going and you'll see."

Doesn't he get it? I don't want to see.

As instructed, I continued with my search. It didn't take long to find what he wanted me to see. In this picture Mandy was front and center, with her hand in the air, and her eyes fixated on her ring finger—a finger sporting what had to be at least a three-carat diamond ring. This would be two carats more than she'd gotten from me. The caption beneath the picture read, "She said yes."

"What the hell?" I growled. "Is this some kind of joke?"

"Scroll back a few pictures," Bobby instructed.

I scrolled back until I landed on what I thought was a wedding invitation, but as I read the words, I realized it was actually a save the date.

Amanda and Baxter are Tying the Knot.
Save the date \ 10.10.18 \ Las Vegas, Nevada
That's a little over a month from now.

What game was she playing? This...picture, this whole damn situation, was absolutely ridiculous. I mean, seriously, had she lost her fucking mind? I tore my gaze from the iPad long enough to find Bobby and Tut watching me, both with expectant looks on their faces.

"She can't do this," I announced.

"She can if the divorce is finalized," Tut muttered.

"I find it kind of convenient that it's right on the heels of your appointed court date. Don't you?" Bobby asked.

Tut nodded in agreement. "Hell yes, I do. If I was you, I would stall." I didn't want to stall. I wanted out, but the hell if I was handing my money over to that cheating bitch and her weak chinned loser of a boyfriend. Still, I felt like I was missing something.

"I don't get it. If she wants money, then why break into Quinn's house and not take anything?" I asked. "And how did she find out I was living here?" The few people who knew would never tell her.

Bobby frowned. "I don't think this was about money. This was the action of a woman scorned."

"Is she still calling you?" Tut asked.

"You know, now that I think about it, she hasn't called since yesterday morning."

"Before the break in," Bobby noted.

"Maybe I should talk to her."

"No, don't. I feel like we're missing something," Bobby muttered.

"Same here," Tut chimed in.

"I don't like it either, but what would you have me do?" I asked.

"I'm not sure, but if you give us more time, we'll figure it out," Bobby answered.

"Done. As long as you're staying, I'll need you to contact the guy who installed Nash's security system. I want the best he has to offer."

"What happens if we prove Mandy did that?" Tut asked, pointing towards the pool house. Oh, she'd definitely done it. Of that, I had no doubt.

"She pays for it," I answered.

"You would actually press charges?" I could tell Bobby was testing my resolve on the issue. Cheating on me and planning to marry another guy, was one thing, but breaking into the place I was living, destroying my things, and scaring the shit out of Quinn, was entirely another. Call me heartless, but Mandy had crossed a line.

"I gotta say, this is some seriously fucked up shit," Tut muttered. I couldn't agree more.

Our conversation eventually drifted from my screwed-up marriage to their crazy friends from Charlotte. Bobby was in the middle of a funny story when we heard a knock on the front door.

"Got it!" Quinn called out, and that's when I realized she wasn't in the room with us. Now that I thought about it, she hadn't returned after her coughing fit.

"Surprise!" a familiar voice shouted from the entry hall. *What the hell?* We all three stood as Olivia and Chaz stepped into the room.

"You are shit at checking your messages," Chaz complained.

"What are you doing here?" I asked.

"You left so suddenly," Olivia answered.

"Without telling anyone where you were going," Chaz grumpily interjected.

Olivia shot him a scolding look before continuing, "Soooo, we decided to cut our trip with Grant and Mallory short in order to make sure you were okay and to see your new place." Her hands flew into the air as she shouted, "Surprise!"

"Bobby, you dickhead!" Chaz roared at the same time.

Poor Quinn just stood there with a panicked look on her face.

"Hellooooo!" All eyes turned as Alex-Ann and Gretchen appeared from the kitchen area. "We're here to see the hot meeen—" her voice faded the second she saw us all standing there. "Holy cowbells," she whispered.

My eyes immediately shot to Quinn.

"Shit," she mouthed, and I couldn't help but laugh.

Shit was right.

CHAPTER EIGHT

"Friends In Low Places"

Quinn

I stood at my kitchen counter with my hands wrist deep in hamburger meat and panicked thoughts traipsing through my head. Alex-Ann, Gretchen, and Olivia chattered in the background. I could hear them, but I wasn't paying attention to what they were saying. My mind was literally spinning. Amanda and Mandy were the same person. The *same* person. How could this be? The woman Alex-Ann and I had made a game out of hating, was not only married to the man living in my house but was cheating on him with my best friend's ex-boyfriend. Correction—was *engaged* to my best friend's ex-boyfriend. Only, she couldn't be engaged to him because she was still legally married! Bigamy might be acceptable in some parts of the world, but it sure as hell wasn't here.

Patty meat squished between my fingers as my mind wandered to the sexy as sin man living under my roof. How in the blazes was a man like Evan Walker married to a woman like that? The Amanda I knew was meaner than a snake, and now, to learn that she was also a cheating hussy... This got me wondering if Baxter knew. Somehow, I doubted it. I thought of all the times that woman had sat in my bar drinking her fancy cocktails and flaunting that gaudy ring as if she'd won the lottery, when all along, she'd been married to another man. Not just any man, either, but Evan Walker. Was she insane? The man was a flippin' rock star, for Heaven's sake!

"Quinn?" Alex-Ann called out.

"Huh?" I asked, glancing in her direction.

"What's up with you tonight? Olivia was talking to you and you're like off in la-la land."

"Sorry," I directed at Olivia, while thinking that I seriously needed to talk to Alex-Ann. She was not going to believe this craziness.

Olivia smiled at me. "No worries. You have a lot on your mind right now. I was just saying that Chaz and I are happy to stay in a hotel." Olivia, with her golden mane of hair, sleeveless T-shirt, and stylish jean shorts, looked as if she was born to be a rock star's girlfriend. You would expect her to be all stuck on herself, but the woman was sweet as pie without a mean bone in her body. That just goes to show, you shouldn't judge a book by its cover.

"Don't be silly. We have plenty of room, here," I told her as I began forming the meat into patties.

"We," Alex-Ann teased with a huge grin on her face.

I shot her a dirty look. "Evan lives here. I live here. That makes we."

"Whatever," she muttered, still smiling like a goof.

"So, you and Evan aren't...together?" Olivia asked, sounding hopeful. She really shouldn't be.

"No, but they should be. Their sexual chemistry is off the charts hawt," Alex-Ann interjected.

"I hate to break it to you, but he's married," I stated, thinking that would shut the conversation down.

"Yeah, but he hates her and they're getting divorced," Alex chimed in...again. I gave her a look of warning. "What? It's the truth," she grumbled.

"He's married," I repeated more firmly.

Now laughing, Olivia said, "Evan is a great guy."

"Not to mention hot as hell," Gretchen remarked before downing her second glass of wine. Gretchen's thick southern accent made words like hell and hot sound more like hail and hawt.

Gritting my teeth in annoyance, I placed the final patty in the dish and turned to wash my hands. I knew exactly who and what Evan Walker was. I lived with the man. I'd cooked for the man. I'd seen him in a swimsuit. I'd thought about him, dreamt about him, fantasized about him. I knew the man a hell of a lot better than they did.

"He totally has the hots for Quinn. She feels the same. She just won't admit it," Alex-Ann continued.

"For shit's sake, Alex-Ann, give it a rest!" I exclaimed, and before anyone could respond, I was out the door and racing up the stairs. I knew exactly who Evan Walker was. He was everything I shouldn't want. He was a tatted rock star, probably didn't even own a pair of cowboy boots, talked all proper, and made fun of my southern twang. He was everything I shouldn't want, but damnit...I did.

I flung myself onto my bed and let out a frustrated sigh. How he'd been married to that hussy of a woman for nine whole years was beyond me. Amanda was a rotten apple. Rotten to the core. Evan was—

My door suddenly swung open.

"I'm sorry, I pushed it," Alex-Ann announced from the open doorway, "but you should see the way he looks at you." The contrite expression on her face made me feel marginally better.

"He's married, Alex-Ann. Anyway, I don't want to talk about that anymore. Where is everyone?"

"The guys just got back from the liquor store and want to go swimming. Gretchen's gone to get our suits and I just showed Olivia and Chaz where their room is. From the sound of it, they'll be there for a while."

"And everyone else?" I primarily meant Evan.

"They're down at the pool house. Bobby was complaining about the police doing a shitty job of getting prints and wanted to collect his own, or something like that, and Evan's helping him clean the mess up. The guy is freaking huge, and have you seen Tut's eyes? Gooooooorgeous," she sang out. God love my sweet friend and her one-track mind.

I patted the bed next to me. "Close the door and come here. I have something to tell you." I waited for her to get comfortable before telling her what I'd learned. When I got to the part about Amanda and Mandy being the same person, her eyes nearly bugged right out of her head.

"Shut the front door," she gasped, her hand latching onto my arm for support.

In a voice low enough for her ears only, I shared what was bothering me. "She broke into my home and destroyed an entire room of Evan's things simply because he took her car away. She's been in my bar, like for months now, pretending to be someone she isn't. She calls the man at least ten times a day and hangs up on him. And clearly, she thinks it's okay to be engaged to one man while still married to another. I shit you not, Alex, the woman is crazier than an outhouse fly." Voicing it out loud didn't make me feel better. If anything, it only made it more real.

"Wait, did Evan or Bobby figure this out?" she asked.

"Bobby."

"How?"

"The night Evan got the car back, he searched it and found a receipt for a man's wedding band. Amanda had signed it, but it wasn't Evan's credit card number. He gave it to Bobby and Bobby traced it to Baxter. When he looked into Baxter's social media accounts, guess who was front and center? Amanda." I didn't bother to tell her I'd eavesdropped, and that's how I knew this last part.

"I should tell Evan."

"No, you should not." Her sharp response caught me off guard.

"But...I knew what was happening—" She cut me off before I could finish what I was saying.

"You're that man's safe haven right now, Quinn. If you tell him, you will just mess it all up. And think about it, what would you say? That you personally know Baxter Keen? That you've been watching his ho of a wife cheat on him for months now? That you were there the night she got engaged to another man, and even offered up free booze in celebration?" My stomach twisted with each word she spoke. She was right. I had done all of the above, but still, it felt wrong not to say something. Then again, what if she was right? I really, really liked being his safe haven. Shoot, if I was honest with myself, I would admit that I really, really liked him.

"Knock, knock!" Olivia called out. She stood in the doorway with her swimsuit on and her hair braided into pigtails looking like she'd just stepped off a runway.

"Girl, look at you," Alex-Ann squealed. A pretty blush spread across Olivia's cheeks as she laughed.

"Sorry to interrupt, but Chaz is already down at the pool and I think he and Evan are going to play for us. I didn't want you to miss out," she announced.

"Shit!" we both shouted and jumped from the bed.

While Alex-Ann went to find Gretchen and her swimsuit, I slipped on a bikini and pulled my hair up on top of my head. We all met back up in the kitchen, and with towels and food in hand, we headed for the door.

The hot August heat hit us the moment we stepped onto the back porch.

"Look!" Alex-Ann exclaimed. At first, I thought she was talking about the music pouring from the pool house, but then I saw the firelight. Those sneaky boys hadn't just gone to the liquor store. Torches, eight by my count, surrounded the pool, their flames reflecting off the water. Against the back drop of the brightly lit pool house and the dusky night sky, it looked magical.

"I love nights like these," Olivia murmured as we made our way down the stone path.

The first thing I noticed when I stepped inside the pool house was how empty it appeared without all of Evan's instruments and gadgets filling it. The second was the man seated behind the piano—a piano I thought was broken, but clearly was not. In a chair next to him sat Chaz, who appeared to be drumming away on what looked like oversized electric stove burners.

Evan's eyes lifted from the keys. I watched as they slowly drifted down my body before settling back on my face. "You good?" he asked. The heat of his stare made me flush.

In an attempt to play it cool, I said, "The torches look nice." His smile widened and my flush deepened.

"That suit looks better than nice." His sexy deep voice all but made my ovaries explode with delight.

"Are we going to play, or are you two going to sit here all-night talking shit and eye fucking each other?" Chaz asked. Embarrassed beyond words, I turned and walked out.

"Dick," I heard Evan say.

Minutes later, the music came to a halt. Not long after that Evan stepped onto the pool decking. He had his phone to his ear, but that's not what held my attention. No siree, I was all about his tatted torso and those black swim trunks that molded perfectly to his lean frame. From the looks of it, I wasn't the only one. Alex-Ann and Gretchen were practically frothing at the mouth. I suddenly had an overwhelming urge to jump into the pool and dunk them both. Before I had a chance to execute that plan, Evan ended the call and his eyes met mine.

"That was the police. They said Mandy had an alibi."

"Did they say who?" Bobby asked.

"She was apparently at a bar with her fiancé," he answered. A gasp of surprise shot up my throat with such force that I had to bite my tongue to keep it from escaping.

"She told them that?" Olivia screeched.

I glanced at Alex-Ann, who was staring straight at me. I needed to say something. As if sensing my inner dilemma, she shook her head and mouthed, "Later."

"No. She told them she was with her good friend, Baxter, and the dickhead corroborated her story. I need a beer," he muttered. Bobby held out a cold one. I watched as Evan walked over to where Bobby was standing and took the bottle.

While the guys huddled by the ice bucket, I got the grill started. Once again, my mind raced with uncertainty. I really should say something.

Chaz eventually broke away from the huddle. As he headed for Olivia, Alex-Ann whined from her pool float, "I thought you were going to play for us?"

"We were until that phone call," Chaz grumbled.

"Well, at least turn the radio on or something," Gretchen slurred.

"I'll put something on," I announced. It gave me an excuse to catch my breath.

I didn't realize he was behind me until I reached the door and saw his shadow looming over me.

"I'm pretty sure I can handle the music by myself, Rock Star," I told him. In a rather stealthy maneuver, his hand slid under mine and latched onto the handle.

"Evan—"

"She lied," he murmured, his voice laced with fury.

"Let's get inside."

He kept talking. "She wasn't with Baxter. She was here, paying me back for fucking up her floor and...for taking the damn car from her." The last part came out in a rush of pent up air. I stared at the door, wondering what to do. Should I run? Should I call for Chaz? He pressed his forehead to my back, right between my shoulder blades, and my heart hammered ninety to nothing in my chest.

"She cheated and lied for who knows how long and I had no fucking idea. What does that say about me?" The vibration from his voice reverberated through my body.

I let out a loud huff, and twisting around to face him, said, "Okay, now you're just talkin' crazy. That woman is nuttier than a porta potty at a peanut festival. She cheated on you, not the other way around. She's the two-timing ho bag, and if I was you, I wouldn't give her a cent of my money." His shocked expression would have been funny if it wasn't directed at me.

"Nuttier than a porta potty at a what?" he asked.

"Peanut festival. You've never heard that before?" His response was a loud burst of laughter. He bent at the waist and dropped his hands to his knees, all while laughing like a loon.

"I need a shot," I muttered, which only seemed to make him laugh harder.

I'd barely made it through the door when I felt his hand on my arm. Suddenly, I was in his arms with my face squished against his chest—his very bare, solidly muscular chest.

"What are you doing?" I asked, only it sounded more like "Whardoin."

"Thank you for being here. I'm sorry I lost my cool earlier and I'm sorry about Chaz. He doesn't have a filter. I promise he's a good guy, but he takes some getting used to." The vibration of his voice made my nipples pebble. He was so warm and felt so good. I couldn't remember the last time I'd been held by a man. *Just this once*, I thought as I slowly wrapped my arms around him and returned the hug.

"I'm sorry about your wife. I know you love her and I'm so sorry you're hurting right now. I wish I could make it better for you." I glanced up as his arms loosened. Our eyes connected, collided, clashed. A ripple of excitement barreled through me followed by a feeling of unease. The look on his face, the heat behind his green-eyed stare, caused my breath to catch in my throat. A million butterflies danced inside my body. We shouldn't be doing this.

"Evan—" He pressed his fingers to my lips, cutting off my words, which was a good thing because I hadn't figured out what to say just yet.

"Let's get one thing straight. Right here. Right now. I cared for my wife. Cared, being past tense. Was I hurt? Hell yes. I spent nine years with her. I'm no longer hurt, though. I'm angry. Before she brought her shit to your doorstep, I was going to give her what she wanted. Now, I'm not." His arms tightened around me. "I know you feel this. To deny it would make you a liar and we both know how you feel about liars." Great, now he was throwing my own words back at me. Note to self: no more heart felt confessions. I tried to break free from his clutches, but the man had a death grip on me, so instead, I settled for a glare. He returned it with a smile, the turd.

"Not tryin' to point out the obvious or anything, but even if I did have feelings for you, which is debatable right at this moment, you're married." His smile widened until it lit up his beautiful face, and the butterflies once again took flight.

"I am, which is the only reason we're still standing here and not upstairs in my bedroom right now." A laugh flew from my mouth. Pretty sure of himself, wasn't he?

"No, the reason we're not upstairs in your bedroom is because I have other things to do, such as turn on some music and down at least three shots. Now, if you'll excuse me, I'm gonna do just that." He released me so fast, I almost toppled over. Before he did something like snatch me back and before I did something like let him, I bolted from the room.

"I'm getting divorced, Quinn," he called after me.

"Good for you," I snapped.

"After that, I'm coming for you." He's *what?*

I bolted back into the room to let him have it but found him already out the door.

"Shit," I whispered. Then I smiled. After that, I went to find the liquor.

CHAPTER NINE

"Soul To Squeeze"

Evan

I'd thrown down the gauntlet. It was shitty timing, but I saw the look on Quinn's face. One minute she was interested and the next she was worried about getting buried underneath Mandy's bullshit. She was right to be wary. I was a married man, and even though I wanted out, I still planned to honor my vows to the bitter end. This way, when I walked away, and there was no doubt I was walking away, I would do so with my head held high and my integrity intact. Once that happened, I would be free.

"Freedom can come at a bitch of a price." Grant once said. I didn't get it then, but I sure as hell understood now. He wasn't talking about money. He was talking about a man's soul. About what one was willing to give up to get what they wanted. I may not have married Mandy for love, but I'd grown to deeply care for her. And even though it had never been overly passionate and all-consuming between us, we'd built a life together. In doing so, we'd formed a solid union. At least, I thought we had.

I couldn't blame it all on Mandy, though. I was far from the perfect husband. I'd lied about trying out for Meltdown and then left her behind when I went on tour. My sin was wanting too much and hers was wanting too little. Irony, the little fucker, was sure as hell getting the last laugh, because while I was busy beating myself up about leaving, Mandy was off screwing someone else. Not only that, but if I hadn't come home during Christmas break, I never would have gone to Margo's with my brother, and I never would have met Quinn.

Six months ago, if someone would have told me I was going to meet a sexy, gray-eyed country girl with the spirit of a lioness and the hair to match, who wasn't afraid to tell me exactly how she felt, I would have laughed in their faces.

Quinn Kinley: bar owner; ego crusher; ball buster.

The woman had single handedly pulled me from the depths of my despair, and in doing so, had somehow managed to capture the one thing Mandy never could—my heart. She was all I could think about. Her humor, her willingness to listen, her unshakable sense of right and wrong, were just a few of the many things that attracted me to her. She looked at me as if I was something special, and for the first time in my life, I felt special. So call me stupid, I was going for it. Well, not going, going. I couldn't do that just yet, but I could sure as shit stake my claim.

Right as I hit the pool area, Chaz took one look at the smile on my face, and shouted, "Someone got himself a little somethin' somethin'!"

"Fuck off," I responded, trying not to laugh. The guy really was a shithead.

"Are you going to play, or do I need to turn on the music?" Quinn shouted from the top of the steps. I detected a slight slur in her voice, which meant she wasn't joking about the shots.

Chuckling to myself, I thought, *something tells me she's done more than three.*

"Play!" the girls all shouted from their pool floats. I glanced over at Chaz and he shrugged.

I guess that meant we were playing.

It took twenty minutes for all of us to make it inside the pool house. This was because pain in the ass, Alex-Ann, refused to sit on the hard floor and insisted on moving pool lounges inside. By the time everyone was situated, Quinn was back with shot glasses and three bottles of liquor.

Staring at Chaz, I asked, "How do you want to do this?"

"I know!" Alex-Ann shouted. "We each get a song selection. If you know how to play it, the selector has to drink a shot, but if you dooooon't," she sang like a goof, "you both have to take a shot."

"I'm pretty sure he was asking me," Chaz stated. Alex-Ann gave him a look.

"I like her idea," Olivia defended.

"Okay, well, what if I know the song and Evan doesn't?" Chaz asked. Leave it to Chaz to fuck with them.

"Then he shoots, and you don't," Alex-Ann snapped, as if he'd asked the most absurd question ever.

"But will you be able to tell? I mean, we're pretty good at improvising." Her smirk faded to uncertainty and Chaz smiled.

"He's messing with you," Quinn said, handing her a bottle of what looked like Tequila. "Here, take a shot." Alex-Ann gave Chaz a scathing look before tipping the bottle and downing a hell of a lot more than a shot. I saw where this night was headed.

"I go firsh!" Gretchen, who was already fifteen sheets to the wind, slurred.

"Wait! Are we adding lyrics or not?" I asked.

"Lyrics!" the girls shouted in unison.

"Laaaaadies, let's not get too crazy here," I drawled.

"If we add lyrics, then we're only responsible for the chorus," Chaz added.

"Fine! I want 'I was Jack!'" Gretchen shouted. At least, I was pretty sure that's what she'd said. I hadn't the foggiest clue what song she was talking about, so I launched into "Hit the Road Jack." Chaz joined in and I almost pissed myself when we got to the chorus and he belted it out in his best Ray Charles imitation. Quinn and Olivia laughed, while the rest of the crowd stared at us in confusion.

"That wasn't my sowng," Gretchen announced, her tone all serious.

"I wanted 'I was Jack.'"

"Well, since you didn't bother to give us the name of the artist, you forfeit your turn. Next!" Chaz called out.

"'Girls Like You' by Maroon 5!" Olivia shouted. Chaz shot me a look, which Olivia intercepted. "What? I love that song," she whined.

"Ooooh, can I do Cardi B's part?" Alex-Ann asked.

"Baby," Chaz murmured. "Come sit on Daddy's lap." Alex-Ann made a gagging noise and Quinn burst into hysterics. Chaz scowled at them both, which in turn, made everyone else laugh.

"I was enjoying Ray Charles," Tut grumbled. Bobby was now crying he was laughing so hard. With a loud huff, Chaz settled Olivia between his thighs, and launched in with a beat. I counted to ten before jumping in. Since both of us knew the words to the song, we didn't bother to wait for the chorus. By the chorus, however, the entire room, including Tut, I might add, had joined in.

"Drink!" Chaz shouted when the song was over and smiled when Olivia took a healthy swig of Jack Daniels.

"Next!" I called out.

"Curtis Mayfield's 'Superfly,'" Tut said with a knowing grin on his face. I didn't even try. I just held out my hand and waited for Alex-Ann to pass over the tequila bottle.

"And here I thought you two were musicians," Tut complained.

"I knew that one," Chaz muttered.

Olivia jerked her head around and asked, "Really?"

"Fuck no," he growled. He held out his hand, and for the first time ever, I saw him take a drink. "Next!" he shouted and then added, "And obscure seventies music is now banned."

"Elton John's 'Tiny Dancer,'" Quinn called out. Of course, my groin responded to her voice. If all it took for me to get a boner was hearing Quinn speak, then I was in a world of trouble. Our eyes connected and we both smiled, the memory of that night still fresh in our minds.

"I love that song!" Alex-Ann shrieked, and began singing the lyrics at the top of her lungs.

"New rule!" Chaz shouted, cutting off her serenade. "You have to wait for the music before singing, or you drink. Drink!" he ordered, pointing his drumstick at Alex-Ann.

"No fair. You just made up the rule," she whined.

"And you broke it. Now, drink." Surprisingly, she did. Olivia, who was still sitting on his lap, didn't look too happy. She turned and whispered something in his ear and he laughed. Then he launched into a slow beat. I caught Quinn's eye and winked. Then I began playing. Chaz, sensing the song meant something to the two of us, let me sing it.

As the last note was played, no one said a word.

"I could just sit here for days and listen to you sing," Alex-Ann murmured through a breathy sigh.

"Thank you," Quinn mouthed.

"Drink up," I mouthed back, and she laughed. With every look, smile, and laugh, she pulled me deeper into her universe.

"Shit, I'm druuuuuunk," Gretchen moaned.

"One more," Bobby called out. "I want Queen's 'Bohemian Rhapsody.'" I flicked my eyes to Chaz and he smiled. If Bobby was trying to stump us, he'd picked the wrong song to do it with.

"Yes!" Olivia shouted as she clapped her hands and bounced up and down on Chaz's lap. We both knew that Chaz was about to blow their minds.

We started off slow, just to get warmed up. One thing people didn't know about Chaz Jones, is his amazing voice. The moment the tempo sped up, the girls shot to their feet and began dancing around the room. Chaz and I played off of each other, him singing the high notes and me the low. Hell, even Bobby and Tut joined in. When the song was over, everyone drank.

Later, while Bobby was grilling burgers, my brother called. We hadn't spoken in weeks, mostly because I'd refused to return his calls. Being that I was already halfway to hammered, I answered the call, and in conversation, told him we were having a party and to stop by. He took me up on the offer and even brought Jason and Mike with him. Jason immediately latched on to Alex-Ann and Mike headed straight for the alcohol. After saying a few words to Quinn, Ehren found me.

He dropped down beside me onto the pool lounge. "Are you ever going to speak to me again?"

"Not if you're going to keep criticizing my life choices," I responded.

"I'm not. I just want to make sure you're okay."

Glancing sideways at him, I asked, "Do I look okay? 'Cause I've gotta say, I feel pretty damn good."

"Is that the booze talking, or the truth?" he asked, his lip twitching with humor.

"Right now, it's both." His chuckle made me smile.

"Mandy's getting married," I lobbed at him.

He jerked his eyes from a half-naked, passed out Gretchen back to me. "You got the divorce?"

"Nope."

His brow furrowed. "I don't get it."

"You know she was cheating, right?" He nodded. "Well, apparently, she's engaged and planning on getting married in Vegas in October."

"What the hell? She can't do that!" he exclaimed. I loved when little brother got all bent out of shape about shit.

"Can I tell you something? I wish she would, because then I would be free of her."

"What are you two over here whispering about?" Quinn asked.

"Nothing," Ehren quickly responded.

"You," I said at the same time. She narrowed her eyes at me and I smiled.

I wasn't quite sure when the party went off the rails. I just know that one minute we were all hanging out by the pool drinking, and the next, Quinn and I were wasted off our asses in the kitchen making chocolate chip cookies. After eating them all, we stumbled upstairs.

"Night, Rock Star," she slurred. I watched her stumble to her room.

"Night Country," I whispered back. *One day*, I thought.

The sound of Alex-Ann's laughter woke me.

"Make her stop," Ehren groaned from beside me. Quinn's best friend topped the Richter scale as the most annoying human on the face of the planet.

For fear of my head exploding in my skull, I slowly turned it in his direction, and asked, "Why are you in the bed with me?"

"Where else was I supposed to sleep?"

"Uhhh, your own place," I responded, as if the answer wasn't obvious.

"After doing like a million shots with Bobby, I wasn't about to drive home. That guy is a drinking machine, by the way. I was practically licking the floor and he was just getting started. Jason got the sofa, so I all but crawled up the stairs and took the other half of your bed. You're right, this mattress is the shit."

"Stop talking," I warned.

After a long pause, he said, "You really like her." I thought about what to say and settled for the truth.

"I've barely scratched the surface and already feel more for her than I ever felt for Mandy."

"Ouch," he muttered.

"I know. It's sad, but it's true. Mandy didn't know me. She never even tried. She took the few things she liked and threw away the rest. Not Quinn. She wants it all and I want to give it to her."

"I'm happy for you, bro." I could tell he meant it.

"Hold your happiness until I'm officially divorced, then you can let it fly," I muttered. He laughed.

With a groan, he pulled himself up to a seated position. I wasn't ready for such a bold maneuver, just yet.

"Have you spoken to Mom and Dad lately?"

"Mom called the other day, but I was busy. Look, just so you know, someone broke in here this past weekend and took a tire iron to my shit. If you ask me, it had Mandy's name written all over it, but she conveniently has an alibi. I don't want Mom to know what's going on. I'll try my best to stop by the house and tell them both about the divorce, once it's official, but until then, they're on a need to know basis.

"In other words, they don't need to know a damn thing," he

111

filled in.

"You got it."

In a jerky motion, he pushed off the bed and shuffled to a standing position. "I gotta go," he announced, once he was steady on his feet.

"Help me up and I'll follow you out."

After Ehren and the guys took off, Alex-Ann and a still half-drunk Gretchen left. Chaz and I were hanging in the kitchen drinking coffee while Quinn and Olivia made grilled cheese sandwiches, when Bobby strolled in. I could tell by his expression that something was wrong.

"What?" I asked.

"Are you aware that there's no marriage license filed for a Mr. and Mrs. Evan E. Walker in the State of Texas?" His question made the room go silent.

"What do you mean there's no license? Mandy and I filed it together. In fact, I distinctly remember that a good friend of hers named Serena worked at the County Clerk's office. She filed it for us. I'm pretty sure that's the law, right?"

"It wasn't filed," Bobby shot back at me.

"You're sure?" Chaz asked.

"Positive," he confirmed.

What the hell?

CHAPTER TEN

"All My Ex's Live in Texas"

Quinn

I was in the middle of flipping the grilled cheese sandwiches when Bobby and Tut walked in. I could claim I was trying not to listen to the conversation in the other half of the room, but as it concerned Evan and that heifer, Amanda, I was all ears. I swear, that woman's cheese had slid all the way off her cracker. She'd better not step foot back in Margo's. Actually, I take that back. I hope she did. That way, I could finally give her a piece of my mind.

"There was an actual license?" Bobby asked.

"Yes," Evan answered, a confused look on his face—confused and hung over. Weren't we all...I was pretty sure Alex-Ann hooked up with his brother's friend last night. I caught them half-naked on one of the pool lounges when I went down to deal with the torches.

My attention snapped back to Bobby when he asked, "Do

you happen to know where it is?"

"It's in one of the boxes in the garage. Why? What are you thinking?"

"Nothing yet," he answered, and then repeated, "You're sure it's in the garage?"

"Why?" Evan demanded. I could tell he was getting irritated.

"We need it," Tut said. He was leaning against the door-jam with his hands shoved deep in his jean pockets. I couldn't quite figure him out. He was a large, imposing man with tattoos all over his body, even on his shaved scalp. He didn't talk a lot and had the most amazingly expressive eyes—well, maybe not the most. Evan's were pretty darn amazing and expressive, not that I was trying to compare or anything. Unlike Evan, Tut had zero bullshit. My daddy would have called him a straight shooter.

"Mandy's living in the house," Evan pointed out, as if Bobby wasn't already aware of that fact. My lip curled at the mention of that woman's name. Mandy shouldn't have been anywhere near that house, and what kind of name was Mandy anyway?

Tut's brow shot up. "Does she own it?"

"No, but she lives in it."

"As long as you own it, it's your home, even if she lives there," Bobby informed him.

Chaz pushed back from the table, and said, "It looks like a good day for a little B and E, boys." Bobby shook his head.

"It's not breaking and entering if we are authorized to enter by the owner of the house, and there's no way in hell I'm taking you with us. In fact, neither of you are going.

Scowling at Bobby, Chaz said, "C'mon, man. How 'bout this, I'll keep an eye out for the bitch while you two break in." I let out a quiet snort as I transferred the sandwiches to the platter and started on two more. I could see why Evan and Chaz were close. The guy was loyal to a fault, and even if he was a bit abrasive, he was funny as all get out.

"How about this, you sit here on your ass with your hot little mama and leave the professional shit to...the professionals," Tut countered.

"Awww, he thinks I'm hot," Olivia cooed. Chaz glowered, Tut smiled, and Olivia giggled. Okay, maybe Tut did have a sense of humor after all.

"What? You're just going to open the garage and take the boxes?" Evan asked.

"Pretty much," Tut answered. Bobby shot him a look and he dropped his eyes to the floor, but I still caught the smile.

"We're going to wait until she's not at home, so there is no possibility of a breach of the peace. Then we're going to access the garage and retrieve the box," Bobby explained in a slightly more professional manner, before asking, "How many did you say there were?"

"Two," Evan replied. "You won't be able to tell them apart, so just grab both." Bobby nodded in understanding.

"In other words," Chaz butted in, "you're going to break into the garage and snatch the boxes." Tut's eyes were still trained on the floor, but I could see his shoulders shaking.

Evan stared at Bobby with a look on his face I couldn't quite read. Apparently, Bobby couldn't either, because he felt the need to say something. "Look, Tut and I want to see if the license is legit. Once we have it in hand, we'll need to track down the minister who officiated, and then decide where to go from there."

"Mandy's cousin married us," Evan told him. That didn't sound good. From the look on Bobby's face, he didn't think so either.

"Shiiiiit," Tut drawled.

"Is he authorized to perform weddings?" Bobby asked.

"I assume so. He's some sort of lay minister with a wing nut congregation out in the sticks. He married another cousin of hers earlier that year, and because we didn't have time to plan, we used him."

"Okay, first thing's first. We need to discuss the logistics, starting with the lay out of your garage." While the men discussed the details, I finished making the sandwiches.

We ate quickly and then Bobby and Tut took off on their mission. Chaz and Evan disappeared to the front porch, while Olivia and I did the dishes and cleaned up the kitchen.

"What if they don't find the marriage license?" she asked. I'd been asking myself that same question.

"What I want to know is why they can't find a copy of it on file?" Neither of us had any answers, so we dropped the conversation and went to find the guys.

Evan was on the porch talking to someone on the phone, but Chaz wasn't with him.

"Chaz?" Olivia mouthed when he looked her way. He pointed upstairs, and she took off. I was about to leave when he nodded to one of the rockers, indicating he wanted me to stay.

"Who was that?" I asked as soon as the call ended.

"The insurance guy. He wants to take another look at the piano before he tells me how much they're willing to give me." He dropped onto the rocker next to mine and grumbled, "What a fucking mess."

A minute or so of silence passed before I got up enough nerve to speak. "Can I ask you something?" His head turned and those striking green eyes were all I could see. Damn, but they were potent.

"You know you can ask me anything. What do you want to know?"

"Why did you marry her?"

He looked away, off into the horizon somewhere. "Because

she was pregnant, and it was the right thing to do." I opened my mouth to respond, but quickly closed it when he kept talking. "We didn't have any money. Her parents didn't have any either. Mine did, but they refused to acknowledge that I was getting married, much less pay for it." He laughed and shook his head.

"What?" I asked, wanting in on the joke.

"Mandy insisted on an extended honeymoon in Hawaii. There we were, poor as shit, and she wanted that damn honeymoon. I should have known then." The bitterness behind his words made me tense. This wasn't funny at all. It was just plain sad. I wanted to touch him, to take his hand or squeeze his arm, but I was afraid of his reaction. As far as emotions go, I couldn't tell my head from my ass. I'd had boyfriends and lovers along the way, but the intensity of what I felt for this man scared the pants off me. He said he was coming for me, but what did that mean? I wasn't sure I could handle being his bed buddy, not without losing my heart. Hell, that ship was already pulling away from the dock.

"I had my little brother go to my mother and ask her for money," he continued, thankfully interrupting my inner tizzy. "She went behind my dad's back and gave it to me." His eyes slowly drifted to mine. "Mandy lost the baby in the first trimester. We'd only been married for two months."

"I'm sorry. That had to be awful for you both," I said, while at the same time wondering why he stayed with her.

As if reading my mind, he asked, "You're wondering why I stayed, right?"

"I'm sure you had your reasons." Knowing her, she cast an evil witch spell on him.

He lowered his elbows to his knees and stared off into the trees. He looked as if he was lost in thought, but I could tell he was choosing his words, trying to decide what and what not to say.

"She was a mess after the baby, all freaked that I was going to bail on her and shit. I just didn't have the heart to leave her like that."

"But—" I started to ask if he ever wanted more and decided to just leave it alone. What did it matter now anyway?

Angling his eyes back on me, he asked, "What?"

"Nothing."

"No, ask it," he commanded, the bitter tone back in his voice.

"Didn't you want more?"

"Not until you." I blinked. The pin was out, and the grenade lobbed...right into my lap.

"Evan—"

"I grew up in a loveless house. I'm pretty sure neither of my parents even know how to love. To them, life is more of a business transaction. We never took family trips because my father couldn't break away from his job long enough. I've never been to Disneyland. I've never been skiing. Hell, the first time I saw the ocean was when I was thirteen and got invited to the beach with a friend. I was this kid with music in his blood living in a tone-deaf world."

My heart ached for both the boy and the man. I couldn't imagine how lonely he must have been. My house had been filled with so much love.

"Mandy fit right in. Like my parents, she was flat and colorless and perfectly happy in her tone-deaf world. From the moment I laid eyes on you, I knew you were different. You're vibrant, funny, and full of life. I bet you raised hell as a kid. Shit, what am I saying, you're still raising hell." I couldn't help but laugh. He wasn't wrong. I'd always been a hell raiser.

"Who you are and what you stand for speaks straight to this." He placed his hand over his heart. Dang it, my eyes were burning. He held out his hand, palm up, as if inviting, no, daring me to take it—to take him. My daddy always used to say, "If you want somethin', take it." Well, he didn't raise no dummy. I wanted it and I was taking it. Our eyes clashed and held as I placed my hand in his, and I knew right then and there that this... whatever this was, was bigger than the both of us.

A breathtaking smile spread across his face. "I don't know where this is going, Country, but wherever it is, it'll have you and me in it, okay?"

"Okay," I whispered, smiling back at him.

We sat there for the longest time, just holding hands and rocking in our rockers. I was full to overflowing with happiness, and I knew that if something was to happen and this was all I ever got of Evan Walker...it would be enough.

CHAPTER ELEVEN

"Ball and Chain"

Evan

This is where I'm supposed to be. I'd gotten so used to the big things in life—the band, the fame, and the money—that I'd forgotten to cherish the little things, such as sitting on a porch in the middle of nowhere Texas with a woman who was slowly stealing my heart. A woman I felt a soul-deep connection with...a woman who made the little things mean more than all of the big put together. I'd never had this with Mandy. I had no idea *this* even existed.

The sound of wheels on gravel pulled me from my thoughts. Bobby and Tut had returned. With them came a sudden feeling of dread. Had they found the boxes or did Mandy stop them? Quinn didn't say a word. She just quietly released my hand. In a whiplash of emotion, the feeling of dread morphed into anger. Anger at Mandy. Anger at myself. Anger at the whole damn situation.

"One day, you won't feel the need to let go," I uttered before pulling myself from the rocking chair and making my way down the steps to greet Bobby and Tut.

Frustration sat heavy on my shoulders as I waited for Bobby to exit the car. "Did you have any trouble?" I asked.

"Nope." His curt reply felt like salt on an already festering wound. I was on the verge of losing my cool when he popped the trunk and I saw the boxes sitting there. This is what nine years of marriage looked like.

The thought of going through Mandy's things, of having to relive what I was trying so damn hard to forget, made my head ache. I'd already done this once. I wasn't planning on doing it again. Yet, here we were.

Once I'd kicked Mandy out of the house, I moved my stuff into the guest bedroom, where I discovered the closet filled with her things. After lugging her clothes over to the master bedroom and dumping them on the bed, I carried the boxes down to the garage. In my haste to get it done quickly, I missed the bottom step, which caused one to topple from the other and crash to the floor. The cleanup included an excruciating trip down memory lane, along with several wedding photos and a manila envelope containing our marriage certificate...

"Here," Bobby said, shoving one of the boxes into my arms. With a grunt of acknowledgement, I turned to find Quinn waiting on the porch. She had a look of anticipation on her face. Whatever was in these boxes, be it good or bad, didn't need to affect her in any way.

"I want her gone when we do this," I muttered low enough for Bobby and Tut to both hear.

"Not a problem," Bobby replied. "John and his team are thirty minutes out. It'll take them about four hours to install the alarm system." *Good. Quinn would be at work by then.*

"Let's drop these in the living room. We can deal with them once they've gone," I said loud enough for her to hear.

"Who's gone?" she asked.

"The guys will be here to install the security system in a few minutes," I replied as I passed by her.

"I have to work later." I heard the disappointment behind her words but didn't respond. Instead, I continued into the living room where I set the box on the floor.

"That it?" Chaz asked from the doorway. Shit. I'd completely forgotten he was here.

"Yep," Tut responded as he set the second box next to its mate. While they discussed what had gone down at the house, I scrambled for a way to get rid of Chaz and Olivia for the evening.

As if reading my mind, Chaz asked, "What's the plan?" I could tell by the challenging gleam in his eyes that I wasn't getting rid of him. That didn't stop me from trying.

"The security guys are about to arrive. Bobby estimates it'll take them four hours to install the system. I was thinking that you and Olivia could head over to Margo's with Quinn and the three of us will meet you there after they take off."

He studied me for a minute before countering, "Or, we could send Olivia to Margo's with Quinn and the four of us could meet up with them after we go through the boxes." I started to tell him no but what was the point? I wasn't going to win. Underneath Chaz's harsh exterior was a heart of gold and a will of steel. There was no way he would let me face this alone, and if the tables were turned, I wouldn't let him either.

"Fine," I snapped.

The fucker had the nerve to smile at me.

"Olivia and I are going for a swim. If you need me, you know where I'll be." He turned to leave.

"Chaz," I called out. His head swiveled around, and he shot me a questioning look. "Thanks," I muttered.

"Anytime," he replied before walking out the door.

Minutes later, John and his team arrived. Directly on their heels was the insurance appraiser. The two may have kept me busy for the next few hours, but they didn't erase Quinn's look of disappointment from my mind. How did I stop my past from affecting my present? I wasn't sure I could, but I sure as hell was going to try.

Quinn eventually found me down at the pool house discussing security logistics with John. I immediately zeroed in on her tight T-shirt and her way too short shorts. By the look on John's face, he did too.

"Sorry to interrupt, but Olivia and I are about to leave for Margo's," she announced, then turning to John, said, "Can I steal Evan for a minute?" I could tell by her pinched expression that she was unhappy.

John shot me an enjoy-the-doghouse look and I smiled in return. "Be right back," I told him. On the way out the door, I zeroed in on Quinn's stiff spine and bunched shoulders. Yep, she was mad.

"Country—" I started to say but came up short when she pivoted around and seared me with an angry glare.

"We're friends, right?" Her stormy gray eyes bored into me. I hesitated to answer, but only because in my mind we were more than friends. As if reading my thoughts, she added, "Friends above everything else."

"We are," I answered, wondering where this was going.

"Well, in my world, friends don't shut each other out, but that's exactly what you're doing. You talk about us being together in one breath and in the other you shut me out. I hate to break it to you, Rock Star, but that's not called being a friend.

That's called being an asshole. Now, I have to go to work. Have fun with your boxes."

Before she could storm off in a snit, I reached out and tagged her by the back of her neck. "I need to go," she huffed as I slowly reeled her in to where I could wrap both of my arms around her.

Dropping my mouth to her ear, I said, "You're right. I was being an asshole, but I didn't intend to be. Let me explain where I'm coming from."

"I'm listening." Her curt reply would have been funny, if not for the situation.

"I have no idea what's in those boxes. The last thing I want is for Mandy's twisted bullshit to affect us anymore than it already has." Her head snapped back, and she leveled her eyes on mine. She opened her mouth, probably to blast me, but I cut her off. "I'm not saying I'm going to keep you in the dark. I just need to take the first look, okay?"

Her expression marginally softened. "I want to be here for you," she grumbled. My chest constricted to the point of almost pain. No one had ever said those words to me before. The urge to drop my head and taste her lips, to take what we both wanted, ate at me.

"And I promise to let you, but I need to do this my way." What I needed was to make her understand. I also needed for her not to feel my erection pressing against her stomach.

"Fine," she huffed, "but I expect to see you at Margo's after with a full report."

"You will," I assured her.

She dropped her head to my chest, and murmured, "I hate that woman." An image of Quinn beating the hell out of Mandy popped into my head.

"I'll have to make sure you two never meet." I felt her shoulders tighten, but then she sank deeper into my arms, and all I could think about was how good she felt. That, and my boner.

When her entire body tensed, and she let out a little groan, followed by a "Jesus help me," I knew I was busted.

Instead of addressing the elephant in my pants, however, she attempted to distance herself by taking a step back. "I have to go," she announced, her voice thick with what I hoped was desire.

"I know."

"I'll see you later?"

"Promise," I answered. As I watched her walk away, I was reminded of those damn short shorts. "We're going to have to reevaluate your work uniform!" I called after her.

"That'll happen after we discuss that thing in your pants!" she called back. Her reply left me speechless. Then it made me laugh. I mean really laugh.

An hour later, the laughter was gone, and the dread was back in full force. It was time to face my past.

The first box contained pictures, journals, and things from Mandy's life before we met—nothing of which pertained to us or our marriage, so we all agreed to set it aside.

I immediately recognized box two as the same box I'd tipped over.

"In nine years, you took like twenty pictures together. What gives?" Chaz asked.

"We weren't really picture people." I tried not to sound defensive, but he'd hit a sore spot. Mandy hated having her picture taken. I'd always blamed it on her being insecure, but I now had my doubts. She certainly had no problem posing for Baxter's Facebook page.

Bobby held up a manila envelope. "Mind if I take a look?" Relief washed over me. I was worried she'd removed it.

"That's it," I told him, and watched as he pulled the document from the envelope and scanned over it. I waited for him to say something. When he handed it over to Tut and then slid his hand back inside and pulled two more things out, my pulse accelerated. It wasn't the same envelope. Tut let out a whistle, indicating surprise, and my stomach jumped into my throat.

My eyes darted back and forth between the two of them. "What?"

"Show him," Bobby said. Tut handed me the piece of paper and they both waited for my reaction. It was a marriage certificate, but not ours. This one was for Amanda James and Baxter Keen. "Notice how it's already filled out?" Bobby asked. I scanned past Amanda and Baxter's names to the bottom of the page, and sure enough, he was right. It even had her cousin's signature as well as her friend from the clerk's office, which made no sense, as the wedding had yet to occur. Chaz held out his hand.

"I don't get it," I said, passing it over to him.

Bobby handed the other items in the envelope to Tut, who scanned over them before handing them to me. One was the save the date and the other was the wedding invitation. I was obviously missing something, because we already knew about the wedding.

Bobby pulled a second manila envelope from the box. I watched as he opened it, scanned over it, and passed it to Tut.

"Hmmmm, notice they're both the original documents," Tut murmured.

"Yep, but look at what's missing," Bobby responded. I had to grit my teeth to keep from snapping at them. Here they were playing twenty questions yet giving no answers. I wanted fucking answers, and I wanted them now.

"The clerk signed it but there's no stamp or seal," Tut finally answered before handing it over to me.

"It can't be filed without a stamp or seal?" Chaz asked, and suddenly I began to catch on.

"If it had been properly filed, there would be a stamp or seal to show it. That way someone like us couldn't come along and contest it," Bobby answered.

As I stared down at the piece of paper in my hands, the only legal proof that Evan Walker and Amanda James were ever married, the severity of the situation slammed into me. "Her friend didn't stamp it," I said.

"Nope," Tut replied.

"Nor did she file it," I continued.

"Nope," Bobby and Tut both replied.

I stared at them both, thinking holy fucking shit. "Which means that if there's no official record of a wedding, then we were never legally married?" I asked.

"That's what we're thinking," Bobby responded, then added, "From what I know, the person officiating the wedding is responsible for filing the certificate." My thoughts shot in a million directions as I tried to grasp what this meant. I wasn't legally married and never had been?

"What the fuck? So the bitch lied about being married to him for nine years and is now planning on doing it to someone else?" Chaz asked. I was too stunned to speak.

"Don't go celebrating just yet," Tut warned.

"Yeah, we need confirmation," Bobby added.

Still reeling, I asked, "What kind of confirmation?"

"First, we pay Cousin Edward a little visit. Then we find the friend who signed the document," Bobby answered.

"What happens if they were never legally married?" Chaz asked.

"How about we deal with one thing at a time." Turning to me, Bobby asked, "Do you have Cousin Eddie's address?"

It took me a minute to find it. After assuring us they'd be in touch as soon as they had something, Chaz and I followed Bobby and Tut out the door and watched them drive away.

"I can't deal with this right now—" I started to say.

"Fine, but if I leave you alone, I need to know you're not going to do something stupid," Chaz shot back at me.

Shaking my head, I whispered, "Nine years."

Chaz tapped his fingers against the doorframe. "You want to know what I think? I think you should trap her in her own game." I gave him a questioning look and he explained. "You're supposed to go to mediation in what, a week?"

"Two weeks," I said.

"I think you should cancel it. Tell your lawyer that you want to make a go of the marriage."

"Fuck no!" I growled. The last thing I wanted was to be anywhere near the lying bitch.

He held up his hand. "Hear me out. If you refuse to divorce her, then she can't marry the other dude without breaking some major laws."

"No laws will be broken if we're not legally married," I pointed out.

He let out a snort of disgust. "The bitch falsified documents and led you to believe something that wasn't true for nine years. Trust me, some laws had to have been broken somewhere along the way."

"Why?" I asked.

"I don't know, but if you go through with the divorce, you're allowing her to do it to someone else. Is that what you want?"

I thought back to our wedding. Did her family know what she was doing? Were there clues that I just didn't see? "No, offense man, but I need to get out of here."

"Fine, I'll go with you."

Scowling at him, I replied, "No. I need to be alone. Tell Quinn I'll see her later. I just need to think."

"Be smart and remember, Mandy's not worth losing what you have," he warned. The screen door slammed behind him as he headed inside the house.

I wasn't sure where I was going. I just had to get away. My intention was to clear my head, but the more I thought about what Mandy had done, the angrier I became. Why didn't her friend stamp the certificate? Why didn't her cousin file it? Was this her plan all along? If so, why? There was only one person who could give me the answers, and I was going to find her.

My phone rang as I turned onto her street. My brother's name flashed across the screen and I quickly silenced it. As I neared the house, it rang again. This time it was my father. Shit. For him to be calling, something must be seriously wrong.

I pulled between two parked cars and answered, "Hello?"

"Evan, it's Dad. Your mother had a bit of a fall this afternoon and has been admitted to Presbyterian Hospital. That's where we are now. I just thought you might like to know." Old wounds ripped wide open at the sound of his voice.

With the shake of my head, I pushed the bitterness back down and focused on what he was saying. "How bad is it? Is she going to be okay?"

"She hit her head and has some internal bleeding. They've taken her into surgery a—"

"I'm on my way now," I replied and hit disconnect.

Before leaving, I made sure to text Chaz and Bobby to let them know what was up. Chaz immediately replied asking if I needed him to meet me there. I told him no and not to say anything to Quinn. I didn't want her to worry. I would have to deal with Mandy later.

On arrival at the hospital, I found both Ehren and Elaine in the waiting room. It had been years since I'd seen my sister. She looked older, more grown up. Guilt at how I'd treated her reared its ugly head. All those years ago, she'd told me Mandy was cheating and I'd called her a liar. She was only trying to protect me. Her eyes lifted from her phone screen and widened in surprise when she saw me standing there.

"You came," she said.

Ehren, who was also staring at his phone, looked up and scowled. "I tried to call you, dickhead."

"Dad called," I replied, and both of their mouths dropped open in shock.

"You actually answered a call from Dad?" he asked.

Ignoring his question, I dropped down onto the chair across from them, and said, "Tell me what happened." They both launched in at the same time. From what I could gather, Mom was coming down the stairs with the laundry basket in hand, had miscalculated the landing, and missed the bottom three steps. On her way down, she hit her head on the entry hall cabinet.

"She was just lying there bleeding everywhere. I didn't know what to do. Dad wouldn't answer his phone, so I called 9-1-1 and then Ehren," Elaine recalled.

"Speaking of Dad, where is he?" I asked.

"Where do you think?" Ehren grumbled.

Elaine gave Ehren a scathing look. "He stepped out to make a call."

"Is he still seeing her?" I don't know what made me ask it. Call it the devil on my shoulder or maybe the fact that I was sick and tired of all the fucking lies. Either way, I needed to know if the old man had changed or if he was the same bastard he'd always been.

Ehren mumbled something that sounded a lot like "Cheating prick."

To both our surprise, Elaine piped up. "It's been over for about a year now."

My brother's eyebrows nearly shot off his face. "Why didn't you tell me?"

She shrugged. "You never asked." Elaine had always been able to hold her secrets.

As usual, Ehren pushed for more. "Well, what made him dump her?"

She smiled. "Mom threatened to leave him and take half of his money if he didn't drop the bitch."

"It's about time," I muttered.

"Believe it or not, he's actually trying. Mom even has him playing Bridge with her two nights a week." Ehren and I both laughed. "I'm serious," she said. I'd believe it when I saw it with my own two eyes. Her gaze drifted from Ehren to me. "A famous rock band, huh? I always knew you'd do something amazing with that talent of yours, but I've got to say, Meltdown pretty much takes the cake."

"Well, you know, Dad always said I would amount to nothing. I had to prove him wrong," I half joked.

An amused grin appeared on her face, reminding me of the Elaine of our childhood. "You certainly did that."

"Dad's really trying?" Ehren asked.

Elaine's expression sobered. "I think he realized he was going to lose her." Her eyes drifted to me. "I shouldn't have done what I did that night. I was drunk and so angry. I—"

"This isn't the time or the place, Elaine," Ehren cut in.

"If not now, then when?" she retorted. "It's not like we ever see each other."

"It's fine," I told Ehren, then turning my focus on my sister, said, "You went about it the wrong way, but I should have listened. I took her word over yours without question and I was wrong."

Understanding hit and she gasped. "Oh my God, I wasn't imagining it, was I? She was cheating."

"She was, and our marriage is over. Ehren knows, but I would appreciate it if you not tell Mom and Dad. I'll talk to them both once Mom is better and everything is finalized."

Elaine opened her mouth to respond when a familiar voice cut in, "Hello, Son. I'm glad you made it." The three of us looked up from our semi-huddle, and I had to admit, our father looked good for a man nearing his seventies. Truth be told, he looked healthier than I'd ever seen him.

Before we had a chance to talk, the doctor stepped into the waiting room and called us over. He explained that Mom was going to be okay and that they'd managed to stop the bleeding but wanted to keep her for a few days for observation.

"Can I see her?" I asked and was surprised when no one objected.

"Sure. I'll take you to her now." Without so much as a backward glance, I left the three of them standing there.

The doctor made small talk as he led me down a long hallway. I replied but couldn't tell you what was said. All I could think about was the conversation I'd just had with my sister and how relieved I was that my mother was going to be okay.

As we stepped inside the room, I paused. I'm not sure what I expected. I knew she'd been hurt, but to see her lying there with her head covered in all those bandages...

"She looks a little banged up, but she's going to be just fine," the doctor assured me.

Swallowing deeply, I shuffled over to the chair beside her bed and took a seat. My mother had always been delicate, but I was surprised to see how pale and fragile she appeared lying there in bed.

"You can take her hand," he urged. Slowly, I reached out and grasped her hand. It felt cold and small beneath mine.

"I'll be back to get you in a little while," I heard him say but was too busy staring at my mother's face. She looked so... old. I tried to recall how long it had been since I'd seen her. A year? Surely not. My eyes stung as I stared at the woman who had given birth to me and wondered where the time had gone. I always thought she was weak for not standing up to my father. Weak because she knew about his cheating and allowed it. Weak because she didn't force him to be a better man...a better dad. She stayed because she loved him that much. I stayed out of guilt. She wasn't the weak one. I was.

"I'm sorry," I whispered. Then I dropped my head to the bed and wept.

CHAPTER TWELVE

"It Ain't My Fault"

Quinn

The minute I walked through the door and spotted the dirty tables and the glasses piled up in the bar sink, I knew it was going to be a rough night.

"Fuck a duck!" I exclaimed. I suppose this is what I get for asking Gretchen and Helen to close on Saturday night.

"What's that?" Olivia asked from behind me.

I stepped aside so she could see. "Look at this mess! Damn Gretchen! She was at my house for hours yesterday. Did she say a word about leaving my bar a mess? No. She. Did. Not."

Her eyes scanned over the mess before landing back on me. "Gretchen was the drunk one, right?"

"Drunk and stupid," I grumbled as I rounded the bar and turned on the water. I sincerely liked Gretchen, but the woman was pushing it. Just because we were friends didn't mean she could pull this shit. Helen was new and was most likely following Gretchen's lead. Either way, it was shitty and just plain wrong.

"I'm sorry she left you hanging. What can I do to help?"

"Here." I handed her a wet towel. "Could you wipe down those tables?"

A few minutes of silence passed before she asked, "Does Gretchen do this often?"

"Too often for my liking. It's not like I don't take care of my people, because I do. It just seemed so much easier when my dad was around."

"Oh? Where did he go?" she questioned. Without even thinking, I told her about Dad's cancer. It was after I'd finished that it hit me. I'd talked about my father without wanting to cry. I wasn't sure if this was good or bad.

"I'm sorry you lost your dad, Quinn, and no offense, but running a business sounds rough."

I snorted. "I bet running a gaggle of rock stars is worse. By the way, how did you happen to land that job?"

With a huge smile on her face, she told me about the crazy things that happened on Meltdown's latest tour. When she ended it with how happy she was with the band's recent unanimous decision to go back on tour, my stomach dropped. Evan hadn't mentioned it. In fact, he hadn't said a thing about his weekend away. Then again, why should he? It's not like we were dating or anything. This made me feel even worse. Here I was, living with a man I wanted but couldn't have. I'm pretty sure there was a word for this—Pathetic, loser, downright crazy. Maybe I wasn't meant to find love.

"You okay?" Olivia asked, interrupting my internal pity party.

"What? Oh, yeah. That's awesome about the new album and tour. When does it start?" Somehow, I managed to keep my voice calm when what I really wanted to do was cry.

"Who knows? Mallory still has to pop out that baby and we have to get through Nash and Rowan's wedding before any big decisions are made."

I was mulling this over when the door swung open and Al-ex-Ann walked in. Following on her heels was Gretchen, who took one look at my face and knew she was up shit's creek with no paddle.

"I'm sorry Quinn. Please don't fire me," she begged.

"You do this again and that's exactly what I'm gonna do."

"I meant to come back and clean, but then you invited me to hang out with the rock stars and the time got away from me." The rock stars? Lord help me. I needed a cigarette.

"Well, what are you standin' over there for?" I pointed to the remaining glasses and messy bar. "Get your ass over here and clean, woman." She hustled over as fast as her short legs could carry her.

"I really am sorry," she repeated. I had nothing good to say, so I left her there to stew in her juices.

An hour later, Chaz walked in. Not Evan. Just Chaz.

Before I could ask, he said, "Evan needs some time alone. He told me to tell you he would catch up with you later."

A million questions popped into my head. I settled for, "Is he okay?"

"Not really, and before you ask, it's not mine to tell, so don't bother."

"I should go home and check on him," I muttered, more to myself than to anyone else.

"If he wanted to see you, he would've come with me, but he didn't, so you need to just let him be," Chaz snapped back at me.

"Chaz!" Olivia hissed.

"What? The man wants privacy, so she needs to honor that

and give it to him." Before I did something crazy, like plant my shoe in his groin, I exited the bar and headed for the back door.

"Where are you going?" Olivia called out.

"To smoke! You and Mr. Rude go ahead and grab a stool. Gretchen will be happy to pour you a drink!" I called over my shoulder.

Sam was waiting for me with a scowl on his face and the entire pack of cigarettes in his hand.

"Knock yourself out," he grumbled.

"I plan on it," I snarled back at him.

Right as I pulled open the door, Chris Stapleton's "Broken Halos" started playing. Heaven help Alex-Ann and her love of sad songs. I was in no mood tonight.

"Change it!" I screamed. Three seconds later the song switched to "Flatliner."

"That'll work," I thought as I stepped outside and into the muggy night. In my attempt to extract a cigarette from the pack, another slid past it and dropped to the ground at my feet.

"This just isn't my damn night," I grumbled, and bent over to retrieve the stray cigarette. Suddenly, the door swung open and smacked me square on the ass. "Shit!" I screeched. In my attempt not to plunge head first off the ledge, I flung my arms out, which sent the rest of the pack sailing off into the wide blue yonder.

"Oh my gosh, are you okay?" Alex-Ann gasped.

"Does it look like I'm okay?" I shouted, somehow managing to regain my balance.

"What is up your ass tonight?" she shouted back at me.

"What do you think is up my ass? I come to work at my bar, a bar which I entrusted to my employees, and discover that it hasn't been cleaned since Saturday night! Then, I want to smoke one cigarette and look!" I pointed to the parking lot, "They're all contaminated with car juice!" Alex-Ann's attempt to hold in her laughter made her eyes bug, which in turn made her face puff up like a frog. Unable to help myself, I burst into laughter.

"Car juice?" she asked through loud guffaws.

"What would you call it?"

"Not car juice." This got us laughing all over again. Together we plopped down onto the ledge and dangled our legs over the side.

When the laughter finally subsided, she asked, "What's really bothering you?" What isn't bothering me should have been the question. "I know you're mad at Gretchen and Helen, but it's not like you to fly off the handle like that. Is it Evan?"

"No. Yes. I don't know. He promised he would be here to-night."

"I know you care for him, honey, but I worry about you. The guy has some serious baggage." When I didn't respond, she con-tinued, "I always pictured you settling down with a sexy cow-boy. A man who knows how to use his hands, if you catch my drift." She elbowed me, and I pushed her away. "But here you are, chasing after a famous guy who's married and all...tattoo-ey."

"Tattooey?" I asked, trying not to laugh.

"Not that there's anything wrong with tattoos or anything," she amended. "They're just not my thing. I didn't think they were yours either."

Evan had great hands, and even though he was all tattooey, he was so much more. He was funny and kind and too damn hand-some for his own good. He made my heart hitch and my pulse race. He made me want to do something crazy, like take a blind leap into forever. Of course, I didn't tell Alex-Ann this. Instead, I gave her a momism. "Love happens when you least expect it, Double A."

Ignoring my age-old nickname for her, she scoffed, "Love? Is that what this is? You've known the man for all of a month. For Christ's sake, Quinn, you haven't even slept with him yet. For all you know, his penis could be the size of a Vienna Sausage."

"I've known him for eight months, and trust me, it's no Vienna Sausage."

"Quinn!" she gasped, and I knew what she was thinking.

"No, Alex, I haven't seen his penis, but it's kind of hard to miss a giant cucumber when it's pressed against your stomach." She didn't respond for the longest time.

When she did, it was to ask, "How giant?" I showed her with my hands. "Damn," she whispered.

"He makes me feel things," I admitted on a sigh.

"So did Casey, and you saw where that got you." She might as well have slapped me in the face.

Glaring at her, I said, "Evan Walker and Casey Wilson are nothing alike."

Casey Wilson was my one and only love. I was nineteen and he was twenty-three. He was my first real kiss, my first sexual experience, the first to steal my heart, and the first to break it. He was also married. Only, I didn't know it at the time. When my daddy found out, he hunted Casey down and gave him quite the beating. I'd had lovers since, but until Evan, I'd managed to keep my heart out of it.

"Casey was married," she stated as if this made them equals.

"Casey was a liar who led me to believe that he was in love with me. Evan has never lied to me about anything. And for your information, he refuses to cross that line. You wanna know why? Because he's married."

She sighed. "I just don't want to see you hurt again."

"That's not for you to decide, and while we're on the subject of lying, I've been thinking a lot about it and have decided to tell him about Amanda."

She shifted her gaze from the parking lot to my face and narrowed it on me. "Stop feeling guilty. You didn't know who she was, Quinn."

"Well, now I do and I'm going to tell him."

"You shouldn't."

"I am." A minute or two passed before she tossed her arm around my shoulder and pulled me in for a side hug.

"Fine. You know where to come when it backfires on you." I didn't bother to respond. The muffled sound of Lady Antebellum's "Bartender" drifted from beneath the door and we swung our legs in time with the beat.

Finally, not able to help herself, she asked, "Is it really that big?" I gave her a suggestive brow waggle and we both laughed.

A few hours later, Chaz and Olivia took off for home. Evan was still a no show and I was torn between Chaz's words and my feelings. If Chaz was right and Evan didn't want to be bothered, then I was simply going to have to deal. Suck it up, Quinn, I repeatedly told myself for the remainder of my shift.

The moment the clock struck one, I tossed my rag on the bar and told Alex-Ann and Gretchen to shut it down. Then I grabbed my purse from the back and walked out the door.

On the drive home, all I could think about was getting to Evan. What happened with the boxes? It had to be something big for Chaz to react so protectively...so negatively. Shit. I was scared. On top of that, I needed to come clean about the Amanda-Baxter thing.

I found everyone in the house asleep, except for Evan, who wasn't even in the house. I thought about texting him, just to see if he was okay, but the stupid Chaz on my shoulder made me reconsider. Forget the devil. I had Chaz. Yep, I was losing my marbles. Too wired for bed, I settled on a beer.

I'd just popped the top when it dawned on me. Maybe he's in the music room. Snagging a second beer from the fridge, I headed out the door and down the path. Halfway there, I heard the piano.

"Thank you, Jesus," I whispered to the sky, and all but skipped the rest of the way to the pool house.

Not wanting to interrupt, I slowly opened the slider and stepped inside. As I moved to close it behind me the music stopped. I turned to offer him a beer, but the look on his face froze me in my tracks. Something was definitely wrong. I wanted to ask, but intuition told me to keep my silence. I held my breath as the Chaz on my shoulder reared its devilish head once more. If he wants me to know, he'll tell me. *Please tell me.*

In a flat, toneless voice, he said, "My mom fell today and hit her head. If my sister hadn't found her, she would have died."

"Oh my God," I whispered, but he wasn't through.

"And it turns out that my marriage—all nine years of it—was nothing but a lie."

CHAPTER THIRTEEN

"Somebody Told Me"

Evan

"Is your mom okay? And what do you mean your marriage was a lie?" Quinn questioned, her voice laced with anger. Here she was, ready to defend my honor, and she didn't even know why. I slowly took a sip of my beer and thought about where to begin.

"Have I ever told you about my grandfather?" She shook her head. "He graduated from law school at the top of his class and was immediately snatched up by a big New York firm. After six years, they made him partner. By then, he was tired of the big city life. He figured he'd learned enough and was done with kissing ass. With the help of his parents, he moved back to Houston to start his own firm. That's where he met and married my grandmother. Six years later, he had a thriving law firm and a wife and three kids to come home to." I let the words sink in before giving her the rest. "He was also on his third affair..."

Her expression shifted from concern to outrage. "He told you this?"

"When I was fifteen and on the verge of what my grandfather considered 'being a man,' he sat me down and explained what was expected of me. I was going to go to law school, take over the firm when my father retired, and marry a proper lady who would give me children. Love didn't enter into the equation. It was all about duty and carrying on the Walker name. He said it didn't mean I couldn't have a little fun on the side. It was about two months later that I caught my father cheating on my mom." I laughed at her shocked expression, and added, "Yeah, talk about a defining moment in a young boy's life."

"What did you do?"

"I got mad. Then I decided I didn't want to be a lawyer. I wanted to be a musician." A contemptuous snort flew from her lips, making me laugh again. "Anyway, I had an interesting conversation with my sister tonight." I proceeded to tell her what happened at the hospital with Ehren and Elaine, including the part about how healthy and happy my dad looked.

"You're afraid to trust it," she commented when I was done.

"Wouldn't you be?"

"Hell yes, I would."

I was torn. I wanted to help take care of my mom but wanted nothing to do with my dad. I could practically see the wheels turning in Quinn's brain.

"This is why you're so against cheating, isn't it?" she finally asked. Leave it to Quinn to connect the dots.

"In my view, cheating is just another form of lying, and I fucking despise liars. Even if I loved Mandy with all my heart and soul, I would never be able to forgive her for lying to me."

"About that—" she started to say.

"But it goes beyond that," I continued, "What she's done is so much worse than a simple lie." Realizing that I'd rudely cut her off, I motioned for her to continue with what she was saying.

She shook her head. "No. Go ahead. What did she do now?" I told her what we found in the box. When I was done, she asked about Bobby and Tut's visit to the cousin.

"It was a dead end. Bobby said the poor guy didn't have a clue. He claims he left the certificate with the clerk the Monday after the wedding and that she was supposed to file it. They showed him the second certificate and said he looked genuinely shocked. He told them he had no knowledge of another wedding and thought we were still married and going strong."

The bottle had barely touched her lips, when she jerked it back. "Wait, but didn't he sign it?"

"He said the signature looked similar, but definitely wasn't his. He denied ever having seen the document before tonight and apparently kept calling her a troubled child, but when they asked what he meant by this, he gave them some mumbo jumbo about her parents giving her the world and how nothing was ever enough...all shit I already knew."

"God, Evan, this is the kind of crazy you read about in the tabloids."

Sighing heavily, I gave her the truth. "You know, I don't even care anymore. I'm so damn tired and just want it to be over."

On that note, she stood and held out her hand. "I know you are. Come on. Let's get you up to bed."

"Oooh, now there's an idea." I gave her a wink and let her pull me from the bench.

"Oh, behave," she replied in a damn good Austin Powers imitation. Even though we both laughed, I could tell something was bothering her.

After setting the alarm, we headed back to the house. We made it all the way to the kitchen door when she suddenly released my hand.

At my questioning look, she said, "Maybe we shouldn't do this."

"What? Hold hands?" I half-teased, when what I really wanted to do was pull her to me and kiss the doubt from her lips.

"You're married," she whispered. The emotion behind those two words made me hesitate, but only because I couldn't tell if it was anger or hurt. "I've had one serious relationship in my whole life and it ended with me getting my heart broken." Shit. I wasn't sure what bothered me more, that she'd been in a serious relationship or that he'd broken her heart.

Not able to stand the distance any longer, I reached my hand out and cupped the back of her neck. Slowly, I pulled her to me and pressed my lips to the side of her head. Damn, she smelled good. My cock rubbed painfully against the metal teeth of my zipper, a constant reminder of what I couldn't have.

"Evan." She whispered my name on a sigh, and I fought the urge to give her what we both so desperately wanted.

"How did the fucker hurt you, Quinn?"

"He was married." She now had my full attention.

"What?" I growled, pulling back so I could see her face. *Why was I just hearing about this now?*

"I didn't know he was married, but that's just it. I was so blinded by my feelings that I made really poor decisions. This—" she made a back and forth motion between us— "hasn't even gone anywhere yet, but it's eons more than I ever felt for him."

"And the problem is?" I asked, thinking it was a good thing.

Her eyes flashed with emotion, making them look more silver than gray. "The problem is, you've been with someone for nine years. Do you really want to jump back into another relationship? Because that's what it would be, a relationship. I can't do casual, not with you. And then, if we do pursue this and it goes bad, what then? Plus, it's not like you'll even be around.

I'm not exactly needy, but I'm not sure I can handle months on end without you." When she realized I had no clue what she was talking about, she elaborated. "Olivia spilled the beans tonight about Meltdown going back on tour." Shit! With all the crazy happening, I'd completely forgotten about that.

"I meant to tell you."

"Well, you didn't."

"Look, I get it. You're scared, but you're letting your insecurities rule you a—"

She cut me off with a growl. "My insecurities? Seriously? Let's get one thing straight. I'm not in the least bit insecure. I'm cautious and concerned. I know you want me." She lowered her hand to my junk and latched on. I let out a grunt of surprise and her brow shot up in an I-told-you-so look. "It's kind of *hard* not to miss this when it's pressed against you. I'm not insecure, Rock Star, I'm smart. Just because we can, doesn't mean we should, and right now, I'm thinking we shouldn't." With a huff of anger, she released my dick and stormed inside the house. Clearly insecure wasn't the right word to use.

"Good job, dumb ass," I muttered. I knew if I went after her, it would lead to a fight...or sex. I wanted to avoid the first and drown in the last. I was well and truly screwed.

An hour later, I was sitting on the living room floor, a bottle of Jack in one hand and a third manila envelope in the other. An envelope I'd discovered while searching through the box we'd set aside. I found it at the very bottom, hidden underneath all of the pictures. I thought about waking Bobby and Tut before opening it, but as it was already late, I decided against it. My gut twisted with angst as I stared at the ticking time bomb in my hand. Whatever was in this envelope was going to change everything. I wasn't sure how I knew this...I just did.

Liquid courage, I thought as I lifted the bottle to my lips and swallowed the alcohol. Fire streaked down my throat, turning to warmth as it emptied into my stomach. After two more chugs, I placed the bottle on the floor next to me and ripped open the envelope. Just like the other two, this one held a marriage certificate. I stared at the names; Amanda Lynn James and Ned Colliard. Who in the hell is Ned Colliard? The date read May of 2007. This was a little over a year before we hooked up. The State of Virginia caught my eye. Mandy went to college in Virginia. Across the top corner was the word "Copy." Sitting right next to it, as plain as day, was the County Clerk's stamp. Not the original, but a copy. If this was a copy, then where was the original? On file in Virginia? This was beyond messed up. It was insane.

Dropping my head back, I screamed, "Fuuuuuuuuuuck!" Then I picked up the liquor bottle and hurled it against the wall. After that, I went to wake Bobby and Tut.

Fifteen minutes later, the entire house was up. While the guys poured over the document, I leaned against the wall and watched Quinn. She was quiet. I could tell she hadn't slept. I could also tell she was still mad at me.

"I say we fuck her world up." This was the fifth time Chaz had suggested this.

"That's enough," Olivia scolded.

"Fuck this," he muttered. Olivia shook her head as he stormed off in a huff.

"Sorry," she said before going after him.

"As much as we'd like to go balls to the wall on the bitch, that wouldn't be smart. She's obviously up to something and the best way to beat her, is to figure out what game she's playing," Bobby stated.

Quinn's eyes narrowed in anger. "What does that even mean?"

"It means we do this the right way. She had to have had help in all of this. First, we pay a visit to the County Clerk. After that, we'll focus on husband number one," he answered. Quinn muttered something about coffee and walked out of the room.

"How did I not know she was married?" I quietly asked, but we all knew that wasn't the real question. The real question was how had she managed to perpetuate this lie for nine whole years. Suddenly, a thought popped into my head. *The baby*. The same night I told her it was over, she told me she was pregnant. My lungs seized in my chest.

"What?" Tut asked.

"The baby."

Bobby's brow furrowed in question. "What baby?"

"I married Mandy because she was pregnant, but was she really? Shit," I angrily bit out, "If the marriage wasn't real..." I couldn't even say the rest.

Tut grunted in amusement. "And the plot thickens."

Bobby frowned at him, before turning his attention to me. "Those are good questions and definitely ones we'll look into, but first, I need for you to trust us and the process, okay?"

I took in a deep breath and slowly let it out. "Yeah, okay. Do you want me to call Stan?"

"Why don't we see what the clerk and husband number one have to say before we get the lawyers involved." I nodded, and he gave an encouraging smile. "Good, now go get some coffee and something in your stomach. You look like you're about to drop."

Bobby and Tut left for the County Clerk's office around nine. This left me with Chaz, Olivia, and a still angry Quinn.

Just as I'd finished cleaning up the remainder of the broken bottle, Chaz appeared in the doorway. "Come on, sissy boy, let's blow this joint."

"Sissy boy? I'm not the one who's pussy whipped," I pointed

out.

"I'm more than whipped. I'm owned," he admitted on a laugh. "Now, let's go. I have something I want to show you."

"Let me grab my wallet and tell Quinn."

"You don't need your wallet and Quinn already knows," he shot back at me. With that being said, I really had no argument. I did, however, need to touch base with my brother. Earlier, while I was in the shower, Dad called and left a brief update about Mom on my voicemail.

On our way out the door, I tossed him the keys. "Here, you drive. I need to check in with Ehren."

Ehren reported that Mom was doing better than expected and would most likely be released later today. I told him to tell her I would stop by the house either tonight or tomorrow before ending the call.

"Is she okay?" Chaz asked.

"She will be."

"Are you okay?"

"No."

Sensing that I needed space, he turned on the radio and dialed it to the local Classic Rock station. Zeppelin's "Going to California" played as I leaned my head against the door and closed my eyes.

"Hey, fuck face, we're here," I heard him say sometime later.

"Hmmm?" I lifted my head from the window and tried to focus on the building in front of us. I spotted the name Madden Daze on the door and froze.

My gaze snapped to his as I pointed to the sign and said, "You know Madden Daze?" Madden Daze was one of the best custom guitar designers in the business. Grant and Nash each had one of his guitars. Grant had even let me play his a time or two.

A hint of a smile touched his lips. "We've met. Let's go, or we'll be late." Talk about vague. Too excited to argue with him, I pulled the handle and opened my car door.

A blonde-haired beauty met us at the door, and after gushing all over us, she escorted us back to what she called the "Design Room."

Sitting on a rustic looking bench was none other than the man himself. I'd seen him in magazines, but this was the real deal. His head lifted from the guitar he was working on and a smile spread across his face. He stood and moved in our direction.

"Chaz, it's good to see you again. I see you met my daughter, Liliana."

Chaz nodded at Liliana. "Madden, this is Evan Walker, Meltdown's newest member and the best fucking keyboardist you'll ever hear," he introduced. My face flushed with pride as I held out my hand.

"Nice to meet you, Evan. Chaz tells me you also play guitar," Madden replied as he shook my hand.

"Guitar is my second love," I explained, while trying not to piss my pants with excitement.

Clapping, Liliana exclaimed, "I'm so excited! Brady and I saw you guys in Ohio and you were amazing!" I gave Chaz a questioning look.

"That was the night you covered 'Creep.'" Oh, yeah. I'd completely forgotten about that.

"It was better than the original," she gushed.

"Thanks," I muttered.

"Is that it?" Chaz asked. I followed his line of sight to the back of the room where a lone guitar sat on a silver floor stand. A guitar that looked identical to the one I'd purchased years ago with my allowance money. The same guitar that Mandy had destroyed in her petty fit of rage.

"Holy shit," I whispered. Dragging my eyes from the guitar

back to Chaz, I asked, "What did you do?"

"Chaz, here, gave me a call after the unfortunate incident at your house. He told me what he wanted, and I just happened to have some spare time on my hands," Madden explained.

Chaz coughed and muttered something that sounded a lot like "Extortion," and Madden broke into a fit of laughter. I had no idea what they were talking about and I really didn't care. All I could focus on was the guitar. It was beyond cool. It was fucking amazing. I couldn't believe Chaz had done this.

Madden waved his hands towards the guitar. "Well, whatcha waitin' for? Go get her." Grinning like a kid in a candy store I walked across the room and lifted the guitar from the stand. My gaze flew to Chaz and he nodded in understanding. He knew. Without me even having to say a word, he felt the depth of my gratitude.

After thanking Madden and getting practically squeezed to death by Liliana, we were ready to go. I couldn't wait to show Quinn.

We were almost to the car when Madden called after us. "See you in October!"

"I can't wait!" Liliana squealed.

I waited until we were inside with the doors shut before asking, "What's in October?"

"A wedding," Chaz vaguely replied.

"Whose wedding?"

"Liliana and Brady's." It took me a minute to catch on.

"You told them we would play?"

His eyes cut to me. "You like your guitar, don't you? Well, that was the only way you were getting it. Now, say thank you, Chaz."

"Fuck you, Chaz," I grumbled. A minute passed before I admitted, "It is pretty damn amazing."

His face split into a smile. "That's not a thanks, but it's close enough."

"Thanks, asshole," I said through laughter.

We weren't even five minutes into the drive when my phone rang. Glancing down, I saw the words "Unknown Caller" roll across the screen. It had been over twelve hours since her last attempt. Twelve peaceful hours. I seriously considered answering it. God, how I wanted to fucking blast her into next year, but Bobby was right. We needed to figure out her game. If I tipped her off that we were on to her, who knows what she would do.

Chaz's eyes darted to the phone and his lip curled in disgust. "Mandy?" he asked.

"Probably."

"I'll give it to her; the bitch has balls." My phone rang again, and again, I sent it to voicemail. "Aren't you going to listen to it?"

My eyes slid from the phone to his. "It's kind of hard to listen when your voicemail is full." We both smiled. When my phone rang a fourth time, I powered it off.

Chaz shook his head. "I don't know what I would do if I found out that Olivia was fucking around on me with another guy."

"I'm pretty sure you would kill him." His lip twitched with humor.

"You're right, I would. I've got to say, though, I'm surprised you're playing by the rules. If it was me, I would have hunted this Baxter joker down and taught him a lesson by now."

Shrugging, I said, "Baxter is a victim of circumstance. Think about it. If a woman you'd shared years of your life with decided to punish you for following your dreams by spreading her legs for another man, who she planned on marrying behind your back, only to discover that she was already married to a third dude, would you hunt him down or would you hunt her down?"

"Oh, I would definitely make her pay, but I'd make sure he felt the backlash."

Leaning my head back on the seat, I let out a sigh. "Honestly, I just want it to be over."

"Did you ever love her?"

"At some point, I thought I did. I sure as hell tried."

"And now?"

"I'm living with a woman I haven't even touched yet, and I already feel more for her than I ever felt for Mandy. What does that tell you?"

"It tells me you need to get laid."

"No shit," I snapped, and we both busted into laughter.

CHAPTER FOURTEEN

"America's Sweetheart"

Quinn

"No, Mom, now isn't a good time for a chat."

"Knock-knock!" I heard Alex-Ann call out from downstairs. Crap! She and Gretchen were here early.

"Upstairs!" I shouted down to them.

After my thing with Evan last night—followed by no sleep, because I was worrying about my thing with Evan—I was in a rotten mood. I couldn't shut off my brain. I'd tried to tell him, but then he started talking about lying and how he could never forgive Mandy for her gazillion transgressions, and I couldn't think straight.

Alex-Ann's face appeared in my doorway. I beckoned for both she and Gretchen to come in as I continued to listen to my mother blather about how I didn't have time for her anymore. I wasn't the one who'd left.

"My mother," I mouthed when Alex-Ann made a face at the

phone.

"Because I have a houseful of guests right now and don't want to be rude," I answered, to her question as to why I couldn't talk. "Look, Alex and Gretchen just arrived. We're going to soak up some rays. I'll call you this weekend." Before she had the chance to lay into me, I said, "Love you, Mama," and disconnected the call.

"Poor Mama K," Alex-Ann uttered.

Olivia appeared at my door. Smiling at the three of us, she asked, "Who's Mama K?"

"Quinn's mom," Gretchen told her.

"Do you think she's having second thoughts about leaving?" Alex-Ann asked.

"No. I think she loves it there but is feeling guilty for how she left things with me. I'm just letting her stew in it for a bit."

A wicked grin appeared on Gretchen's face. "Yeah, but if she hadn't of left, you wouldn't have Mr. Hot as Hail rock star living with you." I couldn't help but scowl. Rock Star was in the dog house. He'd called me insecure; the exact same word he'd used to describe his lying, cheating hussy of a—I couldn't exactly call her his wife, now could I?

Zeroing in on my frown, Alex-Ann asked, "What's wrong?" I wanted to tell her what happened, but I didn't want to hear her gloat, so I opted to evade the question altogether. Plus, I didn't dare say anything in front of Olivia for fear she would say something to Chaz.

"Nothing's wrong. At least, nothing that a float in the pool won't cure. I made some iced tea for us. Alex-Ann, can you grab the cups?" Surprisingly, she dropped the subject and did as I asked.

"Chaz and I were up kind of late last night. Do you mind if I skip the swim and take a nap?" Olivia asked. The three of us smiled knowingly at her and she laughed.

While Jake Owen sang about his girl named Sheila who went batshit on Tequila, we floated in the pool.

"Any news on crazy bitch?" Alex-Ann asked. I shot her a shut-the-hell-up-in-front-of-Gretchen-look and she rolled her eyes.

"I'm with Alex-Ann. I don't think you should tell Evan you know Amanda. In the end, it will only complicate things," Gretchen commented. My eyes shot to Alex-Ann, who was staring at Gretchen as if she was a glitter sprinkled unicorn. I glared at my now ex-best friend. Wow, talk about not being able to trust someone.

Catching my glare, Alex exclaimed, "What? I didn't tell her!"

Gretchen let out a snort. "Here's a little secret for you, ladies. If you act like you don't have a brain, people treat you like you don't have a brain. They're also more likely to say shit in front of you."

As I contemplated this new side of Gretchen, Alex-Ann asked, "What else do you know that you're not supposed to?"

"I know I want in that man's pants," she murmured low enough for only us to hear. We followed her gaze to the top of the steps to where Tut stood. "Right there is a chocolate fudge Sunday and I want to be his cherry on top," she continued, and then in a much louder voice, called out, "Hey, sexy! Come swim!" He gave a wave that he'd heard us before disappearing back inside.

A few minutes later, he was back with Bobby.

"Yee-fucking-haw," Gretchen commented when she saw them heading down the steps in their swim trunks.

They hit the pool deck and Bobby immediately started bitching about the music. Tut cannonballed into the pool, making the three of us squeal in outrage. He resurfaced, only to let out a deep rumble of laughter on confirming that he'd soaked us.

I wanted to ask about their visit to the clerk's office, but wasn't sure it was my place. This was just one of the many things I found so frustrating. Evan and I had all of the trappings of a relationship, but without the main ingredients. I really needed ingredients.

As Gretchen flirted with Tut and Alex-Ann shamelessly crawled all over Bobby, I floated on my bright green pool float—all alone, while thinking about how nice Evan's ingredients were.

Everything was going along just dandy until "Islands in The Stream" came on the radio.

"That's it. I'm changing it," Bobby announced as he hefted himself out of the water.

"I'll come with you. I have to pee," Alex-Ann said.

"Can you make more tea while you're up there?" I asked.

"Sure. Where are the tea bags again and how long do I do that thingamajiggy?" she questioned.

"Never mind. I'll do it."

"Put on something good," Tut told Bobby.

"Hey, don't das on Dolly," Gretchen said, toeing his float.

"It's dis," he told her, and she busted into giggles. I had to give it to her, Gretchen had this dumber than dirt thing down pat.

On the way to the house, I thought about Chaz and Evan's secret errand. Knowing Chaz, it could be anything.

Leaving Bobby and Alex-Ann to deal with the music, I worked on the tea. When I was done and ready to head back to the pool, they were nowhere to be found. I didn't call out for fear of waking Olivia. After a few minutes of waiting, I decided to leave without them. Knowing Alex-Ann, they were probably already down there.

Bobby and Alex-Ann weren't at the pool. From the looks of

it, neither were Tut and Gretchen.

"Well, shit," I muttered as I stepped inside the gate. Just as I'd set the pitcher down on the table, I heard a noise. At first, I thought it was the filtration system, but then I heard it again. It sounded like it was coming from inside the pool house. So that's where they were.

As I neared the sliding doors, I noticed they were partially open. Then I heard Gretchen say, "Harder, baby." At least, I thought it was Gretchen.

Don't do it! My brain screamed, but did I listen? Heck no. I crept right up to the slider and peered inside. Tut was a sexy mountain of a man, but Tut with his naked backside on display with his muscles flexed as he nailed Gretchen to the pool house wall, was something to see. Tingles danced up and down my spine and a deep ache set up residence in my lower abdomen as I watched him pump in and out of her. Gretchen was no small woman, yet with one giant man hand on her ass and the other tangled in her hair, Tut made her seem like flipping Twiggy.

"I've been wanting this pussy for days now," he said in a low, guttural sex voice, and I literally felt my insides spasm. Goosebumps sprang up all over my body as I tried to wrangle in my out of control hormones. Where was the Chaz on my shoulder when I needed him?

I started to pull away when Gretchen let out a moan, followed by, "I want you behind me." Before I knew what was happening, Tut pulled out and lowered her to her feet. Holy shmoly. He. Pulled. Out. He was huge. He was bigger than huge. He was a freaking megadick, a hosscock...a stallion. The man was hung like a damn horse.

They moved to shift positions and I quickly stepped out of view. With my back pressed to the side of the pool house, I tried to catch my breath, but couldn't. My body was on fire and it was all Evan Walker's fault. The man had me hornier than a three peckered billy goat.

Gretchen let out a long, drawn out groan and I squeezed my eyes shut. Devil take me, but I needed relief from this unbearable ache. *No one's here. They'll never know,* I thought as I slid my hand under the waistband of my bikini bottoms. A part of me was ashamed that it had come to this. The other didn't care. I needed release and I needed it now. It didn't take long. Just a few finger strokes and a few quiet moans and I was there. Gods above, I. Was. There.

A shush of relief escaped from my lips as I opened my eyes and retracted my hand from my suit bottoms. *There, all better now.* Before making a move to leave, I scanned my surroundings, and there he stood, watching me with those sexy green eyes. My face flamed with mortification at the realization that he'd just watched me do...that.

Bobby and Alex-Ann walked through the gate at the same time that Tut and Gretchen stepped out of the pool house.

I didn't know what to say...what to do, so I asked, "Does anyone want some tea?"

"I'll take some," Alex-Ann replied.

I moved to pour it for her and heard Evan say, "Do you have news?" Bobby answered him, but I was too far away to hear his response. The next thing I knew, Evan, Tut, and Bobby were walking toward the gate.

"Where are they going?" Gretchen asked.

"Bobby has news," Alex-Ann replied. As much as I wanted to hear that news, I wasn't about to go after them. Not after what had just happened.

"I just had the most amazing sex," Gretchen said once they were out of earshot.

"Same here," Alex-Ann gushed.

"I just got busted giving myself the business," I confessed out loud, and then burst into tears.

CHAPTER FIFTEEN

"If It Makes You Happy"

Evan

I was furious. Furious and so turned on I couldn't see straight.
Good thing I was in the lead, or Bobby and Tut would see my
cock straining against my shorts. Painfully straining, no thanks
to Tut. Is that what Quinn wanted? Flashes of her standing there
with her hand between her legs traipsed through my brain. Jaw
clenching jealousy ripped through me. That she was turned on
enough to take care of herself in broad daylight, where anyone
could see, made me see red. I wanted to beat Tut's ass. He may
be bigger, but I had anger on my side.

From behind me, Bobby asked, "Where did you and Chaz
run off to?" Ignoring his question, I ripped open the door and
stormed inside the house. "What the fuck is his problem?" I
heard him say. My problem? Try problems. Tut wasn't the only
one screwing around on the job. When Chaz and I entered the
house, we heard Alex-Ann—and it was clearly Alex-Ann—

shouting Bobby's name. It definitely wasn't in anger, either. At the time, we thought it was funny. Now, not so much.

I steered them into the living room, and in an attempt to keep it professional—when what I really wanted to do was lay into them—I asked, "Did you talk to the clerk?"

"What's your problem?" Tut growled. There was that damn question again.

"My problem is that I'm paying you two to do a job, not to fuck Quinn's friends." Bobby's face blanked of all expression.

Tut's brows shot up. "You got a thing for Gretchen?"

"No."

"Alex-Ann?"

"No."

"Then why do you care who we fuck? If you'd been here, we wouldn't have been fucking anyone. We would've been offloading information, but since you weren't..." he leaned forward, and in a menacing tone said, "we were having a little fun. So, I'll ask again, why do you care?" He was right. I was being a dick. He didn't know Quinn was watching. He didn't know anything. Fuck!

Unclenching my jaw, I took two short steps back, dropped to the chair, and lowered my head to my hands. "You're right. I'm sorry. This shit with Mandy is messing with me."

"You're not the only one. Why do you think we needed to blow off steam?" Tut questioned.

"You're right," Bobby cut in. "We're here to do a job and took it too far."

"Speak for yourself. If anything, I didn't take it far enough," Tut grumbled. I lifted my head in time to see Bobby mouth for Tut to shut the fuck up.

Before they started beating the hell out of each other, I asked, "Did you learn anything?"

RB HILLIARD

"Boy, did we. It's a damn good thing you're sitting or this would knock you back a few feet," Tut responded. And like that, the unease I'd been feeling shot to the oh-shit zone.

Bobby tossed him a look of warning, before answering, "The clerk—Serena is her name—didn't file the marriage certificate because Mandy paid her not to."

I waited for them both to take a seat before asking, "Why would she do that?"

"Start at the beginning," Tut told him.

"You remember when I called the County Clerk's office and asked about the certificate, only to discover one hadn't been filed?" I nodded, and he continued, "That was Serena. I knew it the second I stepped inside the office and heard her voice. Just so you know, it's a felony for a government official to tamper with public records."

"The bitch could go to jail for not filing that document," Tut clarified.

At my confused expression, Bobby said, "I told her who we were and what we wanted. When she started to lie, I simply reminded her that she'd already broken a few laws."

Chuckling, Tut murmured, "Talk about diarrhea." Bobby scowled and the chuckle morphed into a laugh. I was about to ask if they'd scared her into shitting her pants, when Tut shared, "You should have seen it. The second Bobby threatened her, those lips loosened right on up." Bobby let out an exasperated sigh.

Dragging his gaze from Tut back to me, he explained, "According to Serena, Amanda called her roughly twelve weeks before the wedding. She told her she'd moved back, was excited they were living in the same town, and wanted to do lunch sometime. Serena was surprised, because she and Amanda didn't exactly get along in high school. Regardless of the past,

163

she took her up on her offer. Over lunch, they talked mostly about Serena's job. She said Amanda didn't talk about herself at all, which she found strange. When Serena let it slip that she was still trying to pay off her student loans, Amanda pounced." Something about Bobby's story bothered me.

"Did you say twelve weeks before the wedding?"

Bobby nodded. "That's what she said, why?" The gears in my head shifted and then ground to a complete standstill.

"That would put it right around the first night we slept together...before she even knew she was pregnant. Are you sure you have the right date?"

"She was pretty clear about the timing," Tut answered.

I sat in stunned silence, while trying to make the pieces of the puzzle fit together. If Mandy had lunch with Serena before we were even together, then... Understanding hit, and I closed my eyes.

"She planned it," I rasped, my throat thick with emotion.

Slowly, I opened them back up to find everyone staring at me— both with understanding and sympathy mired in their expressions.

Lowering my head back to my hands, I whispered, "Mother fucker, she planned the whole thing." A minute passed before I gained enough composure to ask, "Why?"

I could see the slow boil of anger simmering in the depths of Bobby's eyes. For some reason this made me feel better, like I wasn't completely alone in this fucked up nightmare.

"We'll get to that in a minute, but first let me finish with Serena. She claims that Amanda paid her a thousand dollars to sign, but not to file, the marriage certificate, and at the last minute, she decided not to stamp it."

"Did she say why?"

"Because somewhere in that stupid little brain of hers, she

thought that if she didn't stamp it, she would still be able to lie her way out," Tut answered. "Serena isn't exactly the sharpest knife in the drawer. It was hard not to feel sorry for the girl."

"Did she tell you why Amanda wanted her not to file it in the first place?"

Bobby let out a harsh breath. "Get this, Amanda told Serena your parents didn't approve of the marriage and that if your dad found out, he would disown you. She said she loved you too much to let that happen." I shook my head in disgust and he continued, "She told us she let Amanda take the certificate home with her. They stayed friends after that but rarely saw each other. My call apparently caught her off-guard. That, and her boss being in the office that day, made her nervous, which led her to mess up the plan."

"What? The fuck over Evan plan?" I asked, my words dripping with sarcasm. "I mean, seriously? If this was all for revenge, then Mandy definitely wins the award."

Bobby's brow furrowed. "Revenge?" he asked.

"What revenge?" Tut responded simultaneously. Shit. I forgot they didn't know about high school.

"Mandy and I dated in high school." Clearly neither of them was pleased by this little newsflash.

"You've been holding out on us," Tut growled. I bristled at his accusatory tone. Fuck him. We held each other's gaze, neither of us flinching, until Bobby cut in.

"Are you gonna tell us?"

"Yeah, sure," I said, still staring at Tut. He finally looked away and I began to tell the story. "We started dating when Mandy was a senior and I was a junior. Out of bed, we were a horrible match, but in bed, we lit up the sheets. For me, that was all there was to it. She was great in bed. I wasn't stupid. I knew she wanted words of love and shit, but that wasn't me. She did stuff to try and make me jealous, but then caught on that I didn't care and stopped."

"What happened?" Bobby asked.

"I wanted out. I was going to college and wanted to be free."

"You dumped her," Tut accused. Bobby glared at Tut, but Tut was too busy misinterpreting my words to pay attention. No wonder Bobby always looked pissed off. The guy was a real dick.

"No, I waited for her to get home for summer break and I let her down easy."

"I bet she didn't think it was easy," he mumbled. What was with this guy?

Speaking over Tut, Bobby asked, "How did she take it?"

"She pretended to be cool with it, and the reason I say pretend is because once we were married, she harped on it."

"As in how?" he asked.

"As in anytime we had a fight, she threw it in my face."

"Is there more to the story or is that it?"

"That's it. I saw her a few times over the next four years, but only in passing." Bobby nodded his head as if it all made sense. However, I was still waiting for him to enlighten me.

"Okay, well, that was off subject but good to know. As far as the plan went, Mandy told Serena that if anyone was to call looking for the marriage certificate, Serena was to stall them and then call her immediately. Mandy would bring the certificate, Serena would stamp it and file it, and no one would know the difference." A tiny ray of hope flared deep in my belly.

"She messed up."

A small smile appeared on Bobby's face. "She did. She called Mandy and when she told her what she'd done, Mandy went ape-shit on her. Get this, that was the same day as the break-in." And another puzzle piece clicked into place.

"Mandy didn't know I moved the boxes to the garage. She uses it for storage, not for parking. She thought I took them with me."

"Which explains her motive," he surmised.

"Tell him about Virginia," Tut urged. Bobby and I both stared at him and he scowled. "What?"

Bobby eventually complied, but I could tell he was getting fed up. "On the drive back this afternoon, I put in a call to the County Clerk's office in Richmond." His words scored through me and I sucked in a deep breath. "They confirmed they have a wedding certificate for Amanda James and Ned Colliard on file in their office." The breath whooshed from my lungs. I didn't want to hope, but there it was.

"Mandy was married..."

"She still is," Tut confirmed, before adding, "and it's not to you, my brother."

"So...I'm free?" I asked, thinking there had to be a catch.

A commotion in the entry hall caught our attention and the room went silent.

"Where's Tut?" we heard Gretchen ask.

"In here," Tut called out. Gretchen, Alex-Ann, and Quinn suddenly appeared in the doorway.

"You left me," Gretchen whined, her bottom lip jutting about three inches over her top. Alex-Ann snorted and Quinn rolled her eyes. What she wouldn't do, was look at me. She wasn't looking at Tut either, I noted.

"Come on or we're going to be late for work," Alex-Ann griped.

Tut leaned forward and whispered something in Gretchen's ear, making her respond with a breathy giggle. This time it was Alex-Ann with the eye roll, while Quinn turned a pretty shade of pink.

The more I stared at her, the more she resisted looking at me. Naughty, sexy country girl was playing a dangerous game. At least she was wearing a cover up. Not that it covered up much. Her legs were on full display and I could see a sliver of those damn bikini bottoms peeking out through the front opening. I'd just discovered that my wife of nine years was a bigamist and all I could think about was stripping the swimsuit from Quinn's body and erasing all thoughts of Tut from her mind. What the fuck was wrong with me? My eyes grazed back up her body and halted on her gray-eyed stare. A stare that narrowed dangerously in on my now smiling face.

"Here, let us walk you out," Bobby drawled.

As the crowd moved towards the front door, Alex-Ann and Gretchen both called out, "Bye Evan!"

"Later!" I replied.

"Where's Quinn?" I asked on their return.

Bobby shrugged. "Showering, I think. Now, to answer your question from earlier, there is no legal documentation to back that you were ever married to Amanda James, but that doesn't mean you're out of the woods just yet. You're due in divorce mediation in two weeks. We still have to find the husband and you need to explain everything to your lawyer. Even then, this will likely have to go before a judge, where both parties will be forced to present evidence."

"No fucking way. That could take months," I clipped.

"Your lawyer will be able to tell you if there's a way around it," Bobby advised.

"Fuck that. I'm calling my dad. He knows every judge in the State of Texas."

"Now we're talking," Tut growled. This earned him a scowl from Bobby and a smile from me.

"Talk to your dad, but right now, we need more time." Bobby's words reminded me of my talk with Chaz the other day.

"That's easy. I'll just cancel the mediation."

"On what grounds?" they both asked.

"On the grounds that I want a reconciliation." No one said a word.

Tut was the first to break the silence. "I would pay money to see the look on that bitch's face when her attorney gives her the news."

Bobby belted out a laugh. "I've got to say, that's pretty fucking brilliant. She's been playing the role of victim to her lawyers this entire time. You giving her what she's been asking for will not only send her scrambling but will buy us the time we need. Which reminds me, right before the crew came in, I got an email confirming that the husband is back in Richmond. Tut and I were already heading that way this weekend, so this makes our job a hell of a lot easier."

"You want to hear something funny? Three months ago, I would have given my left nut to see Mandy incarcerated. Now, she could be the princess of polygamy, for all I care. I just want her the fuck out of my life." I pointed at the ceiling. "You know that woman upstairs? I want her more than I've ever wanted anything. That includes Meltdown, or hell, even music, for that matter. If there's the slightest chance that I can be held to my marriage vows, I need you to tell me, because the one thing I can't do, is hurt Quinn."

Bobby's face split into a smile. "Here's how I see it. Without a properly documented marriage certificate there is no marriage. I would be worried about Mandy pulling a fast one, such as trying to get Serena to stamp and file the original certificate, or even attempt to claim a common law marriage existed, but being that Serena's boss immediately sent her home and vowed to have the County attorney investigate right away, and the fact that Mandy is already married, neither of these would hold up in court. You still need to call your lawyer and cancel the mediation and we want you to follow through with your dad to see if he has a better solution, but as far as Quinn goes, my view is that you're free to do as you please."

"Someone's coming down the stairs," Tut warned. His words barely had time to settle when Chaz appeared in the doorway. Quinn was in his wake, but instead of stopping, she continued past the room and out the front door. Glancing down at my watch, I realized she was leaving for work. The fact that she was doing so without saying so much as a goodbye was not cool at all.

"Fill Chaz in. I'll be right back," I told them, and sprinted from the room.

Quinn was almost to her car when I caught up with her. As she made a move to open the door, I slapped my hand against it—at the same time pressing my front to her back, which forced her up against the side of the car. Her gasp told me she felt it, and trust me, there was a hell of a lot to feel. I'd never been this hard, never felt this way, never wanted something so damn much. Never. Fucking. Ever.

Dropping my lips to her ear, I whispered, "Do you feel it?"

"Evan—"

"Answer me," I growled.

"Yes." It came out as a half-whisper, half-groan.

"Is this what you wanted from Tut this afternoon?" I regretted it the minute I said it.

"No, you stupid man, it's what I want from you," she snarled, and I could tell that my little hell cat was getting fired up.

"What do you want, Quinn?" I needed to hear her say it.

"You," she whispered in a barely-there voice.

"I can't hear you." God, I wanted to rip off those fucking

short shorts and bury my cock deeper than deep. I wanted to brand her, own her...make her mine.

"You!" she all but shouted. "Now release me so I can go to work!"

I did her one better. Using both hands, I spun her around and pressed her back to the car door. Gorgeous gray eyes stared up at me as I tangled my fingers in her hair, dropped my mouth to her lips, and gave her everything I had.

CHAPTER SIXTEEN

"Ask Me How I Know"

Quinn

I wasn't expecting his kiss. In truth, I thought it would never come—that we were meant to be together, yet destined to remain apart. But then his lips were on mine—soft, warm, sexy man lips—and suddenly, I didn't know what to do. My body screamed jump him, but my conscience demanded answers.

As if sensing my hesitation, he loosened his grip on my hair. "Don't be mad," he murmured against my mouth.

Before that magical tongue got its hooks into me again and my conscience went on permanent vacation, I slid my hands to his chest and pushed him away. Away, being a half a step back—just far enough for me to gather my bearings, yet still close enough that I had to tilt my head to see his eyes. Dang, but those emerald green eyes literally turned me inside out.

"You can't just...kiss me like that." His brows drew together and I inwardly sighed. Great, Quinn. The words sounded fine in my head, but stupid out loud. A jolt of frustration slashed through me and I pushed him back a step, hoping to gain a little more perspective.

"I can't be the other woman. I just...can't, and it's not because I don't want to, because I do. I really, really do, but I know me. I'm already ten kinds of gone for you and if you keep kissing me like that, it'll only make it worse." I would have kept going if not for the distraction of his hand trailing down my arm. Down it went, until slowly, he entwined our fingers together, turning me into a complete puddle of mush. With a slight yank of his arm, he jerked me forward.

"Evan!" I gasped as my chest bumped against his. Before I knew what was happening, he had his arm wrapped around me. His lips grazed across my neck, causing my insides to ignite. I sucked in a deep breath, thinking, I can worry about my conscience later.

Softly in my ear, he said, "Bobby and Tut just confirmed it. Mandy is legally married to the guy in Virginia."

My heart pitter-pattered like crazy inside my chest as my breath exploded in a loud, "What?" Tilting my head back, our eyes collided and I could see that he was telling the truth. I also saw heat—boiling hot, sexually intense...heat, brewing beneath that green-eyed stare of his.

"I still have some minor issues to take care of, but it's over. I'm free of her, and you know what that means?" I knew what I wanted it to mean. "It means I'm coming for you Quinn." Once again, I found myself pressed to his chest with his lips hovering at my ear.

"Watching you take care of yourself this afternoon nearly killed me. I want to take care of you. I want my hands, mouth, and cock—on you, in you, and all fucking over you, woman." Lust dripped from each word he spoke and I fought back a groan.

"But first, you have work and I have to check in on my Mom. I'll come by the bar after." Before I could reply, his lips were back on mine. Holy cow, the man could kiss! With one hand circling the nape of my neck and the other pressing against my backside, he all but devoured me. Sparks of desire bolted through my body, lighting me on fire. Burn baby burn, I thought as I shoved my fingers into his hair and gave him everything I had.

Had he not broken away, I would have let him take me right there. In front of God and his horn dog friends, I would have shucked off my shorts and shown him the way to the promised land. It was a good thing he chose that moment to walk away, because I wasn't sure I could. Not now. Not ever.

Hours later, I was going crazy. If I heard one more word about Tut's anaconda or Bobby's meat cleaver, I would lose my ever-loving mind. I was so irritated that I couldn't even enjoy the rowdy crowd as they sang along to "Follow Your Arrow," which just so happened to be one of my favorite Kacey Musgraves' songs of all time.

"Girl, you are strung tighter than a willy in the wrong hole! What is with you tonight?" Alex-Ann asked.

Not in the mood for conversation, I said, "I'm going for a smoke break. Hold down the fort."

"Cigarette!" I snapped at Sam on my approach to the service window.

Scowling, he said, "I thought you quit?"

"Do I look like I quit?" His eyes narrowed dangerously on me when I snapped my fingers at him. He glared. I glared. He sighed. I smiled. Moments later, I was outside, perched on the ledge with a cigarette between my fingers.

I got two measly puffs in, before the door opened and out stepped Evan. Of course, his gaze immediately dropped to the cigarette.

"I swear, I quit," I blurted.

He dropped down beside me. "Really? It doesn't look like it."

With a sigh, I flicked the remaining cigarette across the parking lot and slid my fingers inside my short's pocket to retrieve the piece of gum I'd stashed, on the off chance that Evan showed up and busted me smoking. "How's your mom?" I asked.

"She's better. At least, she looks better."

I held up the stick of gum. "Want half?"

"You know what I want." The smoldering deep tone of his voice made me all gooey inside.

"Yes, well, as good as that sounds," and it did sound so very good, "that's not going to happen here."

"Can I at least kiss you?" If he kissed me, it would lead to naughty naked stuff. He knew it and I knew it.

"Noooo. How's your dad?"

He exhaled loudly. "I told him about Mandy. He agrees with Bobby and Tut in that we need more time." My stomach dropped. *And here's where he takes it all back.*

"For?" I asked, nearly choking on the word.

"According to him, the marriage needs to be legally declared void, in that it happened under false pretenses. This means I need to get before a judge as quickly as possible, because regardless of whether the certificate was filed or not, we had a marriage license and a ceremony within the sixty-day requirement period." My eyes smarted as I waited for the other shoe to drop...and crush my heart to smithereens. "However," he continued, "he said that in light of her previous marriage, no judge in the State of Texas would disagree with me, and just so you know, he's friends with them all, so this is more a formality than anything."

Blinking back the tears, I asked, "A formality?"

"It means that I need to contact my attorney and tell him that instead of mediation, I want to set up a time to meet with Amanda to talk about a reconciliation."

"Are you serious?" I hissed, spearing him with a glare.

"Relax, it's just a ploy to buy us more time. Bobby and Tut are leaving for Virginia tomorrow. They're going to get a copy of the marriage license and have a chat with the husband. In the meantime, my dad is on the hunt for a judge that can get us on his docket as quickly as possible." My shoulders slumped with relief.

Swallowing my brief mental meltdown, I said, "This all sounds really good, Evan." He shifted beside me and then began scooting back. Once his back was to the wall, he leaned forward, grabbed me by the hips, and pulled me between his legs.

"It's better than good," he murmured against the back of my head. As he pulled me to his chest, I came to a decision. I wasn't going to tell him that I knew Baxter and Amanda. Alex-Ann was right. It would only complicate things, and Lord knows we didn't need any more complications in our lives. With that settled, I relaxed back against him, breathed in the night air, and let the happiness fill me.

About that time, Garth came on the jukebox. "Ask Me How I Know" was one of his newer songs; a song I liked, but hadn't really taken the time to listen to. That is, until Evan started singing it. With his arms wrapped tightly around me, he sang about a man so set in his ways, that even when he met the girl that changed it all, he was too proud to admit it and too scared to hold on, so he let her go. Even though it was depressing as all get out, I loved hearing Evan sing it.

When the song was over, he placed a gentle kiss on my neck, and whispered, "What a fucking idiot."

Glancing back at him, I asked, "What would you do if you were that guy?"

"I am that guy, Country. Do you see me running?" My breath hitched in my throat. Oh, God, was this really happening?

Staring straight at him, I whispered, "I'm crazy about you." He smiled. Then he tried to kiss me, but the angle was awkward, so I sat up, flipped around, and crawled back into his lap. Now, straddling his legs, I could feel every temptingly hard inch of him pressed against me. He watched me with a hungry expression on his face, and I thought, Jesus take the wheel, because I'm about to be a very bad driver. Then his lips were on mine and all I could focus on were the tiny beats of pleasure coursing through my body.

Evan made a noise in his throat, somewhere between a growl and a moan and I couldn't stop myself from rocking against his erection. Jerking me in tighter, he deepened the kiss and we both groaned. If he wasn't careful, this spring-loaded gun was going to come unsprung right in his lap.

We were seconds away from stripping each other naked, when the door flew open and Alex-Ann stepped out.

She took one look at us and shouted, "Ha! I knew you were riding that wild baloney!"

Evan buried his head in my neck and we both burst into laughter.

Margo's was packed that night. College was back in session, which meant that summer was officially over. Evan took up residence at the end of the bar, but we were so slammed that I could barely talk to him. At some point, I looked up to find Chaz, Olivia, Bobby, and Tut circled around him.

It took me a minute to make it down to their end of the bar to take their order. That's when Chaz informed us that he and Olivia needed to get back to New York.

"When are you leaving?" I heard Evan ask as I poured their beers.

"Tomorrow afternoon," Chaz answered. My eyes brushed over Evan's face as I lowered the beers to the bar top, and I knew what he was thinking. With Chaz and Olivia gone and Bobby and Tut in Virginia, it would just be the two of us...all alone...for who knows how long. His mouth slowly lifted into a wicked smile—a smile filled with dirty, sexy promises. A smile that made my insides quiver and my nipples stand at attention. Lord, what this man did to me.

"Is it just me or does it suddenly feel hot in here?" Olivia asked on a laugh.

"Shaw, this ain't nothing," Alex-Ann cut in. "You should have seen them outside earlier. They were seconds away from playing bury the boner." My face flamed with embarrassment as everyone burst into laughter. Alex-Ann bolted to the other end of the bar before I could slap her with my bar towel.

I was standing at one of the tables gabbing with a few of my regulars when some of the college kids recognized Chaz and Evan. All of a sudden, things went a little crazy. I knew it was bound to happen, I just didn't expect it right then. It was easy to forget they were famous, but super exciting to watch them in action. They didn't just sign autographs, they actually talked to the kids and made them feel special. Watching Evan in his element only made me want him more. Evan the rock star was just another piece of Evan the man—a man I both respected and appreciated more than I ever thought possible.

The gang took off a few hours before closing. Bobby and Tut wanted to run through some things before they left. I was shocked when Evan pulled me across the bar and kissed me. In front of a crowd of people, he kissed me!

"See you at home," he murmured.

All eyes were on me as I watched him walk away. After that, several of the girls set up residence at my end of the bar, and each time I was within talking distance, they bombarded me with questions. Some of them were downright personal.

It was well into the morning hours when I finally made it home. It was nights like this I wished I had a job with normal hours. However, the promise of Evan Walker overruled the fact that I was dead on my feet.

He did wait up for me. Well, kind of. I found him asleep on the downstairs sofa. I stood there for the longest time, just taking him in. Amanda James was a stupid woman, but I was not. Her loss was my gain.

With a smile on my face, I tiptoed to the hall closet, where I had an extra blanket stashed away. After covering Evan up, I went to bed.

CHAPTER SEVENTEEN

"I Will Wait"

Evan

I woke with a jolt. Thinking I was in my bed, I rolled over to look at the clock and nearly faceplanted onto the floor. It took a minute for the cobwebs to clear. Glancing around the room, I saw the boxes shoved against the wall, and suddenly, it all came back. While waiting for Quinn to get home last night, I must have fallen asleep. My eyes darted to the front window and a feeling of dread took hold. The sun was barely up, which meant it was early morning. Where was Quinn?

In a rush of fear, I bolted from the sofa and shot into the kitchen, hoping to find her purse sitting in its usual spot on the counter. Relief whooshed through me. It was here, which meant she was home, so...why didn't she wake me? This thought followed me all the way up the stairs and into her bedroom. A bedroom, I might add, that was spotlessly clean... as in scary clean... so clean that the thirty second rule could easily extend to the three-day rule. Pushing that thought aside, I advanced across the room to her bed. Somewhere, buried under the jungle of comforters, was Quinn. How many comforters did the woman need? There had to be at least three.

"I can feel you staring," a sleepy voice mumbled from beneath the pile.

Smiling at her early morning crankiness, I lifted the comforters up to slide inside and nearly pissed myself. Lying on her stomach with one leg cocked to the side, one arm above her head, and one half of a breast on full display, was a very naked Quinn. My cock shot up so fast, it nearly knocked out a tooth. The knowledge that my dream woman slept in the buff was almost too good to be real. It also elevated her status to future wife.

"That better be you checking out the goods, Rock Star, or we're going to have some issues."

Fighting back a laugh, I said, "Hmmm, could you roll over, please. I'd like to test drive the car before I buy it." At the sound of her girly giggle, I lost the fight, and while laughing with her, I thought, *I'm the luckiest bastard alive.* I made a move to join her in bed, but paused when she said, "Fine, but if I roll over, I better be seeing some cock." My brows shot to my hairline. Surely she was kidding. When she suddenly flopped over onto her back, I was caught so off guard that I swallowed my spit down the wrong pipe. While coughing like crazy, I ogled her gorgeous body. Anyone with eyes could see that Quinn was fit, especially wearing that work outfit that we still needed to have a chat about, but a naked Quinn was out of this world...perfect.

"Drop 'em," she ordered, and just like that, I was smacked by a wave of doubt. What if I didn't measure up, and I wasn't talking about my junk, because I knew that was impressive. I'd just pissed away nine years of my life on a woman who'd done nothing but lie to me. I felt like a wild animal that was finally freed from its cage. Gun shy was a good word to describe it. Scared was another. Was I wrong to have doubts? My thoughts must have shown on my face, because Quinn was suddenly on her knees and crawling to the edge of the bed.

"Hey, I'm sorry. I haven't done this a lot, I—" I placed my fingers on her lips to silence the rest of her sentence.

As she stared up at me with those sleepy gray eyes and that wild hair, I just had to know. "Tell me this isn't a mistake." Her face clouded with worry and I wanted to kick myself for ruining the moment with my insecurities.

"Do *you* feel like it's a mistake?" she asked. I could slowly see her withdrawing from me.

Now, mad at myself, I blurted, "I feel like you're the most important thing that's ever happened to me."

Her eyes sparked with emotion. "I feel the same way about you. Look, I know you're overwhelmed right now. I completely get it. So, how about we just take it one day at a time?" I wanted more, but for now this would have to do.

Reaching for her hand, I laced our fingers together. "One day at a time, huh? Tell me, Country, what do you have in mind for today?" I loved making her laugh. It made me want to do it over and over again.

"For starters, I'd like to not be the only naked person in the room."

"But naked looks so good on you." I was teasing her, but damn if it wasn't the truth.

Her laughter faded into a cock-throbbing smile. "I bet it would look good on you, too." She was taunting me and I liked it. I liked everything about Quinn Kinley.

In lieu of a response, I let go of her hand, and with the flick of my fingers, I unbuttoned my shorts. They landed on the floor with a thud. Trapped in her heated stare, I slid my fingers inside the waistband of my briefs and slowly pushed them down my legs.

A rush of air hissed from her mouth and I glanced up to find her eyes frozen on my cock. She kept them there as she shifted from her knees onto her ass and began shuffling backwards across the bed. When her back hit the pile of pillows lining the headboard, she stopped. What she didn't realize, was that in doing this, she opened herself up to me. I'd dreamed about this moment, fantasized about it, jacked off countless times while envisioning it in my head, but nothing could prepare me for the real deal.

Her breath hitched as I lowered one knee to the side of the bed. "I can't believe this is happening," she half-whispered, half-moaned. It was happening, alright. In fact, if I didn't get a grip, it was going to happen all over her pretty little stomach, which reminded me that I needed to grab the condom from my wallet. But first, I wanted a taste.

Surprise flickered in her eyes when I suddenly dropped to my belly, pushed up onto my forearms, and began to slither up the bed. When I reached the V of her thighs, I slid my hands under her ass and tilted her hips. The urge to see her face when I tasted her for the first time had me shifting my gaze up her stomach and past her breasts to her face—a face brimming with hunger. I drank in her lust filled expression as I glided my tongue across her opening.

A very unladylike curse flew from her lips, making me smile, making me only want more. Fuck more. I wanted it all. Jerking her hips higher, I dove in. She tasted like hope, like the promise of a brighter future. She tasted like...a song. I closed my eyes and nearly wept from relief. I could hear it in my head. For months I'd been waiting, wanting, wishing for the music to come. I thought it had died beneath the weight of Mandy's betrayal.

With a groan, Quinn buried her fingers in my hair and began to rock against my mouth. I could tell she was close. I was going to write a million songs for this woman, but first I was going to make her come on my tongue and then...I was going to make her mine.

She didn't scream like I thought she would. She just let out a low, guttural sounding moan. A moan that shot straight to my cock and echoed through my balls. In a flash I was off the bed and scrambling for my shorts and the condom inside my wallet.

Once I had it in my grasp, I turned to find her up on her elbows, watching me with a satiated smile on her lips. Her stare drifted to the condom in my hand, her smile instantly changing to a smirk.

"Well, aren't you just the Ready Freddy," she drawled.

Not wanting her to think that I regularly carried condoms around in my wallet, I told her that I'd stopped off at the gas station on the way home last night and bought three boxes.

Her jaw dropped and then she busted into laughter. "Three? Good lawd, Rock Star, talk about high expectations."

Shrugging, I murmured "High is better than none."

She wiggled her finger in a come-hither motion and burst into laughter when I took a running leap onto the bed and tackled her to the mattress. My cock accidentally rubbed against her slit, causing us both to groan. Chills of pleasure circled my balls and squeezed. I needed to get a move on or I was going to embarrass myself.

Quinn's husky murmur of, "Let me put it on," only made it worse.

"Next time," I told her. She opened her mouth to argue, but it was too late. I was already sliding the condom on. Gray eyes darkened with lust as she watched. Later, I would give her a show, but for now, I just needed to be inside her.

Slowly, I dropped to my forearms, lined myself up to Quinn's entrance, and gently pushed inside. Pleasure rippled through my body as I tilted my hips and added more pressure.

As I gazed down into her eyes, I knew that this was what I'd been waiting for. This was what I'd been missing. I just didn't know it, until now.

In an attempt to take me deeper, Quinn arched her back. At the same time, she made this noise in her throat, somewhere between a groan and a plea. A noise that almost derailed my self-control. I was trying to take this slow, to make it good for her, but she was making it harder by the second—both literally and figuratively.

"Please," she gasped, and that was all it took. The sound of her begging while my cock was inside her was more than I could handle, and in one swift thrust, I was buried as deep as I could go. A surprised gasp flew from her lips.

Our eyes locked and held. "You're perfect," I rasped.

She blinked. Then she craned her neck up and sealed her lips to mine. With a slight cant of my head, I deepened the kiss. At the same time, I pulled out and thrust back in.

"So good," she murmured against my lips.

I broke from the kiss long enough to say, "Legs behind my back." She immediately complied, and I swept my tongue back inside her mouth as I slowly began to build the pace. Neither of us could manage to hold the kiss because we were panting too hard. With each stroke I took us closer to the edge.

"Evan," Quinn gasped, and I knew she was close.

Not about to come without her, I switched it up, and at the bottom of each thrust, I ground my pelvis into her clit. Evidently, this worked, because she suddenly latched her hands onto my forearms and let out a long, drawn out, sexy as hell moan. A moan that catapulted me straight into orbit.

Waves of mind-numbing pleasure racked my body as I was engulfed by a spine stiffening orgasm. I didn't realize I was shouting until someone banged on the door.

"Hey, fucker! Keep it down in there! It's too damn early to be doing that shit!" Chaz shouted.

"Oh, God! I forgot they were here," Quinn whispered. Collapsing on top of her, I wrapped her in a full body hug, and burst into laughter.

"It's not funny!" Chaz yelled, but he was wrong. It was more than funny. It was fucking hilarious.

After a humor filled breakfast, where everyone gave us shit for being so loud, we said our goodbyes. Chaz and Olivia were on their way home to New York, while Bobby and Tut were headed to Virginia. The house was all ours by noon.

The housekeeper arrived shortly after they'd gone, and while Quinn instructed her on what to do, I called my attorney, Stan, and told him what I needed. Needless to say, he thought I was insane.

"You want to what?" he screeched. I explained what Bobby and Tut had discovered, how they were on their way to Virginia to confirm their findings, and that we needed to buy time.

"This is a bad idea," he argued.

"Do you have a better one, because if so, I'm all ears." As far as I was concerned, the guy hadn't done shit except for complain. When he failed to respond, I said, "Just do it," and hung up.

An hour or so later Quinn found me. "You okay?" she asked from the doorway. She had on sweatpants and a black tank top with the words Countryfried written across it in bold pink letters. Her hair was on top of her head in a frizzed-out pony tail and she wasn't wearing a stitch of makeup. She was perfect. My perfect.

"Is Linda still here?" I asked, thinking that if she wasn't, I was going to strip off Quinn's sweatpants and have my evil way with her.

A slow, very knowing smile spread across her face. "It's Lowis, and she's gone." And just like that, my cock was up and ready to go.

Unlike the first time, I planned on taking things slow. Quinn, evidently, had other ideas, because one minute we were talking about how I needed to remember the housekeeper's name and the next she was naked and straddling my lap.

"Quinn—"

Rearing back, she speared me with those amazing eyes of hers and said the words I never thought I'd hear, but had fantasized about. "Fuck me, Rock Star." Well, minus the rock star part, that is. She wanted to get fucked? Who was I to tell her no?

As I dug another condom out of my wallet, Quinn worked on my shorts. In record time, they were unzipped and my cock freed from my briefs. I was going to suggest getting undressed, when the condom was suddenly jerked from my grasp. The sight of her rolling it onto my cock made me lose my train of thought. With lust in her eyes and a look of intense concentration on her face, Quinn lifted up onto her knees and slowly sank down, taking me all the way to the root. Being here, in this house, inside this woman, felt monumental. It felt right...as if my whole life had been leading me to this moment.

Eyes leveled on me, she ordered, "Shirt off, Rock Star. I want to see those tats." Trying not to laugh at her drill sergeant tone, I reached between us, grabbed the bottom of my shirt, and yanked it over my head. With a satisfied smile, she pulled back and lowered her lips to my nipple. Damn, that felt good. I thought I was going to explode when she began to outline one of my chest tats with her tongue. At the same time, she continued to ride my cock. How? I had no clue, but I liked it. When the licks turned into nibbles, I had to take a deep breath. The need to come was riding me hard, but I couldn't tell if she was close or not. Needing her there, I cupped both of her ass cheeks with my hands, and began pumping her up and down my shaft.

"Evaaaaaan," she groaned.

"Please tell me your close," I responded on a pant.

"If you keep doing that, I'm going to be closer than close." Leave it to Quinn to say something funny during sex.

Trying to stave off my orgasm for a few more seconds, I replied, "What if I want you to be closer than close?"

Her whole body tensed. I knew what that meant. Not even three seconds later, she shouted, "Yes! Yes! Yeeeeeees!" And just like that, my orgasm hit. Hard and fast, it slammed into me.

After riding out the shockwaves, Quinn slumped onto my chest with a sigh. A moment of silence passed. I thought she might have fallen asleep, but then all of the sudden, her head sprang up from my chest and she captured me with that gray-eyed stare of hers.

"What would you say if I played hooky from work for the next few days or so?" I didn't want her to get into trouble because of me, but I sure as hell liked the idea.

"Can you do that?"

Smirking, she replied, "I'm the boss. I can do anything I want."

"Oh yeah, and what does the boss lady want?" I asked.

Eyes glittering with mischief, she answered, "I want you." Then she sealed it with a kiss.

CHAPTER EIGHTEEN

"Brace for Impact"

Quinn

Sex with Evan was like riding a roller coaster with no safety bar or skydiving without a parachute. It was the biggest adrenaline rush I'd ever experienced, an addiction with no possible form of rehabilitation...it was everything I thought it would be and so much more.

Take this morning, for instance. He woke me with his mouth. Good gracious, that man's tongue could win the best tongue of the century award, if there was one. After that, he gave me his rock star cock and I'm pretty sure I saw Jesus.

I rewarded him with a pancake breakfast and even made bacon as a side. I'm pretty sure I was the only person on the planet who disliked bacon. Later, when Evan left to visit his parents, I drifted through the house on cloud ninety-nine, so high in the air that when my phone rang, I nearly tripped over my own flip-flop to answer it. So high that I didn't even look at who was calling. I just swiped my finger across the screen and answered, "Hello?"

"Oh, thank God!" the caller gasped. The voice on the other end caught me completely off guard. My mind blanked of all thoughts but one. Why was Amanda calling me?

"Quinn, this is Amanda Walker. Look, I know Evan is living with you...err, at your house," she corrected, "and I know what he's probably said about me, but it's not true. Please, just hear me out." I didn't want to hear her out. In fact, I didn't want to hear her at all. Why was she calling me? We weren't friends. We weren't anything. I'd made peace with my decision not to say anything to Evan. Before she could get another word out, I disconnected the call and had a really bad thought. What if she told Evan she knew me? Or even worse, told him we were friends. Anger, followed by a good dose of fear, swept through me. God, what do I do? Do I tell him? Do I not tell him?

While trying to decide, my phone rang again, causing me to shout in surprise. Thanks to Amanda, my nerves were now shot. Unknown caller scrolled across my screen. Unknown was the wrong word for Amanda. Try Bad caller, or better yet, Bitch calling. With a press of my finger, I sent the call straight to voicemail. My hand shook as I scrolled to my favorites and pressed Alex-Ann's number.

She picked up on the first ring. "For the thousandth time, things are fine. Margo's is fine. Gretchen and Will are fine. Sam is an ass, but he's also fine. I—"

Cutting her off, I said, "Amanda just called me."

I heard her suck in a surprised breath. "You're kidding. What did the bitch want?"

"I don't know. She started to tell me that things weren't what I thought and I hung up on her. She called back. In fact," I paused to check my phone screen, "that's her beeping in right now. Shit, Alex-Ann. What if she tells Evan? He'll think I lied to him." My eyes began to burn. "He hates liars."

"Calm your titties, woman. You didn't know who she was, and when you did—"

"I should have told him," I inserted. "But now that I'm totally and completely in love with the man, it's too late."

A loud sigh echoed through the phone. "You are so overreacting."

"I could lose him," I said through the tears that were now falling freely down my face.

Using her stern voice, Alex-Ann said, "Listen to me. That woman is crazier than a shithouse rat. Evan wants nothing to do with her. The likelihood that he's going to speak to her, much less listen to her spew lies about you, is slim to none. Do you hear me?" I heard her, but the fear of losing the most precious thing I'd ever known, aside from the love of my parents, had a stranglehold on my heart—to the point that all I could do was cry.

"Don't make me drive over there and paddle your cellulite riddled ass," she warned.

"You did not just say that."

"Serious as a heart attack, Quinn, if you don't stop this bullshit right this minute, I will pack up my car and move to your place. You haven't seen cockblocking until you watch me in action, sister." As usual, her ridiculousness made me laugh. Alex-Ann was a nut, but she was my nut.

We talked for a few more minutes before she had to go. This was good as I wanted to hop in the shower before Evan returned.

Of course, he just had to find me in the shower.

"Everything okay with your parents?" I asked as he slid in behind me.

He snagged the body wash from the shelf and squirted a glob of it into the palm of his hand. "Mom's doing remarkable well for having had a brain bleed. My dad's still an ass, though." I started to ask why, but the question died on my tongue at the feel of his soapy hands on my shoulders. In slow, methodical strokes, he began to massage them. When he hit the middle of my back, I dropped my head to my chest, and moaned. Partly because it felt so darn good and partly because of his erection pressing against my lower back.

"Feel good?" he asked.

"Better than good," I mumbled. He pulled back long enough to tackle my lower back. Slowly, he slid his hands to my front. Soap dripped down my stomach as he expertly massaged both of my breasts. Scooping some of the lather in my hand, I reached behind me and circled my fingers around his cock, causing him to suck in a sharp breath. Smiling, I began my own little massage.

"No fair," he rasped. The warmth of his breath against my neck caused shivers to shimmy up my spine. When his tongue traced the shell of my ear, my knees threatened to buckle. His lips drifted from my ear to my shoulder while his fingers slid southward down my stomach. This was a first for me, and I wasn't just talking about the shower, but all of it. I thought I'd been in love before, but I didn't even know what love was. I gasped when his fingers hit the heart of me, and quickly sped up my strokes. Talk about sensory overload. My head was spinning, my hoo-ha was tingling, and my heart was seconds away from bursting.

I was beginning to lose feeling in my hand, when Evan suddenly paused. In a voice three octaves deeper than usual, a voice laced with sexual tension, with...need, he said, "Turn around, I want to watch you come." We broke apart long enough for me to turn and face him. Then our hands were back on each other. As his magical fingers played me, I worked him with both of my hands.

In a matter of minutes, he had me close. His smoldering gaze seared through me, only managing to intensify the thrill of knowing that I was about to fall apart underneath his green-eyed stare.

"Christ, you're gorgeous." Those three words along with his growly sex-voice was all it took. I was there and screaming out my orgasm.

Seconds later, Evan wrapped his hand around mine and picked up the pace. In hard, fast pumps, he jerked our joined hands up and down his shaft. I couldn't look away. I was mesmerized, stupefied...enthralled. Forget taboo, this was...hot. I'm talking hotter than a Georgia whore house on dollar day. A long, drawn out groan spilled from his lips as he emptied himself all over my hand and stomach.

When he was spent, I dragged my eyes to his, and said, "That might be the hottest thing I've ever seen." Laughing, he pulled me in and laid a hard kiss on my lips.

"Are you going to tell me about your dad?" I asked while we were drying off.

"There's nothing to tell." I could tell by his tone that there was plenty to tell, but I didn't push. I simply walked over to the bed, crawled under the covers, and stared at him.

"It's like he's trying to make up for twenty-nine years of mistakes. He's never doted on my mother. Now that I think about it, he's never doted on anyone, but there he was, acting like the dutiful husband. Get this, he even complimented one of my tattoos. The man fucking despises tattoos."

"Which one?" I asked, patting the bed beside me. Long, lean, muscular legs carried him across the room. The knowledge of what we'd just done in the shower, what we were going to do later today, tonight, and in the future to come, made my breath catch in my throat.

Crawling in beside me, he rested his back against the headboard and pointed to the Meltdown symbol tattooed on his forearm. "This one."

I traced my finger over it. "Maybe he's changed."

He scowled. "Men like him don't change, they adapt. My mother threatened him and now he's adapting." His words made my heart hurt. I hadn't met his father, but I could already tell I wasn't going to like him.

"Why doesn't he like your ink?"

"Because it's what low-class people do. That's one thing he and Amanda had in common." Just the mention of her name made me squirm, and I wondered for the zillionth time if I was making a mistake by not saying something. In the end, the fear of losing him stopped me.

"Well, I like them."

"I like you," he whispered in my ear. "I like what we just did in the shower." He traced his finger over one of my rigidly hard nipples. "I particularly like these." Heat exploded through my core when he lowered his lips and sucked it into his mouth. My head fell back against the pillows as I slid my fingers into his hair. He was reaching for a condom when his phone rang. It was right beside us on the bedside table, so we both could see the screen. Bobby was calling.

Evan's gaze snapped to mine. "I can call him back." The phone rang again. The moment was shot. We both knew it.

Planting a kiss on his lips, I said, "No, get it. I'll make us some lunch."

While Evan talked to Bobby, I threw on a T-shirt and shorts and headed downstairs to make some sandwiches.

About half an hour later, he appeared in the kitchen.

"Everything okay?" I asked.

"They found the husband. They're sitting down with him to-night. They'll be back in a few days."

Well...damn. Was it wrong that I didn't want them to come back? That I wanted to stay here like this with Evan forever? That I wanted Amanda to fall off of a steep cliff or get eaten by a rabid squirrel? I'm pretty sure it was, but nevertheless, it was how I felt.

CHAPTER NINETEEN

"Interstate Love Song"

Evan

A few days later, over a lunch of sandwiches, apple slices, and chips, Quinn and I got into a discussion about Mandy. She stood firmly in Chaz's corner in that she wanted Mandy to pay for her lies. I'd be lying if I said a part of me didn't want retribution. Who knew how many men Mandy had scammed. Just the thought that I'd been one of them, that she'd strung me along for nine years, was all kinds of whacked. Chaz made a valid point. If I sat back and did nothing, Mandy would be free to wreak havoc on someone else's life. My father seemed to agree. In fact, earlier this morning, he suggested that I pursue criminal charges in addition to having the marriage declared void. Pressing charges, however, would potentially involve a trial, which would also inevitably bring with it a media shitstorm as well as being hounded by paparazzi. With Meltdown going back on tour, this would be a bad idea. Up to this point, I'd managed to keep my personal life out of the press and under the radar. If I pressed charges, the story would be splashed across every tabloid in the country. After Luke's death, Rowan's kidnapping, and the shit that happened on our last tour, the band couldn't afford to take another hit.

What I didn't tell Quinn, was that my dad had accused me of holding back. He was right. I was holding back. I hadn't disclosed what my accountant had discovered—that Mandy had been syphoning money from our joint account and depositing it into another. I hadn't told anyone, not because I still cared about her, but because I didn't. I didn't give a shit if she stole two dollars or ten million. It was only money. I could make more. I also didn't tell her that Mandy had been blowing up my phone for the past hour. Again, not because it mattered, but because it didn't. Quinn mattered. She was the only thing that mattered.

As I stared across the table at my future, a future so glaringly bright that I was nearly blinded by it, I made a decision. Once the annulment was final, I was walking away. No charges. No payback. Nothing.

"What are you thinking?" Quinn asked. I watched as she took a bite of apple.

"I was thinking that we should continue this discussion upstairs."

"You do, do you?" The sight of her licking her fingers made me want to sweep the dishes to the floor and take her right on the table.

"I was thinking that you could play that new guitar for me. You know, the one you brought back from your secret mission with Chaz and never told me about." Her pouty tone made me smile.

"I was going to show you, but then I caught you with your fingers down your swimsuit, while fantasizing about another man's cock, and it kind of killed the excitement for me." Clearly, I was still jealous.

A crease appeared between her brows as she narrowed her eyes on me. "You just had to bring that up, didn't you?"

"Am I wrong?"

She stood from the table, picked up both plates, carried them across the kitchen, and set them in the sink. Then she turned and gave me an evil grin. "I didn't plan on watching, but once I caught sight of that man's penis, I just...couldn't help myself."

A spear of jealousy blazed through me. I knew she was fucking with me, but still...she was talking about another man's cock. Not fucking cool.

"It was that big, huh?" I asked.

Ignoring my tone of warning, she spread her hands to at least a foot apart, and answered in slow, clipped words, "It was king dong big." That was it. With a growl, I shoved back from the table and stood. As if sensing she'd pushed me too far, Quinn let out a cute little squeak and darted for the kitchen door. She was fast—so fast that I didn't catch up to her until we were right outside of the pool house. I didn't give her time to turn around. I just smushed her flat to the brick façade and held her there with my front flush to her back.

Dropping my mouth to her ear, I said, "King dong?" Even though we were both panting heavily, she still managed to giggle.

"Is something funny?" I asked.

"Yes, you," she shot back at me. "For all I care, that man could have had the biggest dong of the century and it wouldn't matter a lick to me, because all I see is you. All I've seen since the night you walked into my bar and griped about my dirty table...is you." Her words stunned me. She didn't know I was Evan Walker, keyboardist for Meltdown, back then. To her, I was just a man. That hadn't changed. To her, I was still just a man...her man.

Air whooshed from Quinn's lungs as I released the pressure on her back. Taking a step back, I gripped the bottom of my shirt and jerked it over my head. The moment she noticed she was free, she spun around to face me.

Staring at my naked chest, she asked, "What are you doing?"

"What does it look like I'm doing?" She dragged her gaze down my chest to my hands, which were busy unbuttoning my shorts. I hadn't bothered with underwear after the shower, and smiled when I heard her suck in a sharp breath as they dropped to the pavement. "Now, as I recall, this is where I busted you having your little fantasy the other day. Had we not been interrupted, this is what I would have done."

In a flash of movement, I had her back against the wall. Quinn stared up at me with a look of acceptance, a look of want, need...of love on her face. Dropping my mouth to hers, I licked my tongue across her bottom lip. A sexy groan escaped as she opened up for me. Deepening the kiss, I dragged my hands down her torso, where I slipped my fingers into the elastic waistband of her athletic shorts. Her arms shot to my shoulders and wrapped around my neck, and in one quick motion, I lifted her up, jerked her shorts and underwear down her legs, and lowered her back to her feet—all without breaking the kiss. In the process, however, one of my knuckles scraped across the brick exterior. As tempted as I was to lift her back up and plow into her, I couldn't risk the brick scratching up her gorgeous skin.

Pulling back from the kiss, I bent over and snagged my shorts from the ground. Then I took her hand in mine and led her inside the pool house. We barely made it through the door before I was back on her.

"What was wrong with outside?" she asked. Her hair, having

come out of the rubber band, was a wild mane of curls around her face. This, added to her sex-drugged gaze and swollen lips made her even more heart-stoppingly gorgeous.

"Could you be any more beautiful?" I whispered. She blinked. Then she smiled...and then she grabbed my cock. Air shot from my lungs as she took a step forward, pushed up onto her tiptoes, and sealed her lips to mine.

In a matter of seconds, the condom was on and I was lifting her from the ground. With her legs wrapped around my waist and her arms around my neck, I pushed her back against the wall and plunged inside.

"Yesssss," she hissed on an explosive sigh.

"Fuck!" I shouted as shards of pleasure raced down my spine, coiled around my shaft, and squeezed. Quinn's heels dug into my back and spurred me into action. With long, hard thrusts, I took her against the wall. Sweat soaked both of us, to the point I thought she might slip from my grasp. Slowly, I lowered to my knees and shifted my hands to her ass and lower back. This allowed me to go deeper, causing us both to groan. Nothing had ever felt this good. I knew nothing ever would. Not without Quinn.

"I'm coming!" she shouted. The moment I felt her pussy clamp down on me, I exploded. Hell. Fucking. Yes.

Two days later, after a round of sex on one of the pool lounges, Quinn and I were floating in the pool when Bobby and Tut appeared at the top of the stairs. I could see the disappointment on Quinn's face as they made their way down the steps to us. I knew what she was thinking and didn't blame her one bit. For one whole week—the best week of my life, I might add— it had been just the two of us.

I held out my hand. With zero hesitation she took it, and smiled when I linked up our floats. "It's almost over."

"I know. I'm just...going to miss this." I was, too.

"Look at me." I waited until I had her eyes to speak. "As soon as this is over, I promise you a million more, even better weeks, okay?"

"Promise?" she whispered.

"Promise."

The latch to the pool gate clanked.

"Hey guys!" Quinn called out over my shoulder.

"As much as I'd like to join you in the pool, I think we should probably discuss this in front of my computer, so if you two love birds aren't opposed, can we move the party to the main house?" Bobby called back.

"Quit staring at Tut," I warned, low enough for only us to hear.

Her eyes danced to mine. "King dong," she whispered, and laughing, she slid into the water and raced for the side of the pool.

Our moods sobered once we reached the house. Quinn went upstairs to get dressed, while I sat down at the table with Bobby and Tut. Bobby started with the marriage certificate. They verified that the license was valid and made sure that the certificate was in fact a legal document that we could provide as evidence. After this, he moved onto their visit with husband number one, Ned Colliard, or should I say visits.

"The guy wanted nothing to do with us. We showed up on his doorstep, showed him our credentials, and told him why we were there. We didn't get far on that visit. He just told us to fuck off and that his wife wouldn't cheat on him if her life depended on it. Then he slammed the door in our faces."

"What was the house like?"

"I wouldn't say there was anything special about it. It was certainly nothing like the house the two of you lived in, but it was nothing to cry about. We tried again the next morning."

"This time, when Bobby tried to finesse him, I pulled out the marriage certificates and waved them in front of his face," Tut cut in. "That got him talking." I motioned for him to keep going.

"Shit, Tut, you have the tact of a bulldozer," Bobby grumbled.

"Well, if we wait for you to finesse every situation, we'll be here all day." They sounded like me and Ehren when we'd spent too much time together.

"Don't finesse me. Just talk," I directed at Bobby.

Sighing loudly, he said, "Fine. Ned was extremely shocked, to say the least. He said he knew who you were and loved Meltdown and your music. He went on to tell us how he met Mandy their senior year in college. After a few months of dating, she discovered she was pregnant. This was right before graduation, so they waited until after the ceremony to tell anyone. They got married and she lost the baby when she was five months along. I hate to say this, but the guy was nice. Not just that, but he was floored by our visit." As I listened to him talk about the woman I'd spent the last nine years with, I felt detached, as if this was happening to someone other than me.

"That's how she lures them in," I stated.

"Let him finish," Tut said.

"When she lost the baby there were complications and the doctors had to take her uterus," Bobby continued. "This led to depression and other problems in their marriage."

"Back up a moment. Did you say the doctor took her uterus? As in, she couldn't have children?" I asked, hoping that I'd somehow misheard him.

"You heard right. Unless she'd suddenly grown a new uterus, the bitch wasn't carrying your baby," Tut snapped. He glanced at the doorway and I followed his gaze to where Quinn was standing. Her eyes were on me.

"Do you want me to leave?" she asked.

Still stunned, I said, "Mandy not only wasn't pregnant. She couldn't even have children."

She walked over and sat down beside me. "I'm sorry."

"Tell him the rest," Tut urged. All eyes went to Bobby.

"According to Ned, Amanda has never worked a day in her life."

"Bullshit! She worked for a pharmaceutical company," I corrected.

"Did she really?" Tut questioned. "You two kept separate bank accounts, right? I bet that was Mandy's idea. Did you ever see a pay stub, meet any of her co-workers, go to any of her work functions?"

"No, but only because her territory was in four different states."

"Four states other than Texas, correct?"

They had to be wrong. "You don't get it. She told stories about sales meetings and shit all the time." Quinn squeezed my hand and I sucked in a deep breath.

"No, you don't get it," Tut said, his voice sympathetically calm. "Amanda James, Collier, Walker, and soon to be Keen is what we call a pathological liar."

"The job was a cover that allowed her to travel back and forth from Virginia to Texas without getting caught. She took the money that Ned sent home, deposited it into an account, and pretended it was from her monthly paycheck. She did the same with the money you gave her, so if either of you ever looked, you would find a sizeable amount in the account and never question it," Bobby explained. With what I'd just learned from my accountant, this made sense.

"Damn," Quinn whispered. Damn was right. "Ned is in the Army?" she asked.

Nodding, Bobby said, "He claims that's what ruined their marriage."

"What? Him having a decent job?" I inquired.

Bobby's eyes locked with mine. "No, him leaving." And suddenly, it all snapped into place. Mandy was fine until I left to go on tour and she could no longer control me. "You're connecting the dots, right?" he asked.

Quinn looked back and forth between the two of us. "What am I missing?"

"Ned said that Amanda didn't want him to go, begged him not to leave. When he refused her, she left him," Bobby explained.

"Let me guess, she came back."

"She came back a bitter bitch," Tut said.

Bobby nodded. "He said things were never the same after, that she was constantly threatening to leave him."

"Get this," Tut added. "She apparently calmed her tits after he bought her a new car...and the house."

Stunned into silence, I stood from the table and walked out of the room.

CHAPTER TWENTY

"Famous in a Small Town"

Quinn

I started to go after Evan, but Bobby shook his head.

"Give him a minute. This is a lot for him to take in."

"Fucking bullshit is what it is," Tut muttered.

Thinking that Amanda was crazy was one thing. Knowing it was entirely another. She wasn't just crazy, she was devious. My daddy would have called it slicker than greased cat shit on a linoleum floor.

"How did you leave things with Ned?" I asked.

"Let's just say that about right now, Ned is seeing his wife in a very different light," Bobby answered. I bet he was.

I gazed at the door, hoping that Evan would reappear. When he didn't, I asked what was next. That's when Bobby told me a new case had come in, and that he and Tut needed to get back to North Carolina.

This bothered me, enough to ask, "So, what? You're just

going to leave Evan hanging?" Bobby scowled and Tut's lips twitched with humor. I didn't find anything funny about it. They were being paid to do a job, and as far as I was concerned, they had yet to finish doing it.

"To answer your question, no, we are not going to leave Evan hanging. However, Evan isn't our only client. We've been here for over two weeks—two weeks in which we pushed our other cases to our co-workers. Now that Evan knows the score with Amanda, he will be able to get in front of a judge with the documentation necessary to support his claim," Bobby explained.

"When do you leave?" Evan asked from the doorway. All eyes shifted in his direction. He looked tired.

"We're heading to the airport first thing in the morning. Look, man, I know things are up in the air, but there's really nothing more that we can do on our end. If you want—"

Evan cut him off. "I've got it from here. You've gone above and beyond the call of duty for me and I can't tell you how much I appreciate it."

Bobby shook his head as he closed his computer. "I wish things had turned out better for you."

Evan's gaze darted to me. "I don't. Things turned out exactly how they should have." My face flushed beneath his stare.

At Bobby's suggestion, Evan conferenced in both his dad and his lawyer, so they could hear what Bobby and Tut had discovered in Virginia at the same time. They spent the remainder of the night coming up with a plan. Evan's lawyer was going to reach out to Amanda's legal team. If Amanda didn't want to face criminal charges, she would agree to appear before a judge, stipulate the necessary facts, not contest the annulment, and walk away. She would also sign an iron-clad non-disclosure agreement that would prohibit her from speaking to the press, or for that matter anyone, about anything concerning Evan Walker, ever again.

Around midnight, I left them still working through the details and went to bed.

Sometime later I felt Evan's warmth hit my back. His arms snaked around my waist.

Before he could settle in, I rolled over and pressed a kiss to his chest. "You okay?"

A minute passed before he spoke. "For so long, I thought it was me. That I was wired different or just messed up."

I shifted up onto my elbow and waited for him to explain. When he didn't, I asked, "How do you mean?"

"I cared for Mandy, but even from the beginning there was something missing. I watched my friends fall head over heels for their wives. I was there when they said their vows and had their first kids. Hell, I was even there when a few of them divorced. They all had one thing in common...passion. I didn't feel that way about my wife. I married Mandy because I'd gotten her pregnant." A bitter laugh shot from his mouth. "At least, I thought that was the case. From the very beginning, there was no love. She knew it and I knew it. Did I tell you that she blamed me for losing the baby after a fight we had?" My heart squeezed inside my chest.

"No," I whispered.

"We had a knock down drag out fight and I swear, Quinn, I was second's away from walking out." I bit my tongue to keep from responding. I hated that woman before, but I despised her now. She'd tricked him into marrying her and then conned him into staying. What a piece of work!

"I was packing my things and she came in crying. She said she'd lost the baby and I couldn't bring myself to leave. After that, we fell into a routine. I tried to love her, but it was like we were always just on the verge of being over. At some point, I stopped wanting what others had. I convinced myself that what we had was good enough. At least she wasn't a doormat like my mom and I sure as hell wasn't a cheater like my dad. But something was always missing. Music was my outlet. Mandy hated it because it was the one thing I refused to give up, the only part of our marriage she couldn't completely control. The last year we were together, I was so damn tired of it all. In a way, I think that's why I tried out for Meltdown. It's definitely why I lied about it."

"Self-preservation?" I asked.

He let out a soft chuckle. "Either that or self-sabotage."

"Have you ever thought that maybe you sensed what was happening, even if you didn't know the actual details?"

"Looking back now, I see it. I see the lies. I was so blinded by my need to do the right thing that I failed to actually do the right thing. My father asked me to get proof of paternity and I told him to fuck off. He was a cheater and I knew better than him. It turns out I knew shit. My family thought I was making a mistake, but I was so determined not to be like my father—so determined to prove that I wasn't like him, that I spent nine years in a lie—and all because I wanted to be a better father than the one I had."

Not sure my heart could take much more, I dropped my head to his chest, and sighed, "Oh, Evan. You're going to make the best father one day, not because your dad was such a shitty one, but because of the exceptional man that you are."

I felt his lips on the side of my head. "No, Quinn. I'm going to make the best father because I'll have you by my side."

Jerking my head up, I stared deep into his eyes. "I'm crazy about you, Evan Walker."

Without hesitating he said, "I'm in love with you, Quinn Kinley."

"Always gotta out-do me," I grumbled, and pushing forward,

I pressed my lips to his. As usual, it went from zero to scorching in a matter of seconds.

Before I knew it, his lips were on my neck and his fingers buried inside me, while I slowly stroked his cock.

"I want to feel you inside me." The feel of Evan's fingers scissoring in a back and forth motion made the word 'me' sound more like a groan. His lips paused at my neck, but he kept at me with those fingers. "I know you're clean because we talked about it, but so am I. I've been on the pill for years now, a—" Before I could finish my speech, he had me flat on my back.

Hovering over me, he locked his green gaze to mine. "So what you're saying is that you want me to slide my imperial dong, or better yet, my dictatorial dong," he lowered his head to where his lips were hovering no more than an inch above mine, before finishing with, "inside you right now." Clearly, my penis measuring banter from the other day was a bad idea.

"Dwell much?" I asked through my laughter.

"Hell yes. When the woman I love refers to another man's cock as king dong, I take offense." Chills zipped through me. He loved me. Then I thought about the rest of his sentence and mentally rolled my eyes. Men and their egos.

"Hmmm, let me take another look-see. I may have been mistaken." He sucked in a breath when I slipped my hand between us and latched onto his cock. Slowly, I stroked my hand up and down a few times, before giving my verdict.

"I was definitely mistaken. This is the kingliest man dong I've ever had the privilege of touching, the only dong for me." He grunted, as if only moderately appeased, and I broke into laughter. Laughter which quickly morphed into a gasp when he settled the object of our discussion right between my legs and slid inside—all the way inside.

"Evan!" I shouted as he began to pound me to the bed. We'd

had a lot of sex over the past week, but nothing like this. It was punishment and pleasure at the same time.

"Say it!" he ordered. I wasn't sure what he wanted to hear. Did he want me to call him imperial king dong or what?

His mouth lowered to my breast and he sucked my nipple between his teeth, biting down hard enough to elicit a loud groan. Damn that felt good.

A few punishing strokes later, he released my nipple, and growled, "Say it!"

Finally, I just gave in and shouted the first thing that came to mind. "I love you!"

I was pretty sure I'd caught him off guard, because he paused mid-stroke. When he picked back up, it was at a much slower pace. I wondered what he was doing when I felt his hands cup my face. "God, I fucking love you," he whispered. Touching his mouth to mine, he gave me the sweetest kiss I'd ever had. Then he made me come really, really hard.

The next morning, we said goodbye to Bobby and Tut. I was sad to see them go, but at the same time, glad to have my house back.

While Evan was talking with his lawyer, who I was beginning to think was a real jackass, I stripped the sheets from the beds. I'd just thrown them into the wash when my phone rang. I was expecting a call back from Alex-Ann, so I didn't bother to look at the screen.

"Hello?" I answered.

"Don't hang up!" an annoyingly familiar voice called out.

Before I thought better of it, I said, "Girl, you have nerve calling me."

"Just hear me out! He's trying to ruin me with his lies. You know me, Quinn. I—"

"I don't know you...Mandy," I spat out her nickname like it

was dung on my tongue. Before I could say another word, the phone was wrenched from my hand.

"No!" I cried out as Evan placed it to his ear and stalked from the room. Oh, God, she was going to tell him!

For five minutes straight Evan said nothing, and I knew she was telling him everything. Suddenly, his face blanked of all expression.

"Who I fuck is my business, Mandy. Don't call Quinn again or we're going to have an even bigger problem to deal with. Now listen and listen well. When your lawyer tells you to take the deal that I'm offering, you'd be wise to take it." I held my breath as I watched him disconnect the call.

Green eyes blazing with anger stared straight at me. I closed my eyes and waited for it. "I'm sorry baby," he rasped, and pulled me in for a hug. As I hugged him back, I knew what I had to do. Tonight, after work, I was telling him everything.

♪ ♪ ♪

Monday nights were always slow. Normally, I hated them but not tonight. Tonight, I wanted to last forever. I would take a million Mondays if it meant that Evan never had to know. Thank God he wasn't here. His lawyer called right as we were leaving and said he had news, so I left without him. Sensing my foul mood, Alex-Ann and Gretchen had both kept a wide birth. That is, until I decided to take a smoke break.

"I see quitting is going well for you," Alex-Ann teased as she joined me on the ledge.

"I have quit," I replied through an exhale.

"I can see that." When I failed to laugh at her sarcastic remark, she nudged me with her shoulder. "What gives?" Guilt, that's what. I was guilty for not telling Evan about Amanda.

Guilty for smoking the exact things that killed my father. Guilty for feeling trapped by Margo's. Guilty, guilty, guilty.

Sighing loudly, I flicked my cigarette off the ledge and turned to Alex-Ann. "I'm telling Evan tonight."

"Bad idea," she replied.

Sick of her always disagreeing with me, I said, "No, a bad idea would be what you were doing with Baxter. No, make that several bad ideas."

"Oh, so that's how it is. Well, go on with yourself then, but don't say I didn't warn you." I waited for the door to slam behind her before dropping to my back and cursing like a sailor.

On my way back in, some God-awful song was playing on the jukebox. Right as I opened my mouth to scream for Gretchen to change it, I saw them. Baxter and Evan. They were squaring off in front of the bar...in front of my colleagues and friends. In front of everyone. Baxter looked angry and Evan... well, he just looked confused. My heart leapt into my throat, and I felt as if I was going to choke on it. I deserved to choke on it.

"Look, man, I'm sorry she dumped you, but trust me when I say you're better off without her," I heard Evan say as I neared where they were standing.

"You just couldn't let her go, could you? Tell me, what's your plan? To move back in, so you can cheat on her some more? Or do you save that for when you go on tour." His gaze swiveled to me and I flinched. "And you," he spat. "I thought you were our friend. We hung out together. You gave Amanda advice when she needed it. Hell, you even gave the bar free drinks when we got engaged. Talk about betrayal." The entire time Baxter spoke, Evan's eyes remained glued on me.

"It wasn't like that," I told him.

"Oh, it was exactly like that," Baxter spat. "You better watch yourself Quinn. What comes around goes around and I can guarantee you that something bad is heading your way." The bar broke out in pandemonium. Alex-Ann all but tackled Baxter to the floor, while Will and the rest of the patrons shouted obscenities at him. Evan just stood there, a look of heartache and betrayal written across his beautiful face.

"It wasn't like that," I repeated, but to him it was.

To him, it was exactly like that...

CHAPTER TWENTY-ONE

"Rusty Cage"

Evan

I'd never been in love before. Never. I knew this because nothing, not my father's cheating, not Mandy's betrayal, not even discovering that the baby wasn't real, came close to hurting as much as this did. Quinn had lied. She'd been lying all along.

"Tell me, what *was* it like?" I asked.

Her gray eyes...eyes that I'd fallen crazy in love with, studied me, and I wondered if she was thinking up another lie. Probably.

"I didn't know she was Mandy. To me she was Amanda. You have to believe me, Evan. I didn't know—"

"Until you did," I cut in. She didn't respond. She just stood there staring at me. "How long have you known?"

"Please—" Her voice was pleading, begging for what, understanding? Oh, I understood alright. I understood that, like Mandy, Quinn was a liar and couldn't be trusted.

"How long?" I asked again.

"She was protecting you," Alex-Ann called out.

Gritting my teeth, I repeated, "How long?"

"The day Bobby and Tut arrived," she answered, her voice shaking with emotion. "I-I figured it out when we were talking in the living room." Now it all made sense. She didn't leave because she was choking, but because she realized who they were talking about. She'd known for over two weeks and hadn't said anything. Not one word.

"You told me you hated liars. Yet, here you stand. Was it all some sort of joke to you?"

"No! Evan, listen to me. I wanted to tell you, but decided not to because it wouldn't change anything."

"It would have changed everything!" I shouted. "We wouldn't be standing here now if you'd fucking told me. Instead, you've proven that you're just like her!" My chest felt as if it had a fifty-pound weight sitting on it and my eyes burned. This was my cue to leave.

"That's not fair," Alex-Ann defended. "She wanted to tell you and I told her it would only make things worse."

"Evan, just listen to me," Quinn pleaded.

Shaking my head, I said, "You had plenty of time to tell me, but you didn't. I'm done with listening and I'm done with all of this."

I was halfway to the door when I heard her shout, "Evan, please!" but it was too late.

I managed to keep it together on the drive back to Quinn's place. That is, until I hit the front door and saw the two rocking chairs sitting on the porch—the same porch Quinn and I sat and drank coffee on every morning. That's when the enormity of the situation barreled into me. Dropping to my knees, I screamed at the unfairness of it all. Screamed at the endless ache inside my heart. Screamed, because if I didn't...I would cry.

Somehow, I managed to pull it together once more. Forty-five minutes later, I was in my car and headed for the airport. On the way there, my phone pinged with a text. Shortly after that it rang. Grabbing it from the cup holder, I checked to see who was calling. When Alex-Ann's name rolled across the screen, I turned the damn thing off. As far as I was concerned, Alex-Ann had said enough. Sadly, she'd said more than Quinn.

Hours later, I was standing on Chaz and Olivia's doorstep with my bag in one hand and my guitar in the other. I'd turned my phone on long enough to text Chaz from the airport, so he and Olivia were expecting me.

Olivia opened the door, took one look at my face, and pulled me in for a hug.

"Oh, Evan," she sighed, and that's when I completely and totally fell apart. After I pulled myself together, she dragged me inside, plopped me on a dark leather sofa, and handed me a beer.

Surprisingly, Chaz wasn't as accepting of the news that things were over between me and Quinn. First, he wanted all of the details. When I told him what I knew, which admittedly wasn't very much, he called me on it.

"Let me get this straight. Mandy dumped Baxter, so he decided to pay you a visit at Margo's, and that's when you found out that Quinn knew what? Who Mandy and Baxter were? That Mandy and Amanda were one in the same? Was Quinn friends with them?"

"According to Baxter she was."

"I'm sure Baxter is a pillar of honesty." His sarcastic tone wasn't helping.

"I don't know what she knows, Chaz. I just know she lied."

"You don't know, numb nuts, because you didn't give her a chance to explain before you walked out on her." He didn't get it.

"My entire nine-year marriage was a lie, every last bit of it. Then to find out that the one person I felt I could confide in, who really got me—the woman I'm in love with, was also lying to me... What was I supposed to do? Tell her it was alright? Forgive her on the spot?"

"No, but if she means that much to you, you sure as hell could have taken the time to listen. Fuck, Evan, do you think this is easy?" He pointed to Olivia and she smiled. The woman deserved a medal for putting up with his shit. "I'm a dick, and I'm not talking sometimes. I'm a dick all the time. If I got butt hurt every time Olivia kept something from me—because that's what Quinn did, she kept it from you—then we wouldn't stand a chance. You're painting Mandy and Quinn with the same brush, bro, and I'm not sure that's fair."

Seeing my confused expression, Olivia said, "Mandy lied because she's a pathological bitch. Quinn didn't tell you because she didn't want to add to your pain."

"Or so she said," I muttered.

"That's my point," Chaz broke in. "You didn't give her a chance to explain. What do you think, that couples never keep things from each other? Wasn't it you who lied to Mandy before trying out for Meltdown? What if that had been Quinn? In your head, what Mandy didn't know wouldn't hurt her, right? Have you ever thought that Quinn felt the same way?" Well, fuck. Sometimes Chaz actually made sense. In this case, he was right on more than one account.

Olivia held out her hand. "Come on. Let's show you to the guest room. Right now, you need a good night's sleep. Tomorrow you can make things right with Quinn." I took her hand and let her pull me from the chair. Then I did exactly that. I went to bed. Only, I didn't sleep. I just lay there reliving every second I'd spent with Quinn in my head.

The next morning came and I wasn't much better. I missed Quinn. I missed sleeping in her bed, waking next to her, hearing her laugh, watching her face light up whenever I was near. I just plain missed her.

Chaz and Olivia lived in what used to be an old warehouse turned loft. With two bedrooms, two full bathrooms, and a kitchen that opened into a large living area, the place was big for New York.

"So, what's the plan?" Chaz asked over breakfast. I shrugged and told him I didn't have one.

"Come," he said once we were done eating. I followed him across the kitchen, through a door that I didn't even know was there, and into a kick ass music studio.

"Damn, Chaz. You've been holding out on me."

A smile of pride appeared on his face. "This is why we had to get back. The guys were laying the finishing touches and I needed to be here."

"This is awesome." I thought of the pool house studio and felt my chest squeeze.

"Go get your guitar. Let's jam," Chaz suggested.

Ten minutes later, my mind was clear of everything, except the feel of my fingers coursing across the strings. I'd missed this, missed playing with Chaz. For two hours straight, I wasn't thinking about how stupid I'd been. I wasn't worried if Quinn would forgive me or if I'd ever be free of Mandy. It was simply us and the music.

That night, Chaz and Olivia took me to a little neighborhood Italian place. We were immediately recognized, but instead of the usual frenzy, it was way more subdued. After posing for pictures and signing several autographs, we were free to enjoy our meal.

In the middle of picking at my ravioli, Olivia turned to me

and said, "Promise not to be mad at me?"

"Fuck," Chaz muttered.

Placing my fork on the side of my plate, I asked, "Now why would I possibly be mad at you?" Knowing full well that she'd either contacted Quinn and told her about my breakdown or had gone super crazy and done something like arrange an emotional intervention with Mallory and Rowan, which wouldn't surprise me in the least. By the way she was biting her lip, I'd say it was both.

"I texted Quinn and told her you were staying with us."

My brow shot up in surprise. "Is that all? I thought you probably set up an intervention with Mallory and Rowan." She flinched and Chaz busted into laughter. "I'm supposed to call them when we get home tonight, so they can calmly discuss things with you."

As it turned out, we didn't make it to the intervention. The moment I powered on my phone, I was bombarded with a million voicemails, most of them from my attorney, Stan. Alex-Ann left me a few scathing messages, but there was only one text from Quinn.

I'm Sorry, it read. It was amazing how potent those two words could be.

I didn't immediately respond to her text. I wanted to, but I couldn't. At least, not yet. I missed her like crazy and loved her more than anything, but Chaz was right. I was punishing her for Mandy's mistakes. This wasn't fair to Quinn, and before going home to her, I needed to make sure I had a handle on it. We were going to argue in the future. I couldn't pull out the Mandy card every time we did or I would be sure to lose her. That's if I hadn't already lost her. Just the thought made me want to jump on the next plane home to Houston. Instead, I called Stan back. and we spent the next hour on the phone. The judge was going to declare my marriage to Mandy legally void. It was over. Once the papers were signed, the nightmare would finally be over.

As it turned out, Ned Collier didn't appreciate being made a fool of. After Bobby and Tut took off, he hired an attorney. As of yesterday, Mandy was brought up on charges of fraud, bigamy, and intent to commit bigamy. That was probably the reason she'd been harassing Quinn.

After telling Chaz and Olivia, I called both my father and Ehren and gave them the news. The person I really wanted to talk to, however, was Quinn. No offense to Chaz and Olivia, but the only person I wanted to be with, wanted to be sharing this moment with, was a million apologies away, and that's when I knew it was time to go home.

Before crashing for the night, I opened my laptop and booked the first available flight from New York to Houston.

Sometime in the early hours of the morning, my phone rang. Normally, I would send it straight to voicemail, but something made me to check to see who was calling. Quinn's name scrolled across the screen and my gut twisted.

Swiping my finger across the screen, I placed the phone to my ear. "Quinn?"

"Evan—" She was crying.

I sat up and flipped on the lamp. "I'm here. What's wrong?" When she didn't immediately answer, I panicked. "Talk to me, Quinn."

"The bar is gone." My lungs seized inside my chest.

"What? What happened? Are you hurt?"

"There was a fire. No one got hurt. It happened after we left. The whole thing is gone."

"It's okay, baby. I'm on my way home. Okay? I'll be there as quick as I can."

"Hurry," she whispered.

"I'm hurrying. Just hold tight. I'm coming home..."

CHAPTER TWENTY-TWO

"Stay a Little Longer"

*Q*uinn

Margo's was gone. As I stared at what was left of my father's dream, I couldn't help but think that this was my payback, my karmic revenge for not being upfront and honest with Evan, or for that matter, myself. I should have told him.

Last night after Evan walked out, I rushed home from Margo's only to discover him gone. After crying myself silly, I sent him a text. I wanted to explain why I didn't say something, to beg for forgiveness...to bare my soul, but after six tries—all of which sounded silly, I settled for two words; I'm sorry.

To Evan, life was black and white. A lie was a lie and it was as simple as that. To me, it was so much more. Nothing was simple about my decision not to tell him. Was I wrong? Yes. The moment I realized who Amanda was, I should have said something, but it wasn't that easy. I was falling in love. I was scared. I was...a fool. Whoever said love makes you do stupid things hit the nail on the head. In the end, my fear of losing him made me do just that.

You're just like her. Of all the things he'd said, this hurt the most. He was wrong. I was nothing like Amanda James.

I heard my name shouted and turned to see Alex-Ann barreling towards me. The minute she reached me, she threw her arms around me, and I burst into tears. I'd cried more in the past two days than in the past ten years.

"Oh no, Quinny, what happened?"

"I don't know," I sobbed. "The alarm company called right as I pulled up to the house and said that the fire alarm had been triggered and they had a truck on the way. When I got here, the place was pretty much gone. The fireman said liquor bottles acted as an accelerant. Once it hit the storage room there was nothing they could have done to save it."

"Shit. We were just here."

"I know. That's all I can think about. What if it had been my night off or what if Sam had stayed late."

"Have you called Evan?"

After the call from the alarm company, I jumped in the car and sped back to Margo's. Two firetrucks were blocking the parking lot, so I had to park down the street and jog to the bar. When I saw the devastation, I fell apart. It took a nice fireman named Dave to talk me off the ledge. I could tell by the look on his face that he thought I was crazier than a squirrel on crack, but I didn't care. Other than the house, the bar was the last thing I had of my dad. When he asked if there was someone I could call, I thought of Evan. Evan, who now hated me. Evan, who I still loved more than anything in this world. Evan, who was currently on his way home to break my heart into a million tiny pieces.

Of course, I didn't say any of this to Alex-Ann. I simply said, "I called him and he says he's coming home."

Thinking about Evan brought on a fresh batch of tears. He may be coming home, but we both knew the score. It was over. I'd broken his trust. I'd broken us.

As I cried on Alex-Ann's shoulder, she rubbed her hands up and down my back, while chanting "I don't believe this is happening," over and over again. I couldn't either. Each time I thought I had a grip on my emotions, something else would set me off. How was I supposed to tell my mother? What was I going to do now? All of Dad's things, the pictures, the memories, all of it, was just...gone.

Eventually, Gretchen, Sam, and Will found us, and as the night shifted to dawn, we watched the blaze die down to nothing but drifts of smoke.

"I'm so sorry. I know how much this place meant to each and every one of you," I told them.

Alex-Ann huffed. "This isn't on you."

"I'm surprised it lasted as long as it did," Sam muttered.

A strangled gasp shot from Gretchen's lips and all eyes swiveled in her direction.

"What?" I asked as I wiped the tears off my face with the bottom of my t-shirt.

"You don't think Baxter did this, do you?" Her question caught me off guard.

Will nodded his head. "I'd be lying if I said the thought hadn't crossed my mind."

"Everyone heard him threaten you, but God, Quinn, this is just..." Gretchen's words trailed off as a police officer approached us. The same one who had questioned me earlier.

He nodded to the group before turning his gaze on me. "Miss Kinley, it appears you left something out in our earlier discussion. I was talking with Mr. Grange, here, and he tells me that a Baxter Keen caused quite a scene at your bar last night." My eyes cut to Will. Yes, Baxter had threatened me, but only because he was upset. As far as I was concerned, he had every right to be. Amanda had played him just like she'd played everybody else. Did I think he burned down my bar? No. That was more Amanda's style, which made me wonder, where was she tonight?

"Baxter was upset," I explained.

"Did he threaten you?"

"His fiancée had just broken off their engagement and he was upset by this."

"Yes, but did he threaten you, Miss Kinley?" he repeated more forcefully. I thought about telling him no, but then remembered Evan and how that had turned out.

"He did, but I don't think he meant anything by it. If anything, you should look into his fiancée."

At the mention of Amanda, everyone started talking at once. The officer listened patiently to what we had to say before telling us he would look into both Baxter and Amanda.

Pending an investigation into the possibility of arson, the police cordoned off what remained of the bar as a crime scene. This meant that I wasn't allowed to see if anything still remained. This also meant there was nothing more for us to do but go home.

"We'll rebuild," I told them. "We'll make Margo's bigger and better. Maybe we can even bring in live bands, you know, like Dad always talked about." No one said a word.

Sam pulled me in for a hug, and I swallowed back a sob. I felt as if my whole world was ending. Evan was gone, and now, so was the bar. "Now's not the time to make plans, darlin'. Now's the time to go home and get some shut eye. We'll have plenty of time to plan later, okay?" All I could manage was a nod.

Alex-Ann sidled up beside me. "Do you want me to come

home with you?"

"No. I'm good. Sam's right. We all need sleep. Love you guys," I called out as everyone began to peel away and head for their cars.

While walking me to my car, Alex-Ann asked, "Do you know when Evan will be home?"

"He didn't say."

"Well, call me when you wake up. I'll come over and we can watch movies or something." I told her I would.

On the drive home, I cried for the loss of my father. While feeding the cats, I cried about the loss of Margo's. In the shower, I cried because I'd hurt Evan, and when I hit the bed, I just plain cried for me.

A warm hand on my back woke me.

"Quinn?" The sound of his voice, the knowledge that he was here...in my house...on my bed, meant everything. Evan reared his head back when I suddenly sprang up and scrambled onto his lap. Hugging him to me, I buried my head in his neck and burst into tears.

"I'm so sorry. I wanted to tell you, but I didn't want to add to your pain. Then I fell in love with you and I didn't want you to leave me. I know it was wrong and I don't blame you for leaving, but please, please forgive me," I sobbed.

"Hey," he cooed, which only made me cry harder. "Baby, stop crying." His hand on my back slid up into my hair and began caressing my scalp. As I pulled myself together, it dawned on me that I was naked. I was naked and sitting in Evan's lap. Evan's very happy-to-see-me lap from the feel of it. Wiping my eyes on his shoulder, I loosened my hold around his neck just enough for me to tilt my head back. Green eyes filled with worry gazed down at me.

"I'm sorry I was a dick. I didn't think, I just reacted. You're nothing like Mandy. I know that. Our relationship isn't even in the same stratosphere. The whole Baxter thing caught me by surprise and instead of letting you explain, I ran." With the lightest of touches, he brushed his lips across mine. "I'm sorry." He kissed me again, this time adding the slightest swipe of his tongue. "Please forgive me." Was it wrong to feel so happy and so sad at the same time? Because that's exactly how I felt. Evan was back, but the bar was still gone.

"I'm sorry," I whispered.

"I know. I am, too."

"The bar is gone, Evan. There's nothing left."

Pressing a kiss to my forehead, he said, "Come on. Let's get you dressed and get some coffee in you. Then we'll talk."

By the time we made it outside to the rockers, it was past coffee and well into beer time. While drinking our beers, Evan held my hand, and as we watched the sun set, I told him about Margo's. When I mentioned what Gretchen had said about it being Baxter and that I thought it sounded more like Amanda, Evan told me about last night's phone call with the lawyer.

"So... what does that mean? It's over?" I asked, my heart thrumming ninety to nothing in my chest.

His head turned, his gaze shifting from the horizon to me. "No, Country. It means it's just begun."

Butterflies took flight in my stomach as he took the beer from my hand and set it next to his on the porch. Then, pulling me from the chair, he led me into the house and up the stairs to my bedroom, where he slowly stripped me of my clothes—one piece at a time. When we were both fully naked, he lay me on the bed, where first, he brought me to orgasm with his fingers. Then he used his tongue. Only when he had me out of my mind with pleasure, did he enter me. Using slow, deliberate strokes, he took me to the top of the world. We came together. We were together. And if I had my way, we would always be together.

The next morning, Evan sat on the porch with me while I called my mother. I had to start and stop a few times, but I finally managed to get it out. I held my breath, waiting for her tears. Surprisingly, they didn't come.

"I'm sorry, baby girl. I know how much you and your daddy loved that place, but I've gotta say, I'm relieved." I sucked in a shocked breath. "We both know Margo's isn't enough. You need to live, Quinn. Now's your chance to spread your wings. If that means running off with your rock star, then do it. If it means moving to Antarctica and chasing after polar bears, then do it. I just want you to be happy.

"I love you, Mama," I said through my tears.

"Love you, too, baby..."

CHAPTER TWENTY-THREE

"Burn the Witch"

Evan

Quinn believes that everything happens for a reason, that by giving good, you will get good back. I grew up believing that good or bad, shit just happened. You deal with it and move on. But then I met Quinn, and in a matter of eight months, everything changed. I was no longer an emotionally crippled man picking my way through this thing called life. I was living it. Feeling it. Loving every second of it. I wasn't necessarily wrong in my beliefs. Shit did happen. Both Mandy's betrayal and the bar burning down were beyond shitty, but sometimes, out of the awful...comes something good. Quinn was my good.

A few weeks after the fire, I received a phone call from my lawyer. Mandy, apparently, wanted to speak to me. At first, my answer was no, but then he explained how she'd been hospitalized after showing signs of instability and that the doctor evaluating her felt it would be a good thing for us to talk. He assured me that she was still being held accountable for her actions and would most-likely spend time in either jail or a facility of sorts. I would be lying if I said I didn't care. I'd spent nine years of my life, even more if I counted high school, with her. That it had come to this, was just...sad.

After several talks with Quinn, I changed my mind. I wanted to know why. No, I deserved to know why.

A few days later, my phone rang. It was Mandy's doctor. She explained that, due to the medication, Mandy may not sound like herself. This caught me off guard. *What medication?* When I questioned it, she said that she would let Mandy explain.

She handed the phone to Mandy, and in a stilted, wooden, very clinical sounding voice, Mandy said, "Hello, Evan. I appreciate you talking to me." *What the hell?* I didn't know what to say, so I just sat there in silence, waiting for her to explain herself. Talk about awkward. Finally, she started talking. She told me she'd been diagnosed with something called Athazagoraphobia, or a fear of being alone. Without me asking, she went on to explain how everyone she'd ever loved had left her. I let her babble for a few more minutes before cutting to the chase. I wanted to know about the fake pregnancy, the fake wedding, and all of the lies. I wanted to know why. Her answer— It was all because of this so-called affliction.

I was skeptical to say the least, but I also knew that something had to be seriously wrong with her. One doesn't go out and collect husbands for the hell of it. But then, she asked if I would vouch for her in a court of law. As in, wanted me to testify on her behalf. Was she nuts? And that's when I got it. She really was mental. She found some poor doctor and conned her into buying into her bullshit lies. Mandy was sick alright, but it wasn't Atha-zawhatsitcalled. It was something much worse. The saddest part of the whole thing was her surprise when I told her no.

As I sat in the upstairs living area listening to her drone on about her newly discovered ailment, I made peace with the fact that I would probably never know why. I decided that I was okay with this. In fact, I was better than okay. I was finally free.

That afternoon, I drove to the phone store and did something I'd been needing to do for months; I changed my number.

Four days later, Quinn got the call we'd been waiting for. Unfortunately, it wasn't what we wanted to hear. According to the detective who'd been investigating the fire at Margo's, neither Baxter Keen nor Amanda James could have been responsible. Amanda wasn't even in Houston that night and Baxter had been with his brother. They were still conducting an arson investigation, but had officially ruled out our only suspects.

At the beginning of September, as promised, Quinn's mother came to visit. I could tell she wasn't crazy about my tattoos, but that didn't matter because she was crazy about me. Even more so, she was crazy about me with her daughter. We spent the better part of a week planting fall flowers around the house. Or I should say, Quinn and her mother did. I helped, but mostly I worked on the song that had been brewing in my head.

While Quinn's mom was in town, Madden Daze called. One of his buddies was selling his sound system and he wanted to know if I was interested in purchasing it. The next morning, I jumped in the car and drove three hours to take a look. It was exactly what I wanted.

Much to my surprise, Madden showed up later that week with the delivery truck. While Quinn helped me with the logistics, her mother showed Madden around the house. That night, he stayed for dinner and we saw him every day after until Quinn's mother returned to Florida.

A little over a month after the fire, my house sold. Even though Quinn and I were already living together, we decided to make it official. We did this by moving my favorite leather sofa and chairs— the ones Mandy hated—my sixty-inch TV, and my two gaming systems into our upstairs living area. After properly christening them, I whooped her ass in Call of Duty three times. Let's just say that Country did not like to lose.

Mallory finally gave birth to a baby girl. They named her Avery Elizabeth Hardy. Grant conferenced us all in so we could see her. We were on for a total of five minutes before Chaz called her a bald alien and Grant hung up on us. Avery had been alive for less than a day and Grant was already neurotic.

One afternoon, Quinn came busting into the studio. By the look on her face I could tell she was upset.

"You're not going to believe this. Sam got another job! Not only that, but Alex-Ann wants to go back to school and Gretchen's thinking about taking a job at The Pole in the Wall." The Pole in the Wall was a strip joint located about a mile past Margo's.

"The Pole in the Wall, really?" I asked, thinking that she could do better than that. Then I remembered who we were talking about.

Leaning forward, Quinn hissed, "Will's been working there since last month." I got that she was upset. I even understood why.

"Babe, they have to work."

"They already have a job," she snapped back at me.

"Come here." Shoulders hunched, she shuffled in my direction. When she got within touching distance, I pulled her onto my lap. "Margo's could take six months to a year to rebuild. With the arson investigation, it's likely to be longer. You can't expect them to wait."

She slumped in my arms, and with tears in her voice, said, "I know, but Margo's won't be the same without them."

"So don't rebuild."

Her chin shot up, her troubled gray eyes landing on me. "If I don't have Margo's, what will I do?"

"Go on tour with me." The words were out of my mouth before I'd even considered them, but the more I thought about it, the more I wanted it. "Seriously. First, help me fix up the studio here. We're supposed to start laying down tracks at Grant's in December. You'll meet everyone at Nash and Rowan's wedding next month. After that, come on tour with us. The girls will all be there. Olivia already loves you. Knowing her, she'll con you into working for her. Trust me, it will be a blast." I could tell she was considering it. "Come on, baby. Say yes," I urged.

Instead of giving a yes or a no, she asked, "Will Tut be there?" At the surprised look on my face, she burst into laughter. Then she kissed me. Then she flung her arms into the air and shouted, "I'm going on tour with Meltdown!"

God, I fucking love this woman.

EPILOGUE

Evan

One month later...

"The wedding was amazing. I loved meeting everyone, but Chaz is still my favorite," Quinn said on a sigh.

We were driving back from Nash and Rowan's wedding weekend in Austin. They'd really done it up. Nash had rented out a beautifully landscaped Austin stone vineyard in the Hill Country and rooms for the guests at a nearby resort close to Lake Travis. Everyone was there. Hell, even Hank showed up. I'd gotten a chance to talk to him last night and learned that he was moving to Charlotte in order to work security at a bar called Dragonfly. We all tried to talk him into coming on tour with us, but he claimed he'd had enough of the big life and was ready for something slightly lower key.

"Chaz is an ass," I said, as if she didn't already know this.

"Which is why he's my favorite. Every time he referred to Avery as a mutant mushroom, I thought Grant would explode."

The sound of her laughter made me smile. Still giggling, Quinn said, "Oh, I forgot to tell you. Guess who Alex-Ann is nailing?"

"Do I really want to know?"

Of course, she told me anyway. "Her calculus professor."

"Alex-Ann is taking calculus?" Surely she was joking.

"I'll have you know that Alex-Ann is a mathematical genius," she answered. Huh. Talk about unexpected.

The moment I turned onto our drive, my hands began to sweat. Shit. My nerves were riding high by the time I pulled the car to a stop in front of the house.

"Stay," I said, and could feel her eyes on me as I circled the front of the car.

Taking a deep breath, I opened her door and held out my hand. This cute little crease appeared between her brows. "What are you up to, Rock Star?" I didn't bother to answer, I simply wiggled my fingers. Smiling, she placed her hand in mine. Sweat trickled down my spine as I pulled her from the car and led her down the path to the studio. I'd done this a million times, but never like this. Once we were inside, I steered her over to our new sofa and motioned for her to sit.

Focus on the song, I told myself as I made my way over to the piano. It took me a moment to settle in. The second my fingers touched the keys, the nerves disappeared. It was just me and the music—A love song for the woman who'd saved me.

I didn't know I needed her. To me she didn't exist. I was starving but didn't even know it. She was an angel, a dream, my savior...she was my everything. I hit my stride in the chorus.

All those lonely years of heartache and pain.
Anger and disappointment were nothing new.
The bitterness inside wasn't in vain.
Because it all led me to you...

Quinn's eyes were riveted on me as I gave her my heart in a

song. She was up off the sofa before it was even over. I barely had time to push the bench back and she was on me.

"I love you. I love you. I love you," she chanted between kisses. Pretty soon, the kisses turned to deep, pulsating tongue thrusts. Her hands dropped to my fly as I reached under her skirt. I felt my cock in her hand right as I pushed her panties to the side and buried two fingers inside her. Her head dropped back on a groan and I licked my tongue across her throat. When we couldn't stand the foreplay any longer, she shifted up onto her knees, jerked my cock to her entrance, and slammed herself down on me.

"Fuck!" I barked.

"Yes!" she shouted, and then she started to ride me. I'm talking a bareback, western, take no prisoners kind of ride. It didn't take long. After all, we both were pretty damn primed.

The second it was over, I looked right into those gorgeous eyes of hers and I said what I'd been thinking all along, but could never seem to vocalize.

"Thank you for saving me." She blinked and then she burst into tears.

♪ ♪ ♪

Around the middle of the month, Quinn and I were sitting on the porch listening to music when a car pulled up.

"It's the arson inspector," she said. We both stood and met him at the bottom of the steps.

He nodded. "Miss Kinley, Mr. Walker. I wanted to stop by in person to talk to you about your case." We ushered him inside and into the living room. Once we were all seated, he began.

"Truthfully, there's not much to tell. The evidence is inconclusive at most, but here's what I think. None of the usual signs of arson were present. There were no unusual chemicals or accelerants detected. I think the fire started in or near the office. My guess, it was by a cigarette or a lit candle. However, when I looked for a candle, I didn't find one. That being said, I can't one hundred percent say it was or wasn't a deliberate act." He told us he would submit his findings to the insurance company and we all stood. After thanking him, we followed him out to the porch and watched him drive away.

"A cigarette," I murmured. "You wouldn't happen to know anything about that, would you?"

Innocent gray eyes stared back at me. "I don't know what you're talking about. You know that I quit smoking long before that." Yeah, right. I followed her up the stairs and inside the house.

"Well, at least you won't be wearing that fucking Margo's uniform anymore," I muttered.

"That's what you think," she shot over her shoulder. "I'm bringing it on tour. It's my new concert o—"

I was on her before she got the rest of the sentence out. She squealed as I lifted her over my shoulder and continued all the way up the stairs and into our bedroom, where I dropped her on the bed.

Then I gave her my imperial, dictatorial king dong.

The End

A Note To My Readers

Thank you for taking this wild ride with me! As I was writing Shattered Rhythm, I kept thinking that Evan needed a second chance. I wanted to give you his story, but knew that I wouldn't be able to deliver it in the same manner as the other three books. Enter my country girl, Quinn. I loved writing her and I especially loved her for Evan. Evan and Quinn prove that love happens when you least expect it, and sometimes...things are exactly as they seem.

I appreciate you reading this series and hope you'll take the time to drop a review.

Much love,

~RB Hilliard

Acknowledgments

~ Christian Brose – I think we may finally have this thing down, baby! A million thanks, and all of my love for everything you do.

~ Natalie Weston – I couldn't do it without you! Thank you for your friendship and for understanding where I'm going with my stories, even when I don't...

~A.C. Bextor – Thank you for our funny as hell chats and your friendship.

~ Betas: Danielle Brass, Lyndsey Hodson, Nicola Adams, Jayne Wheatley, Jenn Allen, Tara Slone, Tara Champine, and Jennifer Dagis- Love you ladies! Thank you for reading and for helping to make Evan and Quinn's story AMAZING!

~ Hilliard's Hellions – The BEST group EVER! You ROCK!

~ My Fellow Authors – Keep on keeping on...

~ Bloggers – Thank you for reading, reviewing, pimping, and believing in my stories.

Other books by RB Hilliard

His End Game
Not Letting Go
One More Time
Right Side Up
Keep It Simple
The Last Call
Utterly Forgettable
Gold Digger
Fractured Beat
Broken Lyric
Shattered Rhythm